DEATH BY VANILLA LATTE

I shut off the engine and sat back. Even though the sun still lounged in the sky, albeit on its descent, a gloom hung over the bed and breakfast, one I knew they would have a hard time dispelling. I knew what it was like to have someone die in your place of business. It wasn't pleasant, and it always left its mark.

I got out of my car and hesitated before closing the door. Getting involved in murders was usually how I ended up getting myself into trouble. How much easier would my life be if I'd simply stay home instead of poking my nose in other people's business? But this was my dad. There was no way I was going to leave him hanging.

With head held high, and a mind full of questions, I marched straight for the front door, determined to get to the bottom of Rick's murder . . .

Books by Alex Erickson

DEATH BY COFFEE

DEATH BY TEA

DEATH BY PUMPKIN SPICE

DEATH BY VANILLA LATTE

Published by Kensington Publishing Corporation

Death by
Vanilla Latte

Alex
Erickson

KENSINGTON PUBLISHING CORP.
http://www.kensingtonbooks.com

KENSINGTON BOOKS are published by

Kensington Publishing Corp.
119 West 40th Street
New York, NY 10018

All Kensington Titles, Imprints, and Distributed Lines
are available at special quantity discounts for bulk pur-
chases for sales promotions, premiums, fund-raising, and
educational or institutional use. Special book excerpts
or customized printings can also be created to fit spe-
cific needs. For details, write or phone the office of the
Kensington special sales manager: Kensington Publishing Corp., 119 West 40th Street, New York, NY 10018,
attn: Special Sales Department, Phone: 1-800-221-2647.

Kensington and the K logo Reg. U.S. Pat & TM Off.

ISBN-13: 978-1-4967-0885-4
ISBN-10: 1-4967-0885-7
First Kensington Mass Market Edition: June 2017

eISBN-13: 978-1-4967-0886-1
eISBN-10: 1-4967-0886-5
First Kensington Electronic Edition: June 2017

10 9 8 7 6 5 4 3 2 1

Printed in the United States of America

1

A contented sigh slipped through me as I finished the last page of the book I'd spent the entire morning reading. My orange cat, Misfit, was curled up in my lap, purring softly. A now-cold mug of coffee sat just out of reach on the coffee table, where I'd left it about two hours ago. The soggy cookie inside would end up in the trash, but I was okay with that. This was about as close to bliss as I could come.

My eyes strayed to the wall clock, and I sighed.

"I'm sorry," I said, running a hand down the soft length of my cat.

He glanced up at me and gave me a silent "please don't" look.

"I wish I could stay forever," I told him. "But I have to work." I picked him up, causing him to make a meow of protest, and then I deposited him on the warm spot on the couch where I'd just been sitting. He glared at me once, swished his tail, and then jumped down. He then stretched, gave me one last angry look, and padded his way to the bedroom, where he'd pout for the rest of the day.

I didn't let his sour grapes shake my good mood, however. Whistling to myself, I rinsed out my coffee mug, put it upside down in the sink, grabbed my purse, and headed out the door.

Afternoon sunlight warmed the inside of my car on a day that was just shy of being chilly. I drove, music blaring, and sang along like a fool, even when I really didn't know the words. I passed by Phantastic Candies and waved to Jules Phan, who'd poked his head out the door to see what all the ruckus was about. He returned the wave with a bemused smile.

A few minutes later, I was parked down the street from Death by Coffee, having struggled to find a spot closer. I wondered if there was any way we might buy one of the nearby lots and turn it into a parking lot, but after only a moment's thought, I decided it would probably cost too much. The shop might be doing better than ever, but that didn't mean we could up and spend however much we wanted, even if it might help the business grow.

Besides, the short walk would do me some good. I kept promising myself I'd work out, yet it seemed the only exercise I got these days came in the form of work. Maybe I'd start doing sit-ups next week.

And maybe I'd hit the lottery while I was at it. Both were just as likely.

Only slightly winded, I pushed through the front door. Lena Allison and Jeff Braun were both behind the counter, hard at work. The line was short, but most of the tables were full, telling me it had been a pretty busy morning. Upstairs, Vicki was talking to a pair of middle-aged women near the bookshelves, using her charms to sell a book or two.

"Ms. Hancock!" Lena said as I came around the counter. "It's a great day, isn't it? A really great day." Her grin was a little too wide, and she was dancing from foot to foot.

I cocked an eyebrow at her and then turned to Jeff, who just about tripped over himself spinning away. He started filling a cup even though no one had ordered anything to drink.

"What's going on?" I asked.

"What do you mean?" Lena ran her fingers through her short purple hair and refused to meet my eye.

"You called me Ms. Hancock. You never do that."

She shrugged. "Thought I'd try it out. A little much?"

"A little."

As a customer came to the counter, Lena spun around and let out a big sigh before saying, "Welcome to Death by Coffee! What can I get you?"

I watched her a moment, perplexed, and then with a shrug of my own, I went into the office to deposit my purse. I snatched the apron off the wall by the door, and then headed back to the front to start what was beginning to look like a very peculiar day.

"How did opening go?" I asked Jeff, who was still standing by the coffeepots. Today was the first day he'd opened with Vicki, and I was curious to see how he liked it.

"It was okay, ma'am," he said, lowering his gaze.

"Krissy," I reminded him. "Call me Krissy."

He nodded, still not meeting my eye. "Sorry."

I patted him on the shoulder. "Go ahead and clock out."

He scurried off, seemingly relieved I hadn't kept

him there any longer than I had. He'd never quite gotten over his shyness, but I was slowly trying to break through to him. He was a hard worker despite being something of a slow learner. He was doing just fine, which was a relief, considering how the last guy I'd hired turned out.

I spent the next half hour making sure the coffee was fresh and replacing the cookies in the display case with fresh ones. I whistled while I worked, though I was still worried by Lena's strange behavior. I'd had to run inventory all last week, and boy, let me tell you, that wasn't something I enjoyed. No one had ever told me how hard owning your own business could be, especially when it came to making sure you were fully stocked. I'm forever thankful Vicki handled most of the behind-the-scenes stuff, because if it had been left to me, we'd have closed within months of opening. Let's just say, money and paperwork aren't my strong suit.

The front door opened, and a thin man with flyaway brown hair and glasses entered, carrying two heavy-looking boxes. He was sweating profusely from the weight and looked as if he was seconds from collapse. His eyes flickered my way, but he didn't come to the counter. Instead, he went straight up the stairs to where Vicki was waiting. She relieved him of one of the boxes, and together they carried them to the back.

"Who's that?" I asked.

"Stock delivery?" Lena replied, though she winced as she said it.

"We get our books shipped," I said. "He's not our usual delivery guy."

"Maybe he's new."

"Okay, where's his uniform, then?" I glanced out the front door. "Or his truck?"

Lena shrugged, and then spun on her heel to walk straight into the back.

What in the world is going on here?

I was about to head upstairs and ask Vicki about it, when the door opened again and my answer strode through.

"Hey, Buttercup."

I sucked in a shocked breath and staggered back a step. "Dad?"

James Hancock, retired mystery author, and father to yours truly, smiled as he walked over to me. His beard was trimmed, as was what was left of his hair. He was smiling, and I swear I saw a tear in his eye when he held out his arms to me.

"What are you doing here?" I asked, coming around the counter to give him a hug. "Not that I mind that you came. You never told me you were coming!"

He chuckled—a dry, raspy sound that resonated through my entire body and brought memories of long nights sitting around a crackling fire, him typing away on his typewriter, and then later, laptop, and me reading a favorite novel.

"I had business and I wanted to surprise you." His voice was gravelly from years of trouble with his throat. I always found it fit him just right, made him sound like one of those old-time detectives with a cigarette hanging loose from his lips, calling all the women dames, much like quite a few of his creations did.

"Well, I'm definitely surprised!" And then realization dawned. I turned to find Lena grinning from behind the counter. "You knew!"

She rolled her eyes. "Of course I knew." She was practically beaming.

I turned back to Dad, not quite believing he was actually there. When I'd moved to Pine Hills, I'd left him behind, knowing how much it would hurt to be away from him, but needing the fresh start. It was surprising how good it felt to have him here now, even though I'd been blindsided by his sudden appearance.

"Why are you here exactly?" I asked, suddenly worried something was wrong. "Are you sick?"

He looked surprised for an instant before his smile returned. "No, I'm not sick." He cleared his throat, rubbed at his beard. He looked down at his hands for a second, before looking up and giving me a sideways smile. "I sort of have a new book coming out."

"You what?" I blinked at him. "But you're retired!"

"Semiretired," he countered. "You know I couldn't just up and quit. The story was burning in me for a while now, so I decided to go ahead and write it down." He took me by the arms and looked me in the eye. "I swear I took care of myself this time. No fasting or skipping showers just to finish up a page."

His health was part of the reason he'd retired in the first place. I got my obsessiveness from him. He would forget to eat, forget to change clothes, or sleep, just so he could finish one last chapter. He never mistreated us or totally abandoned his family, though there were some days you could tell he wanted to get back to writing. His dedication is what made him such a good writer, though it definitely took a toll on his well-being.

"When's it coming out?" I asked, and then remembering the boxes that had come in a few minutes before, I added, "Is it out now?"

"No, not now," he said with a laugh. "I'm going to do a reading from the new book and then sign some of my old novels. Rick thought it would be a good idea to make an event of it, and where better than right here, in a store that bears the name of one of my books?"

At mention of Dad's agent, my mood darkened just a little. "Rick? Is he here?"

As if he'd been summoned, the door opened and in walked Rick Wiseman. He was wearing a suit that looked as if it had come off a bargain-bin rack, though he wore it well. His hair was much thinner than when I'd last seen him, but he'd stopped trying to cover it with a comb-over by cutting it short, instead. When he saw me standing next to my dad, he grinned. He was holding a travel coffee mug with his name written on it in big black letters.

"Kristina!" he said, holding out his arms for me. "I'm so glad to see you."

"Rick," I said, not budging from where I stood. One glance at my dad, and I forced myself to turn my scowl into a friendly smile. Rick had just gotten here, so there was no reason to sour the festive mood with my distaste for the man.

"You've grown up so much," he said, seemingly oblivious to how I felt about him.

"I have." I hadn't seen Rick for at least ten years now, and I'd hoped to go another ten or twenty before I ever saw him again.

"We should get together and catch up sometime." He glanced around the coffee shop. "Somewhere nice."

I caught the implication, and my smile grew even more strained. "Want a refill?" I asked, nodding toward his coffee mug. "What are you having?"

He shook his head and grimaced. "Vanilla latte. Made it myself. Brought the machine with me so I wouldn't have to drink something from a package."

I bit my lip hard enough I very nearly drew blood.

"It is quite a quaint little place you have here," he said. "Could use some paint, but I think it'll be fine." His attention snapped over my shoulder. "Cameron! There are five more boxes outside and they aren't going to walk themselves in here."

I glanced back to find the man who'd carried in the boxes hurrying down the stairs, and away from Vicki, who he'd obviously been talking to. "Sorry, Mr. Wiseman."

"Don't 'Mr. Wiseman' me." Rick sighed. "Come on. Let's make sure you don't mess something else up. . . ." He turned back to me. "Nice to see you again. We'll definitely have to talk."

Rick strode out ahead of Cameron, who kept his head down all the way out of the store. The poor guy looked as if this sort of thing happened all the time.

"Why is he here?" I asked Dad, who was watching the display with a frown of his own.

"He wanted to come. When we arranged this with Vicki, I'd thought we'd have copies of the new book, but production got pushed back. I told Rick it wasn't necessary to come now that I'm only selling older novels, but he'd insisted."

"That poor man." I hoped Rick wasn't loading

Cameron down with all five boxes of books at the same time. "Is he Rick's son?"

Dad laughed. "No, not his son. I guess you'd call him his assistant. Cameron Little has been working at the agency for the last year now, though I'm not sure what all he does."

"Why does he put up with him?" I wondered out loud.

Dad gave me a look. "Now, Buttercup, Rick works hard. He can be abrasive, but his heart is in the right place. I'm sure they both get quite a lot out of their working relationship."

I wondered about that, but kept my opinion to myself. Rick had always rubbed me the wrong way. His smiles never felt quite genuine, like he was calculating how he could use you while he studied you. And then with the way he'd insult you without really insulting you . . . I don't know. Maybe he wasn't as bad as I made him out to be, and I should give him a chance to prove it.

The door opened, and I braced myself for another interaction with Rick, but instead, I was broadsided by something far, far worse.

Rita Jablonski made it all of two steps inside before it registered who was standing just inside the door.

"Oh!" It came out as a surprised sound as her eyes widened. Then, her hand fluttered to her chest as she realized exactly who she was looking at. "Is it really . . ." She sucked in a breath, and for a moment I thought she might let out one of those screams teenaged girls make when they see their favorite pop star.

"Rita," I said, hoping to stem the tide before she started gushing, but it was too late.

"James Hancock! It's really you." She started breathing in and out like she might hyperventilate. She fanned herself off as she hurried over to where we stood. "I can't believe it. You've finally come after all this time. It's a blessing, I tell you. A downright blessing straight from heaven, sent to me on this most blessed of days."

"Hi," Dad said, holding out a hand, polite as ever. "I *am* James. You are?"

"Oh, dear me." Rita was flushed as she took his hand. "Rita Jablonski. I'm your number one fan."

I just about choked. We went from overexcited teenager straight to *Misery*. Could this get any worse?

"It's very nice to meet you, Rita," Dad said, practiced smile in place.

"We've met before," she said with a wave of her hand. "I got your autograph from a signing you held a few years back. I traveled quite a ways to meet you then." Her eyes widened. "Are you doing a signing here in Pine Hills? Please tell me you are! I can't imagine what other reason you'd have to come to our little town."

I cleared my throat, but I might as well not have been there.

"I am," Dad said, his smile turning amused. "It won't be until this weekend, however."

Rita just about glowed with excitement. "That means you'll be here all week!" I could see the wheels spinning behind her eyes and knew whatever she was thinking couldn't be good.

"Rita," I said, forcing her to look at me. "Dad and I haven't seen each other for a few months now. We'd like to have a few minutes to catch up, if that's okay?"

"That's fine, dear," she said, actually shooing me away. "You'll have plenty of time to catch up, I'm sure."

Behind her, the door opened and Cameron came in, three boxes in his arms this time. Rick trailed behind, carrying only his coffee mug. The least he could have done was to offer to carry the last two boxes, but apparently physical labor was beneath him.

"I have an idea!" Rita said, clapping her hands together and startling me. "We hold a writers' group meeting every Tuesday night. You should come and talk to our members!"

"I wouldn't want to intrude," Dad said, for the first time sounding uncertain.

"Nonsense!" Rita patted him on the hand. "It will be a special meeting, one held in your honor. I'll let everyone know you're going to be there and they can prepare for it. I bet we'll have at least three times as many people show up, all because of you! It's going to be fantastic!"

And before my dad could protest, Rita spun away. Her cell phone was in her hand even before she reached the door. As she stepped out on the sidewalk, I could hear her say, "Georgina! You won't believe who I just ran into!" And then the door closed, and she was gone.

"What just happened?" Dad asked, a bemused expression on his face.

"You don't have to go," I said. "Rita gets overexcited at times and forgets that people sometimes like to make up their own minds about what they do."

"She seems nice enough."

"She is," I said. "But if you let her, she'll have you

paraded all over town. You won't have a moment's peace."

Dad patted me on the arm. "I'm in town, so I might as well go. I'd like to get to know the people here and the writers' group seems like the perfect place to start."

"Are you sure?"

"I am."

A crash and a pained yowl caused us to turn. Cameron lay sprawled on the floor, the boxes of books spilled before him. The store cat, Trouble, sat a few feet away, licking his back foot and glaring at the poor assistant like he'd stepped on him on purpose.

"Be more careful with those!" Rick shouted. "What is wrong with you?"

"I'd better go help out," Dad said with a sigh.

"Yeah."

He kissed me on the forehead. "It's good to see you, Buttercup."

"You too, Dad."

And then he was running up the stairs in a vain attempt to calm his raging agent and to help the battered assistant get to his feet. Vicki was there to comfort her poor black-and-white kitty.

My mind raced wildly as I watched from my place by the door. Between the sudden appearance of my dad and Rita's obsession, who would comfort me?

2

"I don't know what I'm going to do!"

Will chuckled on the other end of the line.

"It's not funny! My dad is here and I'm terrified Rita is going to drag him off somewhere and force him to marry her. She was practically drooling all over herself when she saw him. It was a wonder she didn't make any more of a scene than she did."

More laughter, followed by, "You really shouldn't worry so much about it, Krissy. Nothing horrible is going to happen. Enjoy the visit. Spend time with your dad. Even if Rita makes a pass at him, I'm sure it will all work out just fine."

I groaned as I turned onto the main drag. I was on my way to the writers' meeting and was hating every second of it. I didn't know what to expect when I got there, but I was sure I wouldn't like it. Rita was probably busy setting up that cardboard cutout of Dad she kept in her bedroom even now.

Just thinking about it was giving me heartburn. "My day started out so nicely."

"It'll be fine." I could hear the amused smile in

Will's voice and wanted to smack him for it. He had no idea how obsessive Rita could be. "It's natural to be nervous. His arrival was a surprise and you weren't prepared for it. You should make the best of it and be happy he's here. There's a lot of people who don't get to see their parents much."

"I know, but . . ." But what? I was actually pretty happy to see my dad, even if his appearance did come as a shock. It wasn't like when my ex-boyfriend, Robert, had shown up, wanting to get back together even though he'd arrived with another girl on his arm. Now that was the kind of surprise I'd like to avoid.

I sighed. "You're right," I said. "I'm being silly."

"You are. And I find it rather cute."

"Shut up." I grinned as I spun the wheel and turned into the church parking lot. "I've got to go. . . ." My eyes widened, and I came to an abrupt stop. "Holy crap."

"What?"

"Nothing." I cleared my throat, which had gone dry. "I'll call you later." I hung up before Will could reply.

Normally, there were six, maybe seven cars at the most, in the church parking lot on group night. And lately, we'd been lucky to have four since Lena had been working a lot and Adam hadn't been coming like he used to.

But not tonight. There had to be at least a dozen, if not upward of twenty cars in the lot.

My stomach did a slow flip as I started forward again and coasted down the rows until I found an empty space. I parked and shut off the engine, heart pounding like I was the one who was about to get bombarded by a horde of slavering wannabe authors.

"Dad, what did you get yourself into?"

I got out of my car and headed for the door, all the while trying to come up with some way to talk Rita out of making such a big deal about my dad's visit. I knew she was excited, but I had a feeling she was going to take it too far. Why couldn't she have a normal meeting where Dad could speak about writing, answer some questions, and then maybe sign a book or two? I was almost positive I was going to walk in on something that would end with someone getting hurt.

The sound of excited chatter echoed down the hall as I entered the church. The old painted steps creaked as I strode up them. I reached the top of the stairs and peeked into the meeting room to find it nearly packed with people. I recognized Andi, Georgina, and Adam right away. They were hovering near where the chairs they normally sat in would have been on a normal night. Now, there were rows of metal folding chairs, and the group members didn't seem to know where to stand. I didn't see Lena or Chief Patricia Dalton anywhere—the two other regular members of our group.

"Krissy!" Rita saw me as soon as I stepped into the room. She rushed over and grabbed me by the arm as if she thought I might turn and flee. I had to admit, it would probably be a wise decision, because I wanted to be as far away from here as I could get. I wasn't a fan of big crowds.

"Do you know when James will arrive?" Rita asked, dragging me into the room. "Everyone is so excited. Many of us have brought our best manuscripts with us in the hopes he'll read them and pass them on to his publisher." She abruptly stopped, spun, and hugged me. "This is so exciting!" And then, before I could gasp out that she was squeezing too hard, she released me and hurried off without waiting for me to reply.

Composing myself, I glanced around the room in search of more familiar faces. The local librarians, Cindy and Jimmy Carlton, were standing in a corner, Jimmy clutching a thin stack of papers close to his chest like he thought someone might try to steal it from him. Next to them stood a few members of the Cherry Valley book club. Albert Elmore glanced my way and said something to Sara Huffington, who tugged on her pearls while she scowled at me. The elderly Vivian Flowers patted her on the shoulder as if consoling her, and then winked at me.

I was actually surprised to see them here. As far as I knew, Albert didn't get along with Rita. Actually, I'm not sure anyone from Cherry Valley got along with her. Anytime I'd ever seen them together, there was usually an argument of some sort, but I guess a chance to meet James Hancock trumped petty squabbling. Then again, Albert had talked poorly about one of my dad's books. Maybe he was here to tell him how he would have done it better.

"Hi, are you Kristina Hancock?"

I turned to find a middle-aged man in a fleece sweater standing behind me, holding his own sheaf of papers. He was wearing a hat that looked suspiciously like the battered fedora one of my dad's most popular characters wore, right down to the black smudge on the brim.

"I am," I said. "But you can call me Krissy."

His face lit up, and he freed a sweaty hand to grip mine vigorously. "I'm one of your father's biggest fans." He blinked at me rapidly, like he was trying to keep from crying. "I'm Joel, by the way. Joel Osborne."

"It's nice to meet you, Joel," I said, extracting my hand from his own and wiping it on my jeans. "Nice turnout, huh?"

"I'm not surprised," Joel said, eyes scanning the room. "When Rita called me, she told me she was going to let everyone know about tonight's festivities. I'm surprised more aren't here already."

"Are you from here in town?" I asked, not having seen him before. Since the Cherry Valley people were here, it wouldn't surprise me to learn he'd come from somewhere else close by.

"I'm from Pine Hills, born and raised." Joel snorted a laugh. "I don't really get out that much, but this was too big of an opportunity to pass up." He touched the brim of his hat, almost reverently.

I glanced around the room then, wondering how many more people were from here in town. There were quite a lot of faces I didn't recognize, including a thin woman who had joined the Cherry Valley group. With the way she talked to Albert, I wondered if he'd started dating again. From what I understood, his wife had left him a while ago.

"Do you know when he'll be here?" Joel asked, bringing my attention back to him. "I'm anxious to know what he'll think about my novel." He held the sheaf of papers out toward me, though he clutched at them carefully, as not to let one flutter away.

"I don't know," I said. "And I'm not sure he'll be able to look at your novel."

Joel's face fell. "Rita told everyone to print out

a copy of their books and bring them with us. She assured me there would be time to show him our work tonight."

I winced. This wouldn't be the first time someone asked Dad to look at their novel. And like every time before it, he would have to tell them no. He had to be careful about these things because not everyone was on the up-and-up. He'd told me once about a writer friend who'd looked at some woman's novel and then was promptly sued by her when a book he'd recently written contained a character with the same last name as the one in her own unpublished book. The case was thrown out, but it did serve as a warning, one my dad took to heart.

"He'll probably listen if you were to read it, but I don't think he's going to do whatever it was Rita promised."

Joel's shoulders sagged, and he nodded. "I guess I understand. He's a busy man." He gave me a sad smile and then wandered over to a chair beside a box that appeared to hold a few more fedoras, all with the same black mark on the brim.

I felt bad, but I wasn't going to let him get his hopes up too much. Rita should have asked before she went and told everyone Dad would read their novels. There would be a lot of very unhappy people by the end of the night, I was sure.

"Krissy, dear," Rita said, hurrying over with a couple in tow. "I have someone I'd like you to meet."

"Barrett Drummand." A man who had to be my dad's age, but with a fuller head of hair, spoke, voice raspy as if he'd spent a lifetime smoking. He didn't offer to shake hands or even do more than speak his name. In fact, he didn't look all that happy to be here.

"Barrett and his wife, Theresa, are thrilled about meeting James," Rita said. "Barrett is a very good storyteller and I'm sure he'll be a star someday."

The woman, Theresa, stood behind her husband, head slightly bowed. She looked to be about ten years his junior, though she was dressed as if she were older. She had on a plain brown dress that went all the way down to her ankles and hid every last curve of her body. She wouldn't meet my eye, no matter how hard I tried to catch her gaze.

"It's nice to meet you both," I said, though I had no idea why Rita wanted us to meet.

Barrett only nodded as if he thought he was doing me a favor by standing in my presence. His wife barely even glanced up at me before staring down at the back of her husband's legs again.

"I do hope James arrives soon." Rita fussed with her hair. "Everyone is getting restless. I was hoping he would be here already so I could prepare him for tonight's activities, but I suppose I shouldn't be surprised he hasn't arrived yet. He is a very important and busy man."

I kept from rolling my eyes and chose to glance at the clock, instead. It was still a good ten minutes before our normal start time, but I refrained from pointing that out to Rita.

"There's Amy Goldstein," she said. "I wonder why her husband isn't with her tonight?"

I caught a glimpse of a woman who looked a little uncomfortable about being there, before my attention was drawn to a nearby shout.

"*The Blind Canary* is a far superior Drake story than *The Tarred Peacock!*"

"You're out of your mind!" A fat man was practically standing on Joel as he shouted at him. "*The Blind Canary* has got to be the weakest of the bunch! The solution took no effort, whereas Drake has to use every ounce of his detective skills to solve the case in *The Tarred Peacock*. That clearly makes it a better novel."

Joel was clutching at what I was starting to think of as his "Bobby Drake" hat, his face turning red.

"Now, now, Harland," Rita said, rushing over, as I followed in her wake. "No need to fight."

"He's wrong!" the fat man—Harland, I assumed—said. "Just because he made those stupid hats, doesn't make him an expert."

"They're not stupid!" Joel looked like he wanted to knock Harland upside the head with one of the hats, but refrained from doing anything more than raise his voice.

The floorboard outside the room creaked, causing every head to turn. James Hancock, followed by both Rick Wiseman and his assistant, Cameron Little, entered the room. A sudden hush fell over the crowd, but it was quickly replaced by excited applause. Even the two squabblers had stopped fighting and were smiling ear to ear.

Dad looked taken aback at first, and then a wide grin spread across his face as he soaked in the applause. He raised both of his hands, looking for all the world like a politician pretending to try to calm his supporters, while really wanting them to cheer louder. Behind him, Rick scowled and took a sip from his travel mug, which likely held another batch of his precious vanilla latte.

"Everyone! Everyone!" Rita blew an ear-piercing whistle. "Make room and welcome our guest of honor, James Hancock!"

More clapping and a few hoots and hollers followed the pronouncement. Rita fanned herself off as if just saying his name was enough to make her overheat.

"Thank you," Dad said, stepping to the front of the room. When he spoke, everyone fell silent. "I'm thrilled so many of you have come to see me tonight. It's my honor to be here and I hope to see every one of you this Saturday when I hold a book signing in my daughter's coffee shop, Death by Coffee." He held a hand out toward me.

All eyes swiveled my way, and I instantly flushed beet red. Thankfully, attention lingered on me for only a few seconds before nearly everyone turned back to my dad. Only Rick continued to stare, a thin smile crossing his lips. He leaned over, whispered something to Cameron, and then handed him his travel mug. Cameron hurried out of the room, presumably to refill it.

"Now," Rita said, "if everyone would take a seat, we can get started." She motioned for my dad to take the chair in the front of the room, which sat right beside her own recliner, leaving the rest of us to sit in the uncomfortable metal folding chairs.

I took a seat in the back, hoping not to draw any more attention my way than I already had. I didn't much care for the spotlight, though my dad enjoyed it. I also had a hard time understanding why everyone was so fascinated with him. I mean, to me, he was Dad. But I guess to everyone else he was a celebrity, as much as a writer can be.

Rick took a chair from the row and dragged it over to the wall, where he wouldn't have to sit next to anyone. Cameron returned just as he settled in, handed him his coffee mug, and then found his own seat at the end of the aisle. I noticed he stared at his boss for a few moments after he sat. I wondered if he was tired of getting bossed around. I know I would have a hard time with it, but that's because I preferred to be my own boss. I don't think I could go back to working where someone else was constantly telling me what to do.

Once everyone was quiet, Rita took control. "I'm sure everyone has a thousand questions for James," she said, patting Dad on the hand as she spoke. "But I thought it might be best if we start with me reading from my novel. Afterward, I do hope you will be interested in reading the rest." She batted her eyelashes at Dad.

"I'm flattered."

Before he could say more, Harland spoke up. "I have a novel for you to read as well."

"As do I!" This from Albert.

And then came the tidal wave of shouts and pleas for Dad to read their every word.

Dad raised both his hands and shook his head as he waited for the crowd to quiet down. "If I could read each and every novel here, I would," he said. "But I cannot." There was a collective groan. For a few moments, Dad looked upset about having to let everyone down, then a mischievous smile crossed his features. "But my agent, Rick Wiseman, is here tonight. I'm sure that after we are done with the meeting tonight, he would be happy to read your novels."

Rick just about spilled his drink as he sputtered out a vain protest. He was drowned out by clapping and more shouts and cheers. I swear I saw Cameron grinning deviously from his seat, though he covered his mouth to hide it from Rick, who was not happy.

Since Dad wasn't going to read the novels tonight, Rita decided to skip reading from her own work, which was a good thing, in my opinion. Her heart was in the right place, but she struggled mightily when it came to putting words on the page. I'd heard enough of it to know, and I would feel bad for her if someone in the audience were to start booing. I had a feeling Albert wouldn't hesitate to embarrass her if he got the chance.

Dad began answering questions like "Where do you get your ideas?" and "How long does it take you to write a book?" I'd heard all the answers before, and quickly grew bored. Dad did a good job of answering without rolling his eyes or getting annoyed by hearing the same thing over and over. He was far better at this than I'd ever be.

It didn't take long before I started to get anxious. I shifted in place at least a dozen times in less than a minute, and the constant creaking of my chair caused a few annoyed eyes to turn my way. I stood and ducked out of the room with muttered apologies. I desperately needed fresh air.

The night had grown chilly, and I hugged my arms around my chest as I left the church. I was trying hard to take Will's advice and enjoy myself, but so far, I'd barely gotten a chance to speak to Dad. I was afraid that he'd be mobbed this entire visit, leaving me to watch him from afar. It actually made me a little sad to think I might not get to sit down and have a real conversation with him without someone else—likely Rita—hovering around.

"You look cold."

I jumped as Rick put his arm around me.

"I'm fine." I stepped away, pulling from his grip with a shudder. "Shouldn't you be inside?" I asked. It came out a bit more accusatory than I'd intended, but I wasn't sorry for it. I didn't like people touching me uninvited, especially when it was someone I didn't like all that much.

"I saw you leave and thought I'd come check on you. Are you okay?"

"I'm fine," I repeated, looking toward the church door and hoping someone else would step outside. The door remained stubbornly closed. "I needed some fresh air. I'm going back in now."

"Wait a few moments, would you?" Rick stepped in front of me, keeping me from the door. "I'd like to talk to you for a minute, if that's okay?"

It wasn't, but I decided to play nice. "Okay," I said. "I have a minute or two."

"Good." Rick's smile was so slimy, it made my stomach churn. "You know, I've always known you'd grow up to be pretty. You were good-looking back when you were this high." He held a hand up to his waist.

"Excuse me?" I took a step back from him, surprised by his directness.

He didn't seem to notice how uncomfortable he was making me. "You were definitely always a very pretty girl, if not a little nosy for your own good. If I'd been your age, then well . . ." He shrugged and then laughed it off as if it were all a big joke. "It's just nice to see you've done well for yourself."

"Thank you," I said, hesitantly, still not sure I wanted to know where this was going.

Rick took a step toward me, glancing toward the church doors as he did. "You know, if you have a novel you'd like me to look at, I'd be happy to take a gander. I'm staying at a local B and B and figure you could, I don't know, stop by and drop it off in person." His eyes moved from my face, down my body. "See where it goes."

His gaze was like a million spiders crawling over me. "Sorry," I said, taking another step back from him. "I don't write."

Rick reached out and put a hand on my arm. "I'm sure you have something I could look at." He practically cooed the words. "I'd really like to see it."

The church doors blessedly opened then. Rick's hand jerked back like he'd been burned. His ever-present scowl returned as Dad led a procession of authors out the doors, a Bobby Drake hat pulled rakishly down over one eye. He hesitated a moment before moving down the stairs. At least a dozen of the prospective authors following saw Rick and immediately started his way, waving their manuscripts at him.

"Not interested!" Rick barked. "Cameron! Let's go. Now!" He spun and went straight for his car, not looking back at the mob, who were pleading with him to take at least one quick look.

"What was that about?" Dad asked, coming to my side.

"What do you mean?"

"With Rick. What were you two talking about?"

I bit my lower lip. I didn't want to ruin their working relationship, but honestly, the guy gave me the creeps. "He wanted to know if I had a novel for him to read," I said, slowly, trying to figure out how to work into it. "And he suggested I come to where he's staying to show it to him."

My dad looked at me, a frown creasing his features as he realized what I really meant. "He did what?"

"I'm sure it was nothing," I said, knowing it was the exact opposite. "He's always made me uncomfortable ever since I was a kid. I was probably reading too much into it." Though I knew I wasn't. He'd been pretty darned clear.

Dad frowned, gazing toward where Rick had gone. He had a contemplative look on his face, one that was slowly turning to anger.

"Thank you so much for coming!" Rita said, coming our way. She was flush with excitement.

"No problem." Dad plastered on a smile as he turned to her. "I'm glad you had me." He leaned over to me and whispered, "Don't worry about Rick. I'll smooth things over." And then he went to join Rita, leaving me to wonder if I'd done the right thing, or if somehow this was all going to blow up in my face.

3

Needless to say, I didn't sleep all that well that night. I kept thinking about how Rick had touched me, of the things he'd said. I'd never liked the guy before, but never once did I think of him as someone who was interested me in that way. I mean, I knew him from before I was a teenager. I kept hoping I'd taken his words the wrong way, yet no matter how I looked at it, I kept coming to the same conclusion.

When I got up in the morning, I was tired, and not looking forward to going in to work. I wasn't due to open, thankfully, but I'd told Vicki I'd come in bright and early so I could help my dad start to set up for the book signing that weekend. Apparently, there were displays, and the books were going to go on sale before the event so anyone interested in one could buy it ahead of time to speed up the lines.

I dreaded having to see Rick, so imagine my pleasure when I entered Death by Coffee and he wasn't there. Dad was upstairs with Vicki, pointing toward the corner where we kept the couch and chairs for people so they could sit and read. After a brief hesitation, I joined them.

"If we set up there, I'll be out of the way," Dad said as he picked up Trouble, who was winding in and out of his legs. The cat immediately started purring.

"I can always move some shelves," Vicki countered. "Put you right up front and in the middle so no one misses you."

"Then I'd just be in the way of your normal shoppers. The corner is fine. I could do the reading downstairs so you don't have to move any chairs."

"If you say so." Vicki turned to me and hit me with her thousand-watt smile. "Isn't this fantastic?"

I lowered my voice so only Vicki could hear and said, "Wait until I invite your parents to town without your knowledge." I followed it up with a playful wink.

She narrowed her eyes at me, but continued to smile. "Now, that isn't very nice." She motioned toward the corner. "What do you think? Should we set him up there? Or should we move the shelves around and put him front and center. You're the deciding vote."

I eyed the bookshelves. They weren't heavy themselves, but that was a lot of books to relocate. And once the signing was done, we'd have to move them all back again. My back ached just thinking about it.

"I think the corner works fine. You can still see him from the door and it would allow our normal shoppers to still look for what they want."

Vicki tapped her chin with a perfect nail and then nodded. "All right, corner it is. Let me go back and check on the signs. I'll have Lena hang them up around town so people know where to find you." She gave my dad a quick hug. "I'm so glad you decided to do this here."

"I couldn't imagine doing it anywhere else."

Vicki spun on her heel and went to the back, where we normally kept our stock, but which had now become a storage space for everything we needed for Dad's signing.

"I'm sorry about last night," he said as soon as she was gone. "I didn't know Rick would do that." He stroked Trouble, who had his eyes closed, clearly enjoying the attention.

"Actually, I should be the one to apologize."

Dad raised his eyebrows at me. "Oh?"

"Rita can come on strong." And that was putting it mildly. "I should have warned you about her the moment I saw you."

"No, she was fine." Dad smiled. "Actually, it was kind of nice to have someone who seems genuine in her enthusiasm about my books. There were people there who only wanted me to take a look at their manuscripts, but who didn't know much of anything about me other than that I am a writer. Maybe I'm getting conceited in my old age, but I didn't like it."

"At least you sicced them on Rick," I said, not without a little malice.

"Yeah." Dad's face darkened, which hadn't been my intent when I'd mentioned his agent.

I glanced around the room. "Where is he, by the way? I figured he'd want to be here to tell you how to set everything up. He was always a control freak about things like this."

"I don't know," Dad said. "And really, I don't care. You won't have to worry about him anymore."

I started to ask him what he meant, but he waved me off.

"Don't want to talk about it."

"Works for me." The less we talked about Rick, the better, in my opinion. I really hoped he'd decided to fly back to New York. It would make Dad's visit so much more pleasant.

Dad set Trouble down, much to the cat's chagrin, and we spent the next twenty minutes discussing the best way to set up the corner for him. Dad wanted to make it as small and unobtrusive as possible, whereas Vicki insisted on making him as visible as she could. If she could get away with flashing lights and arrows pointing at the top of his head, I'm sure she would have done it.

I was fine with something in the middle. Dad *was* something of a celebrity, albeit a small one. He was no Brad Pitt or even Stephen King, but he was a far stretch more well-known than anyone in Pine Hills. People would want to know where to find him, and honestly, he deserved the attention. He was a good man who'd worked hard for what he'd accomplished. He should enjoy it.

The door opened while we were moving the couch to the back of the room, and Cameron came in, looking harried. His eyes fell on my dad, and he practically ran over a customer to get to us.

"Have you seen Mr. Wiseman?" he asked, panting the words like he'd run all the way there.

"Not since last night," Dad said. I nodded in agreement.

Cameron ran his fingers through his hair. "This can't be good." He looked around the store like he thought Rick might be hiding behind one of the bookshelves.

"What's wrong?" I asked, figuring it was the polite thing to do, though I was hoping Rick was long gone.

"I haven't been able to reach him all day." Cameron made it sound like not talking to Rick was a tragedy. "In fact, I haven't heard from him since I left him last night. He was pretty angry and would barely talk to me. I'm afraid he blames me for everything."

"I wouldn't worry about it too much," Dad said. "If anything, he's angry at me. I'm the one who told everyone to bother him with their novels, and . . ." He trailed off with a frown and shook his head.

"I can't lose this job." Cameron practically whined it. "I always pick him up in the morning and if he didn't need a ride, he would have called me. I waited thirty minutes outside that place where he's staying and he never showed."

"Maybe he slept in," I said.

Cameron gave me a flat look. "He never sleeps in. Mr. Wiseman is a very precise man, which is why I'm so worried. If he blames me for last night, he might find someone to replace me."

"Did you go in and ask for him?" I asked.

"Well, no." Cameron flushed. "He doesn't like it when I pry."

Of course he didn't. Rick had probably spent all night making his precious vanilla latte on his own special machine and had lost track of time. It wouldn't surprise me in the slightest if he were to walk in at any moment, screaming at Cameron for not waiting for another hour for him to decide to mosey on out the door.

"Let me try to call him," Dad offered. "Give me

one moment." He stepped aside, taking his cell out of his pocket.

Cameron started pacing, eyes constantly going to the front door every time it opened, and sometimes when it didn't. I was worried he was going to pace a hole in the floor, so I moved to block his path, putting on my warmest, friendliest smile. I might not like Rick, but Cameron seemed like a decent guy.

"How long have you worked for Ri—uh, Mr. Wiseman?" I already knew the answer from my conversation with Dad yesterday, but it seemed like the polite thing to ask.

"A little over a year," Cameron said. He looked ready to pop now that he wasn't pacing.

"Did you always want to be an assistant to an agent?"

Cameron gave me one of those "seriously?" looks. "I went to college for literary theory. Didn't know what to do with it once I got out, so I figured I might try my hand at agenting the next big novel. I like books and it seemed like a good job. I had to start somewhere, so I thought I'd intern with the Wiseman Agency to learn the ropes."

I caught something in his voice. "It wasn't what you expected?"

"Not exactly." He sighed. "I thought I'd read contracts, help with rights and whatnot. Instead, all he has me do is fetch his coffee and run errands. I get to answer e-mails now and again, but that's about it. I don't think he sees me as anything more than his personal gofer."

"So, why not quit? I'm sure you could intern somewhere else."

Cameron shrugged. "There's no guarantee anyone

else would take me on. I am learning some things from watching him, at least." He frowned. "Though now that this has happened, I'm not so sure I'll have a job anymore." He groaned. "What am I going to do?"

"I'm sure it will work out." I patted him on the arm, and he gave me a strained smile.

I felt bad for Cameron. Working for Rick Wiseman had to be terrible. I could barely stand to be in the same room as the man, let alone having to get him his coffee day in and day out. I would have either quit or killed the man after a few weeks of him bossing me around.

Cameron perked up as Dad returned.

"Any luck?" I asked.

"Didn't answer," he said. He looked down at his phone like it was somehow the reason why Rick wasn't answering his calls. "I tried three times. I even went as far as to call his office phone, figuring he would have it forwarded, but he still didn't answer."

"So, it's not just me." Cameron sounded relieved; then his eyes widened. "What if something happened to him?"

"I'm sure he's fine," I said.

My words didn't soothe Cameron one bit. He snatched up his own phone, dialed, and then slammed it to his ear hard enough that it had to hurt. He walked to the middle of the room to pace between the stacks, chewing on his thumbnail while he listened to the phone ring.

"Maybe I should go over there and make sure nothing happened to him," Dad said, frowning after Cameron.

"I could do it." The offer came out of nowhere.

I wasn't even sure why I'd offered, considering my feelings for the man in question. It just sort of popped out of my mouth.

"You don't need to do that," Dad said. "He's probably just sulking."

"It's no bother. We aren't all that busy, and besides, Vicki and Lena have things under control here." They were both standing downstairs behind the counter, talking. Vicki was holding up flyers, more than likely telling Lena where to hang them up later.

Dad gave me a skeptical look. "After last night, are you sure you should?"

"I'll be fine. He said he was staying at a bed-and-breakfast, right?"

"Yeah," Dad said. "I think it's called Ted and . . ." He frowned.

"Bettfast," I supplied. "I know the owners. If Rick doesn't answer, I can have them check on him for me."

"I don't know . . ." Dad looked worried. "If something's wrong with him, I should be there."

"You have stuff to do here," I reminded him. "I can be there and back in no time. You're probably right and he's just sulking."

Dad sighed. "If you're sure . . ."

"I am."

I so wasn't.

The door opened, and for a moment, I was certain Rick had finally arrived. Instead, Rita's voice floated across the room, sickeningly sweet. "Is he here?" Her eyes fell on where Dad and I stood, and she started our way.

"I'd best get going," I said, not wanting to get trapped in a conversation with her, especially since it would likely involve her drooling all over my dad.

"Be careful, Buttercup." Dad kissed the top of my head like he always used to do when I was little. He sounded genuinely worried about me.

"I will." I headed downstairs, passing Rita by, who didn't even acknowledge me on her way upstairs, and went to the counter. "I'll be back soon," I told Vicki. "I need to check on something."

"Okay." She held out some flyers. "Would you mind hanging some of these up while you're out?"

"Sure." If Rick refused to see me, then I could at least accomplish something useful on my trip.

I grabbed the flyers, went to the back to grab my purse, and then I was on my way.

4

I took my time walking to my car, stopping every now and again to hang up a flyer. Most of the businesses on the block were happy to take one and stick it in their window. Would it help get the word out about Dad's signing? I had no idea. I never paid attention to anything hanging in a window unless it said SALE! in big capital letters.

Once I reached my car, I considered going back and telling Dad to forget it. I really didn't want to check on Rick, but I said I'd do it in a fit of insanity. All I knew for sure was, I wasn't going to go into Rick's room without some backup. If I had to drag Ted Bunford up the stairs with me, I'd do it, just so I wouldn't be alone with Rick.

If it weren't for my worry about how Rick was going to take my showing up at his door, it would have been a pleasant drive to Ted and Bettfast. The sun was out, and the breeze was cool. Maybe once I'd finished working for the day, I'd see if Dad wanted to go for a walk. It would give us a chance to talk without other people—Rita, namely—butting in.

The long, twisty driveway to the bed-and-breakfast appeared, and I took it slowly, marveling at the view. The house itself was a mansion that had fallen on rough times. The current owners, Ted and Bett Bunford, had worked hard to bring the place back to something of its former glory, though its age was really starting to show through again. I didn't know if it was the couple's age or a lack of funds that caused the slowdown in the repairs, but it was a shame. I could only imagine how magnificent the house would be if it were to be fully restored.

As it was, the ivy was taking over, and the surrounding flora wasn't being cared for like it used to. The hedge animals lining the driveway looked especially sad, since they hadn't been trimmed in quite a while.

I parked in the lot next to a battered Prius. There were only a couple of other cars in sight. I didn't know what Rick might be driving, if anything, since he'd flown in. Chances were good he'd had Cameron drive him around, though it seemed odd that Rick's assistant was staying somewhere else, not at the same bed-and-breakfast as his boss. I was guessing they both had rentals, but Rick was forcing Cameron to play taxi because he couldn't be seen driving himself anywhere.

It was no wonder Cameron was staying somewhere else. "I wouldn't want to be near him either," I grumbled, getting out of my car. If Cameron were under the same roof as Rick, I bet he'd never get a lick of sleep, having to wait on the man hand and foot.

As I started for the front door, I noted one of the vehicles in the lot. I recognized the truck as belonging to Justin, one of the employees here. It would help to have someone I knew with me if I had to drag Rick out of his room.

I entered and was immediately met by a tall lanky kid with long hair that covered most of his face. I could only see one eye, and it widened when he saw me.

"Hi, Justin," I said, stopping in front of him. He looked just as miserable as when I'd last seen him, which was his standard appearance. His emotional range seemed to go from nervously depressed to shyly miserable.

"Ms. Hancock." His gaze darted around the room as if he were afraid of being seen with me. "What are you doing here?"

I held up the flyers Vicki had given me. "My dad is holding a book signing at Death by Coffee this weekend and I was wondering if it would be okay to hang some of these up to promote it."

Justin shrugged one shoulder. "You'll have to ask the Bunfords."

"Thanks, I'll do that." I smiled. "So, how have things been at work since . . ." I shrugged. The last time we'd talked, Justin had given me a piece of evidence that helped crack a murder investigation wide open. He has, let's call them, sticky fingers, and while I normally don't condone that sort of behavior, it had helped me out a lot.

"Good." He rubbed at his chin, which was acne-free. Apparently, it had cleared up since our last interaction. "Nothing bad's happened since then. And I've stopped. You know." His gaze darted around the room. "I don't do it no more."

"I'm glad," I said. And I really was. Justin seemed like a good kid. He'd stolen from the guests in order to help support his little sister, which is why I hadn't turned him in. I was hoping he'd stopped because he'd found a better, legal way of earning more money, not that he'd moved on to major crimes, instead.

"It's been tough." He scuffed a sneaker on the floor. "But I'm getting by. I was afraid you'd tell on me."

"Hey, you helped me out. I wouldn't rat on you after that."

His lips moved in a way that I thought was supposed to be a smile, but it was hard to tell. "Cool."

I heaved a sigh. I knew I was procrastinating, but I really didn't want to go up and see Rick. A part of me hoped he'd already left and I would find an empty room. I had a bad feeling I wouldn't be so lucky.

"Hey, Justin, do you know if Rick Wiseman is here? He's my dad's agent and I heard he was staying here. No one has been able to reach him all day, so I thought I'd stop in and check on him."

Justin looked down at his shoes. "I don't know. He doesn't want anyone to clean his room while he's here."

I nodded. That sounded like Rick. "Did he come down for breakfast?"

A single shoulder shrug.

"Have you talked to him at all?" It might have come out a little exasperated. I knew Justin didn't like to get involved with the guests, other than his past thieving ways, but he should at least know whether or not they were still around. He *did* work here.

"Not really." He glanced around again and then lowered his voice. "Mr. Wiseman isn't exactly well liked around here. I heard Mr. and Mrs. Bunford talking earlier. They were thinking of asking him to check out early."

"Really? Why would they do that?"

"He doesn't get along with anyone." Justin chewed on his lower lip a moment before going on. "He sent one of the girls who works here home crying because she said something to him he didn't like."

"What did she say?"

"I don't know. I was cleaning another room at the time. All I know is he called her up to his room, spoke to her for a few minutes, and then she said something that caused him to start yelling. He slammed the door in her face and then called Mr. and Mrs. Bunford to complain."

"Geesh." I shook my head sadly, but wasn't surprised. "Did you have any encounters with him like that?"

"No." He sounded relieved. "Don't think I ever want to. He isn't a nice man."

It sounded like Rick wasn't just mean to his assistant, but was an all-around jerk. It made me wonder if he ever treated anyone with respect.

"Do you think Rick is still in his room?" I asked. "You didn't see him leave or anything, right?"

"As far as I know, he's still there. He usually calls down and has someone bring up something for breakfast, but not today."

I lowered my voice conspiratorially. "Would it be okay if I went up and checked on him?" I asked. "Since he knows me, he won't be angry about the interruption. There are some people worried about him."

Justin shrugged. "I don't care. Just don't let Mr. or Mrs. Bunford catch you. They're upset about all the noise lately and don't want anyone bothering the guests."

"I'll be careful."

Justin told me which room Rick was staying in and then wandered off to sulk elsewhere. The kid was friendly when you could get him to talk, but was always so nervous, it actually made *me* nervous. I hoped that once he got past his depressed, awkward stage, he'd finally break out of his shell a little more. He deserved to find someone nice, despite his slightly checkered past.

I walked slowly up the wooden staircase, listening for the sound of anyone approaching. I doubted Ted or Bett would throw me out if they saw me, but I didn't want to have to explain myself, either. The older couple were friendly enough to me before and might want to talk. While it wouldn't be terrible to catch up, I *was* here for a reason and needed to get back to work soon. I'd have to remember to at least drop off the flyers at the desk on my way out.

I reached Rick's room and hesitated before knocking. I hadn't realized it when Justin had told me, but the room was the same one in which a murder victim had stayed a few months back. That guy hadn't been very nice either, but it still gave me the willies thinking about it. He hadn't died here, but still . . . It was creepy.

The room across the hall had a DO NOT DISTURB sign hanging from the doorknob, so when I knocked on Rick's door, I did so quietly. As I waited, I glanced around, taking in the sights. When I'd last visited Ted and Bettfast, I'd paid little attention to the hallways, focusing instead on the people.

Old paintings hung from the wall, or at least, the

paintings were framed to make them look old. I doubted the Bunfords had spent a lot on them, judging by how the manor had started to fall into disrepair again. The carpet was clean, if not worn from years of guests walking the halls. It was actually pretty peaceful as well. Quiet. You could almost feel the history emanating from the walls. It made me wonder who had owned the building before, if it was someone important or just someone who'd come across a lot of money and decided to build a big house.

And then what had happened? Had the previous owners fallen on hard times? Did they suddenly die and leave no heir to claim it?

I promised myself I'd look into it sometime as I knocked on Rick's door again. I might not be a big history buff, but I did find it interesting how certain places ended up the way they did, and the bed-and-breakfast had certainly piqued my interest.

When Rick didn't answer this time, I knocked harder, thinking he might be asleep and couldn't hear my softer tap. "Rick?" I called. "You in there?"

Still nothing.

With a sigh, and a quick look over my shoulder to make sure no one was watching, I tried the door. Much to my surprise, it clicked open. With one last glance over my shoulder, I pushed it open the rest of the way and stepped inside.

The room hadn't changed much from when I'd last been inside. There was a TV hanging from the wall, currently off. The bed was big enough for two to three people and had a trio of pillows stacked as if Rick had used them for support while he'd sat on the bed to read. Heavy curtains hung over the windows, casting the room in a deep gloom that made it hard to see.

"Rick?" I closed the door behind me and then flipped on the light, wincing at how bright it made everything. "You here?"

A desk sat in front of the windows. Atop it sat Rick's precious latte machine and a stack of what I assumed were manuscript pages. I eyed the latte machine and considered crossing the room and tossing it out the window, but decided it likely wouldn't have the desired effect of forcing Rick to buy his latte from Death by Coffee. He'd probably just buy a new machine, instead.

At first glance, everything seemed in order. It looked like Rick had left at some point and was probably on his way to Death by Coffee even now.

And then I saw the travel mug on the floor.

The mug lay across the room, next to the far side of the bed, near the window. The lid was off, and the dark blue carpet was stained a light brown where it had spilled. For the first time, I noticed the room smelled like vanilla and coffee, and something else, something I couldn't quite place.

"Rick?" My heart started pounding as I took a step toward the fallen mug. Had he had a heart attack? If so, I prayed I wasn't too late to help.

Two more steps, and I could see the floor on the other side of the bed.

Rick was lying on his stomach, hand outstretched toward the travel mug as if he'd tried to catch it and then collapsed. His neck was bent at an awkward angle, face concealed by a blanket that must have fallen from the bed when he'd gone down.

I froze, unsure what to do. I couldn't tell if he was

breathing. "Rick?" It came out as a weak gasp. My hands shook as I knelt and reached for his neck.

My fingers touched cold flesh.

I jerked back, hands flying to my mouth as I tried not to scream. Sure, I wasn't Rick's biggest fan, but I didn't want him dead. Even rude jerks deserved a chance to live a long and fulfilling life, just as long as they did it far away from me.

I tentatively reached out and touched him again, just to make sure, and yep, he was definitely dead.

"Oh no, Dad." He was not going to take the news well.

I don't know why I did it, but I reached out and pulled back the blanket covering his face. Maybe I wanted to double check to make sure he wasn't messing with me somehow, or maybe some deep dark part of me knew what I would find, but when I pulled the blanket away, I recoiled back, nearly falling over onto the spilled coffee as I did.

Rick hadn't died of a heart attack.

Not unless he'd somehow put a pen through his eye when he'd fallen, and I was assuming that was unlikely.

No, this wasn't an accident.

Rick Wiseman had been murdered.

5

This was the first time I'd ever discovered a body, and I could say for a fact, I never wanted to do it again.

The first few minutes went by in a blur. As soon as I was certain Rick was a goner, I called the police. I'm not even sure what I said. I was darn-near hyperventilating, and I'm sure I babbled a little before I hung up and went downstairs to let Ted and Bett know one of their guests was currently lying in a pool of coffee and his own blood. Needless to say, they weren't thrilled about my discovery.

"Every time she comes around, someone dies," I overheard Bett say to her husband as they both headed up the stairs to check on Rick.

I wanted to point out that this wasn't my fault, but doubted they'd listen. Heck, their last guest to die had kicked the bucket in my coffee shop. I'm not sure that would have improved how they thought of me in any way. It might just reinforce the idea that I was responsible for all the deaths in Pine Hills, something I was beginning to wonder about myself. I mean, how many people could die near me before it started to become a fatal pattern doomed to repeat over and over again until I packed my bags and left?

Once they were gone, I was left alone downstairs. Justin was nowhere in sight, though he'd been nearby when I'd told the Bunfords about Rick's untimely demise. Right then, I wanted to vanish just as much as he had, but decided it might be best if I stuck around and waited for the police to arrive. I found the body, so they'd want to talk to me. If I left, I had a feeling things would only get harder for me.

I plopped down in a chair and waited, mind racing. How was I going to tell Dad? What did this mean for his new book? And what about poor Cameron? The guy would probably collapse in shock. He'd been pretty upset when he'd thought he was going to simply be out of a job. Now that Rick was dead, he not only wouldn't have a job, but he was out a reference, and quite possibly, a friend.

Well, maybe a work acquaintance. I'm not sure anyone called Rick a friend.

Sirens filled the air as two police cruisers pulled up out front. I could hear more sirens in the distance, telling me the paramedics were on their way as well. Not that they could do much more than gather Rick up and haul him away.

I sighed and stood. I wasn't sure if I should break down and cry or fly into hysterics. Either was just as likely.

The door opened, and the two police officers I knew the best stepped inside the room. One look at me, and both their faces fell.

"Krissy," Officer Paul Dalton said. John Buchannan stood just behind him, glowering.

"Officer Dalton." I kept my voice neutral. We'd once been close to becoming an item and there was still something of a flame between us, a flame I tried hard to ignore. We were both seeing someone else, though I'd noticed lately he hadn't been seen around town with his latest fling, Shannon, much. I tried hard not to care, but couldn't help it. He was good-looking, and those dimples of his knocked me flat every time he flashed them my way.

Of course, I saw no dimples in my future. Now was definitely not the time for smiling.

"Where is he?" Buchannan asked. He had on his cop face, and as usual, it was trained on me. I was pretty sure he would assume I killed Rick until proved otherwise. I had no idea why he had it out for me so much, but there it was. The guy disliked me, and nothing I did seemed to make much difference.

"Upstairs." I focused on Paul as I gave them the room number. He wrote it down, not meeting my eye.

"Okay, everyone stay here," he said. Ted and Bett had come back downstairs and were both looking suitably distraught. Justin had materialized from somewhere and was standing in a corner, trying to look like part of the scenery. "And that includes you," Paul said, pointing at me.

"Of course," I said, only mildly insulted. I did have a habit of showing up exactly where he didn't want me, so some distrust was understandable.

Both Paul and Buchannan went upstairs to check on the body just as the paramedics arrived. I waited and watched while techs and cops moved up and down the stairs. I was in something of a daze, and just stood there like a dope. A cop I didn't know arrived and took Ted and Bett aside and asked them a few questions. They kept looking over at me like they thought I might go and kill someone else if they didn't keep an eye on me. I was itching to tell someone I had nothing to do with Rick's death, but it wasn't until Paul came back downstairs and took me aside that anyone asked me anything.

"He's dead," he said as we came to a stop in a quiet part of the front room.

"I know that," I said with a little heat. Now that I'd been mostly ignored and had gotten over the initial shock, I was a little peeved that someone hadn't said anything to me before now. "I'm the one who found him."

Paul frowned. "What were you doing in his room? Do you know the victim?"

"His name is Rick Wiseman. He was my dad's literary agent. They're in town to have a book signing and I was told no one could reach him. Since I knew the place, and the owners, I offered to come over and check on him. And well"—I shrugged—"I found him."

Paul tipped back his hat, revealing his sandy brown hair, and scratched at his head. "Was his door unlocked?"

"It was." Which should have been my first clue that not everything was okay, but at the time, it didn't even cross my mind.

"Did you see anyone before you went in to see him?"

"Just Justin." I nodded toward where he was talking to the cop I didn't know, who'd apparently moved on from Ted and Bett. "He met me just inside the door. He works here."

Paul's frown deepened. "When was the last time you saw Mr. Wiseman alive?"

"Last night. He came to the writers' group meeting at the church. We talked after it was over. He left shortly after and I believe his assistant drove him back here, but I can't be sure they didn't stop somewhere else first."

"What is this assistant's name?"

"Cameron." I paused and frowned. "I can't remember his last name." My stomach did a little flip, and the entire world started to wobble. I staggered back a step and found myself leaning against the wall, with no idea how I'd gotten there.

Paul was immediately at my side, hand on my upper arm. "Are you okay?" he asked. His cop voice was gone, replaced by concern. "Do you need to sit down?"

"I think that might be a good idea."

He led me across the room to a chair. I sank down heavily and buried my head in my hands. Apparently, the shock *hadn't* worn off quite yet.

"Did you know him well?" Paul's tone was soft, consoling.

"Kind of, I guess." I sucked in a deep breath and let it out slowly. "He's been my dad's agent since forever. I never really liked him, but I knew him. I hadn't seen him for years until yesterday when he arrived in town for the signing."

"You didn't like him?" Some of the police officer was back in Paul's voice.

"I don't know many people who did," I said. I was too upset to take offense at what might not have been an actual accusation. My stomach had calmed somewhat, but I still felt sick. "He wasn't a very nice man."

"I see." Paul seemed to consider it a moment

before he rested his hand on my knee. "Well, I'm sorry you had to find him."

"It's terrible," I said. "I might not have liked him, but that doesn't mean I wanted him to die." Tears threatened. I couldn't believe I was actually about to cry over Rick Wiseman, but here I was, fighting back snuffles.

"You should take some time to clear your head. Get some rest. I could call one of the paramedics over to check on you if you think it will help. They might be able to give you something to calm your nerves."

I shook my head. "I'll be okay. I just need a few minutes."

"Officer Dalton."

Paul stood and turned to find Buchannan standing at the bottom of the stairs with an older woman fidgeting beside him. "You should hear this."

Paul nodded and then turned back to me. "I'll be right back. Try to relax."

"Thanks." What I really wanted to do was get up, get in my car, and drive home, but I knew it was unlikely I'd be allowed to leave until the police were done talking to me. I also should have called Death by Coffee to let Vicki know I was going to be out longer than I'd planned, yet I couldn't bring myself to pick up the phone. I don't think I could have talked to her about it without breaking down completely, and right then, I was trying my darndest to keep it together.

So, I just sat there and watched as Buchannan introduced Paul to the woman next to him. She seemed excited about the prospect of talking to the police, because the moment Paul looked at her, she was off, gesturing and pointing and talking a million miles a minute.

At first, I was happy. If she saw who killed Rick, then things would get back to normal far more quickly. Paul could chase him or her down, arrest them, and I wouldn't have Buchannan giving me the stink-eye every five minutes.

But then Paul glanced over at me, and my happiness fled. He was frowning as he listened to what the older woman said. Buchannan kept sneaking glances my way too, though he didn't stare outright.

"Who is that?" I asked, not expecting an answer, but Justin had moved to stand near me, possibly because I was one of the few familiar faces in a room full of strange people.

"Iris McDonahue," he said.

The name meant nothing to me. "She staying here?"

Justin nodded. "She usually stays for a week once every two months. She's only been here for a few days now."

"She from out of town?"

He shrugged, looked disinterested. "I suppose."

I wondered vaguely if she was from Cherry Valley since their book club stayed here when they were in town. Thinking of them made me wonder if Albert, Sara, and Vivian were staying, and if they might have seen something. I asked Justin about them.

"No, I don't think they're staying here," he said. "I haven't seen them."

I suppose it shouldn't have surprised me. They'd only come to Pine Hills to see my dad. There was no reason to stick around afterward.

Realizing I wasn't going to get much in the way of

conversation out of Justin, I turned my attention back to watching Iris talk to Paul and Officer Buchannan. The more she talked, and the more the two cops kept looking my way, the worse I felt. Dread pooled in my gut, and I wanted to be sick. Whatever she had to say wasn't going to make me very happy.

Finally, Paul thanked her and made the long walk back to where I sat. He had a look on his face like someone had just told him ghosts were real. He looked pale, worried, and I didn't like it one bit.

"Krissy," he said, voice heavy with concern. He licked his lips and fell silent.

"Paul?" I tried to keep the worry out of my voice, and failed miserably. "What did she say?"

He glanced at Justin, who took the hint and slunk away without having to be told.

"Paul?" My voice rose in pitch, and I just about rose from my seat with it. "What did she tell you?"

"I just need to ask you a few more questions," he said, obviously avoiding my own question. I didn't think it was very fair, since his questions came about because of whatever Iris McDonahue had told him. I thought I deserved to know what she'd said so I knew how best to answer.

But Paul wouldn't relent. I knew him well enough to know that.

"Fine," I said, crossing my arms. If that woman had so much as hinted I had anything to do with Rick's death, I was going to knock her a good one upside the head, even if it meant spending the night in jail.

"You said Mr. Wiseman was at the meeting last night, correct?"

"He was."

"And he came back here afterward?"

"As far as I know, he did. He was anxious to get away. I don't think he enjoyed himself very much."

"But you aren't sure he came back here directly?"

"No, I'm not. You'd have to ask Cameron to be sure."

Paul nodded. I could see the gears working behind his eyes. "You went home after this meeting too, correct?"

"I did." Spoken slowly, warningly. I was waiting for him to ask me if anyone saw me at home to verify my alibi. My elderly neighbor, Eleanor Winthrow, makes it a habit to sit by her window and watch me whenever I come and go. It has gotten me in trouble before, but this time, I was sure it would provide me with an ironclad alibi. I wasn't even sure that woman ever slept, which would only serve to help my cause.

But, apparently, my alibi wasn't necessary.

"Your father," Paul said. "His name is James Hancock, correct?"

"It is." I paused, the dread in my stomach growing. "Why?"

"Was he at the meeting with you last night?"

I nodded slowly. "He was the guest of honor. Rita made a huge deal about it. It felt like half the town showed up."

"Did he leave at the same time as Mr. Wiseman?"

"I don't know when he left. He was talking to Rita when I got in my car to go home. Why?"

Paul didn't answer, of course. "So, you didn't see him leave?" And before I could answer, he asked another question. "Is he staying with you while he's in town?"

"I left before he did," I said as a cold chill seeped

through me. "I think Dad's staying in a hotel, so no, he's not staying with me."

Paul's expression turned grave. "Did you have any contact with him after the meeting? Did he call you, or perhaps stop by last night?"

"He didn't."

"Did he have a problem with Mr. Wiseman? Did they have a falling out or a fight with one another?"

"Not that I know of." My mind immediately shot back to when Dad had seen me standing with Rick outside the church. How much had he seen? I hadn't told him exactly what Rick had said, not all of it, anyway. I knew he got the gist since he'd told me he'd smooth things over. And then that very morning, at Death by Coffee, he'd told me I wouldn't have to worry about Rick anymore . . .

The chill turned into an icy cold that very nearly paralyzed me where I sat. Paul watched me, his expression full of concern.

There was no way Dad could have killed Rick. He would never have gone that far, no matter what they'd said to one another.

"What did she say?" I asked, eyes moving toward where Iris was talking to Buchannan. He was writing everything down.

Paul didn't answer right away, which only served to bring back my anger.

"Paul Dalton, you tell me what she said right now or else I'll . . . I'll . . ." There was nothing I could do but stamp my foot and pout, but I'd do it if he made me.

"She saw what happened last night," he said, keeping his voice low so no one else could hear.

"And what was it she saw, exactly?" I asked.

"There was an argument last night. Mrs. McDonahue claims it was loud enough that it woke her up. She went to her door and listened and said she heard someone shout, 'You're fired,' before there was a thump, followed by what sounded like a scuffle. She peeked out the door just as a man wearing a hat stormed out of the room. She says she recognized him as James Hancock."

I swallowed, tried not to show my fear. "How does she know it was my dad? It could have been anyone."

Paul tried to comfort me with a smile, but I was having none of it and glared at him. He lowered his gaze when he answered. "She knows of him, says she's read all his books. She recognized him from his author photo."

I wanted to argue that those pictures of him were old, and that he never wore a hat, but then I remembered the fedora he'd come out of the meeting wearing, the one obviously given to him by Joel Osborne. There were others wearing them by the end of the night as well, but I hadn't paid attention to exactly who.

"Oh," I said in a small voice. And then I shook my head, my determination taking over. "He didn't do it."

Paul winced, but nodded. "I'm sure he'll be able to explain himself when I talk to him."

I started to rise. "Let me talk to her." I started for Iris. "I'll find out who she really saw."

Paul put a hand on my shoulder to stop me. "I can't have you talking to her."

"And why not?"

All he had to do was look at me, and I knew.

Chances were good that if I talked to Iris, I'd end up yelling at her and scaring her half to death. That wouldn't look good for me, nor my dad. I had to play this smart. We both knew if I started investigating Rick's death, I wouldn't be able to stop. I'd get in the way, and would probably somehow make my dad look worse than he already did.

"Can I at least let him know?" I asked, slumping. "Before you go talk to him, can I please tell Dad about Rick?"

Paul gave me a sad smile. "Of course. I'll give you about five minutes to fill him in. I know I shouldn't, but I trust you won't do something you shouldn't." He gave me a warning look before going on. "I'll follow you over."

"Thank you." Five minutes wasn't much time, but it was more than he owed me.

Paul backed up and let me pass. My legs were shaking, and my stomach was back to doing somersaults, but I refused to let it stop me. I wasn't going to let Dad hear about Rick from anyone else but me.

6

I spent nearly the entire drive back to Death by Coffee trying to decide how to tell my dad that the man he'd worked closely with for at least thirty years was dead. Even if he had just fired him liked Iris claimed, there was a history there. You didn't just turn that off. It was going to hurt, and it was going to be hard.

I decided somber and delicate was the way to go. And it would be far better if it was only the two of us. I didn't need the entire town listening in when I told him the bad news. It would be all over Pine Hills soon enough, I was sure. Rita and her gang of gossips would latch on to the news and have it whispered in every ear within ten minutes.

But I refused to let that happen until Dad knew. This was going to be just as hard on me as it would be on him.

I checked my rearview mirror as I neared Death by Coffee. Both officers, Buchannan and Dalton, were in their respective cruisers, following me. I wasn't sure why they both needed to be present, and honestly, it bothered me that Buchannan had decided to come, but there wasn't a darn thing I could do about it, not unless I wanted to make a scene.

Curious faces lined the sidewalk as I pulled to a stop. The cruiser sirens weren't blaring, but it wasn't every day two patrol cars escorted someone across town. Even though I hadn't done anything wrong, I felt like a criminal when I got out of my car and joined Paul on the sidewalk.

"Five minutes," he said. "And then we'll come in."

I nodded, hating every second of this. Just talking to my dad was going to be more than I could bear. Seeing him talking to the police after learning about Rick's fate was going to be heartbreaking. I didn't know if he'd cry, or if he'd put on a strong face, though I was guessing the latter. No man wanted others to see him cry.

"Krissy," Paul said as I started for the store. I paused, looked back at him, but couldn't find it in myself to say anything. "It'll all work out. I promise."

I gave him a weak smile. *I wish I could believe that.* I turned and silently headed inside.

Dad was upstairs by the pair of tables he'd use for his signing. While I'd been gone, they'd been set up and Dad was working to place stacks of books on top. He was surrounded by quite a few people I'd seen at the meeting last night, including Rita. A few I'd recently met, like Joel Osborne and the Drummands, were there as well. They didn't notice me as I entered the shop and slunk my way to the stairs, dragging my feet like I used to when I was little and was told to go upstairs and brush my teeth.

"Is everything okay?" Vicki came to my side just

as I reached the bottom of the stairs. "That man, Cameron, has been beside himself all day."

I glanced to where she pointed. Cameron was sitting at a corner table, head in his hands. His cell was sitting atop the table, his eyes affixed to it like he thought it might ring at any moment.

Somehow, that made me feel even worse.

"Not really," I said, keeping my voice low. Dad was laughing at something Rita said, and he rested a hand on her shoulder. He didn't move it right away, which only served to make her beam around the room like she'd just been anointed queen. "I . . ." I shook my head. I couldn't tell her. Dad first.

Vicki seemed to understand. She could read me pretty easily, which was what made her such a good friend. Not everyone understood my quirks. "Lena and I will hold down the fort," she said. "Do what you have to do."

"Thanks." I glanced back toward the big plate glass window that looked out onto the street. Paul and Buchannan were leaning against Paul's cruiser, watching me. A few of the customers inside had noticed them and were looking back and forth from me to the two officers, waiting for the excitement to start. Paul glanced at his watch, a gentle reminder I was running out of time.

With a sigh, I headed up the stairs, shoulders hunched. I wanted to crawl into a hole and hide until all of this blew over, yet here I was, right in the middle of it again. My life always seemed to revolve around someone dying, and my having to deal with it. This kind of thing didn't happen to normal people, so why me?

Guilt made me flush. This wasn't about me. A man

had died. It was sometimes hard to remember that just because it always happened around me, it didn't mean I was responsible in any way.

I stopped a good five feet from the small gathering. "Dad," I said, voice coming out small and weak.

Everyone turned my way, and my flush deepened. "Yeah, Buttercup?"

I winced at my pet name becoming public knowledge, but plowed on. I didn't have time to fuss over little things. "I need to talk to you for a few minutes."

He must have detected something in my voice or demeanor, because his face went suddenly serious. "Yeah. Sure. I'll be right back." He patted Rita on the shoulder and then slipped past everyone to join me. I led him to the far corner of the stacks, where no one could hear us, dreading every step. How was I going to do this without breaking down myself?

"What is it, Buttercup?" he asked, thankfully keeping his voice low.

I knew I should have led with the bad news, but I needed to make sure he couldn't possibly have had anything to do with Rick's death first. I didn't believe for one second he murdered his agent, but accidents did happen.

"Where did you go last night after the meeting?" I asked, heart pounding in my ears.

"I went back to my hotel room." He paused, frowned. "Why?"

I breathed a sigh of relief. "The police think you went to Ted and Bettfast, the bed-and-breakfast where Rick was staying. I knew you didn't have a reason to go there."

His frown deepened. "Well, I did stop by there later last night. I called Rick once I got to my room, wanting to talk to him about what happened in the parking lot. He was pretty upset about what I'd done, saying the local authors were harassing him. He wouldn't listen to a thing I said, so I went over to confront him about what he said to you in person."

I groaned. "So, you did go there last night?"

"I did." His gaze moved past me, to the front of the store, where Paul's head, including his police hat, were just visible. "Why are the police involved? Did something happen last night?"

I swallowed back an urge to scream at him to run. "It's Rick, Dad." I licked my lips with a tongue that had gone sandpaper dry. "Someone killed him."

"Mr. Wiseman's dead?"

I jumped about three feet straight up in the air at the sound of Cameron's voice. He must have come upstairs to see what I'd learned. He was leaning against a bookshelf, face gone deathly pale as he stared at me.

"Who died?" This from Rita, who must have heard Cameron's exclamation.

"I think he said the agent died," Joel said, sounding stunned.

I grabbed Dad's arm and walked him a few paces away. He looked just as pale as Cameron, but was doing his best to hide his shock. "Someone says they saw you there last night, that you were arguing with Rick before he died."

"Are you sure?" he asked.

"That someone saw you? That's what she said."

"No." He shook his head, brow crinkling. "That Rick's dead."

I nodded. "Found him myself." I shuddered. "The

police are here to talk to you, but they let me come in and break the news first."

He looked past me again, and then straightened. "Then I best not keep them waiting."

"Dad!" But he walked right past me and went down the stairs and out the door without a backward glance.

I felt like passing out, which would have probably been a blessing. If I could sleep through the next few days, it would save me a lot of heartache and stress, I was sure.

"What am I going to do?" Cameron said, sounding much like I felt. He was looking at me as if I might hold all the answers.

"I don't know," I told him. I didn't even know what *I* was going to do.

Death by Coffee was now buzzing with the news of Rick's death. Rita was already on her phone, more than likely calling her gossip buddies, Georgina McCully and Andi Caldwell. The entire town would know of Rick Wiseman's demise within minutes, and I was pretty sure no one would think it an accident.

I drifted past Cameron, who didn't look like he'd be able to stand on his own anytime soon, and headed for the front windows so I could watch Dad's visit with the police. Vicki started my way, but I waved her off. I needed to be alone. I was hoping that Dad would set the police straight and would come back inside and tell me everything was okay, that they'd figured out who'd killed his agent, and that he wasn't a suspect.

Of course, when was the last time something happened just like I wanted?

Buchannan was standing stiff beside Paul, who looked concerned. He kept sneaking glances my way, which only made me feel that much more nervous. Dad's back was to me, so I couldn't read his lips to know what he was saying. He made a gesture toward Paul's car, and then both cops looked straight at me. Neither looked happy.

"Come on, Dad." I shifted from foot to foot, antsy to know what was going on. I wanted nothing more than to rush outside and listen in, but knew I'd be told to go back inside, so I stayed put.

Dad said something else, which brought both cops' eyes back to him. Paul rested a hand on his shoulder, said something, and then turned to his cruiser.

Buchannan opened the back door.

It felt like someone had poured ice water down my spine. I stood frozen, watching as they helped my dad into the back of Paul's police cruiser. Buchannan closed the door, lifted his hat to run his fingers through his hair, and then he walked slowly back to his own cruiser, shaking his head. Paul turned toward the front of his car, and that's when my paralysis finally broke.

I shot for the door, screaming Paul's name as I did. Nearly everyone in Death by Coffee was on their feet, watching in fascination as the visiting author was arrested and his daughter flipped her lid. It wouldn't surprise me to learn half of them had their cell phones out and were recording. I didn't care. I wasn't going to let them take my dad to jail.

"Paul Dalton! How dare you!" I shouted, flying out of the store.

He paused halfway into his car, sighed, and then stepped back out. "Krissy . . ."

"Don't 'Krissy' me!" I couldn't stop shouting. My blood was boiling now, and there'd be no cooling it.

"How dare you take my dad to jail? He didn't do anything wrong! Both you and I know it."

"He's coming willingly," Paul said, trying his best to sound diplomatic, but I was beyond listening.

"Let him out of your car right now or I'll . . . I'll . . . Well, I don't know what I'll do, but you can darn well imagine that it won't be pleasant."

Paul raised a hand, and I noticed Buchannan had started our way, a stern look on his face. He was likely thinking back to when I'd rushed him months ago and punched him on the shoulder a few times. I don't think he ever quite forgave me for that, though I hadn't hurt anything but my pride. I'm not sure *I* forgave myself for acting like such a fool.

"Krissy," Paul said, forcing me to look him in the eye. "We aren't arresting him."

"Then why is he in your car?"

"Because he wants to give a statement and said he wanted to do it at the station."

I frowned. "Why would he want to do that?"

Paul's shoulders eased slightly now that it didn't appear as if I was going to rip his ears off. I, on the other hand, was still undecided.

"It was his choice," he said. "He suggested it. He admits that he was at the bed-and-breakfast last night, in the victim's room. He wants to make sure we get his statement down correctly, without all of this." He gestured toward Death by Coffee and the crowd of onlookers. More than one nose was pressed against the glass.

"Oh," I said in a small voice, before straightening my back. "Then I want to come, too."

Paul shook his head. "Stay here. Let us do our job.

You'll help your dad out far more by staying put and out of trouble than if you insist on getting involved."

There was something in his voice that told me he was thinking about more than my just coming down to the station. Maybe I did have a habit of sticking my nose where it didn't belong, but this was my dad! I couldn't just let it go.

"I don't know what to do with myself," I said, very near pleading. "He's my dad. And I . . . I just can't . . ." Tears threatened, and I silently cursed them with every ounce of my being. "I can't do nothing."

Paul put his hand on my shoulder, leaned in close; much closer than was strictly socially acceptable. Our foreheads very nearly touched. "I'll make sure nothing happens to your dad, okay? He's going to give us his statement and I'll drive him right back here, safe and sound. Don't stress yourself out over this. We'll get to the bottom of this, and your dad's statement can only help."

"But . . ." I'd seen the shows, read the books. How many times did someone tell the police something, only to have it twisted back on them?

But what could I do? As much as I didn't like it, Paul was right. I couldn't help anything by coming along. I'd just get in the way. And if Dad told them the honest truth, then there would be no way they could suspect him of any wrongdoing. He never would have killed Rick.

I simply had to be patient and let the police do their jobs.

Unfortunately, patience wasn't my strong suit.

Paul leaned forward and kissed me on the forehead before straightening. He cleared his throat and looked around at all the watching faces. A flush ran through him as he spun on his heel and hurriedly got into his car. Buchannan watched me a moment longer, as if checking to make sure I didn't throw myself on the hood of Paul's car, and then got into his own cruiser.

I looked into the backseat of the car, suddenly aware my dad had witnessed the entire thing. He smiled at me and waved. I waved back, but couldn't bring myself to smile.

And then both cruisers pulled away, taking my dad with them.

7

Waiting for someone I love to come back from being interrogated by the police wasn't something I ever wanted to do again. Sure, it wasn't an actual interrogation; he'd gone in of his own volition. But it didn't make me feel any better. My dad was still sitting in the police station, answering questions about a murder I was sure he didn't commit.

Everyone in Death by Coffee was looking at me like they thought I knew more than I'd let on. At least they weren't bombarding me with questions, though Rita had tried to pry information out of me between her calls. Everyone else was a bit hesitant about me after my near meltdown outside.

"How long does giving a statement take?" I asked, not expecting an answer, but getting one, anyway.

"I'm sure he's just making sure they get everything right so there are no mistakes later." Vicki stood beside me, behind the counter.

I grunted in frustration. It had been over an hour already. My nerves were fried, my focus on anything but my job. I'd already made five mistakes on simple orders, burned a batch of chocolate-chip cookies, and knocked over an entire pot of coffee. Thankfully, I hadn't dropped it on the floor, so nothing broke. Vicki took over from there, leaving Lena to handle the bookstore duties, and giving me the freedom to worry my little heart out.

I was both grateful and ashamed they were doing this for me. There was a lot going on in my life right now, I'll admit, but that was no excuse for me screwing up so badly. This was our business, and I should be doing my part, not standing around, moping.

"He should be back by now," I said, straightening from where I leaned on the counter, a firm resolution washing over me. "I'm going to go down to the police station to make sure they aren't holding him on some trumped-up charge." Apparently, doing my part was going to have to wait.

"Krissy," Vicki warned. "Don't go mucking things up because you can't be patient. These things take time."

"But what if they arrested him?"

"Did they say they were arresting him?"

"Well, no."

"Wasn't he going in willingly, of his own free will, to give a statement?"

"Well, yeah."

"They aren't going to arrest him unless he confesses to something or they have proof he did something wrong." Vicki held up a hand when my eyes widened in panic. "I don't believe for a second he would do that. Nor do I think the police have anything on him. If they did, someone would have called you by now. Stop worrying. You're going to chew your fingernails right off if you keep it up."

I jerked my hand away from my mouth. "I hate this."

"We all do," she said with a warm smile. "You need to relax. It will work out."

"Easy for you to say," I muttered, burying my chin in my hands as I leaned on the counter again. "It's not your dad at the police station."

Vicki gave me a sour look. "That's not fair. We're all practically family."

I sighed. "I know. I'm sorry. I know you're trying to help."

She squeezed my shoulder. "Don't be. This isn't easy for any of us, and I know how hard it has to be on you. Just try to look at the bright side."

"And what's that?"

She shrugged. "I don't know. But I'm sure there has to be something."

We both stopped talking and looked up as Cameron approached the counter. The poor man hadn't sat down since learning about his boss's demise. And when anyone tried to talk to him, he'd shake his head and wander off, muttering to himself. He looked better than he had an hour ago, but he still looked like he'd just lost everything he cared about.

"How you holding up?" I asked him, pushing aside my own worries. Vicki was right; I needed to try to find the bright side in all of this. Or at least realize that there were other people affected by Rick's death just as much as me, if not more so.

"Not all that well," he said. "Can I get a coffee? Something with a lot of caffeine?"

"Sure," Vicki said. "I'll make something for you that'll knock you right off your feet."

He gave her a strained smile. "Thanks." He looked

at his phone as if he thought Rick would suddenly call him and tell him this was all some elaborate joke designed to see how he'd handle the stressful situation.

Of course, I knew firsthand that wasn't going to happen.

"What are you going to do now?" I asked, genuinely curious. He was only in Pine Hills because of Rick. Now that the agent was gone, Cameron had no reason to stay.

"I don't know," he said. "I feel like I should be doing something." He frowned at the door. "Like, should I go and identify the body or something? Pick up his things?"

"I think he's already been identified." I mean, I was the one who'd found the body, and there was no mistaking it for anyone other than Rick Wiseman. "And I imagine they'll call someone when it's time to get his stuff." I paused and frowned. "Was Rick married?"

Cameron shook his head. "He wasn't exactly the marrying type." He laughed, though it came out sounding off somehow, like it had very nearly popped out a sob, instead. "Rick went out with women a lot, but it was never serious. He liked his freedom, I guess. He wanted to be with women, but not with *a* woman, if that makes sense?"

"Yeah, it does." A vague part of me wondered if Rick chose the bachelor lifestyle by choice, or if his personality was what kept him single. It was a shameful thing to think since he was dead, but I couldn't help it. "So, there was no serious girlfriend or anything? Someone who'd want to know about his death?"

"Not that I was aware of. I don't think he ever went out with anyone more than twice."

So, chances were good we weren't looking for a vengeful ex or a jealous girlfriend. I suppose someone could be angry with him for ditching her after only one or two dates, but why come all the way to Pine Hills to seek vengeance? It didn't make much sense.

"I'm sure his family will take his things, then," I said.

Cameron shrugged. "I guess. Though I don't think he was on good terms with any of them. I never heard him talk about anyone, anyway. No photographs of his parents or a sister or nephews on his desk." He frowned. "Come to think of it, I didn't know much about his personal life, even though I'd worked closely with him this last year."

"Well, you were only his assistant, right? Why would you know?"

He gave me a wan smile just as Vicki returned.

"Free of charge," she said. "I'm sorry for your loss."

"Thank you." Cameron picked up his coffee and took a sip. His eyes widened, and when he swallowed, he practically gasped. "Wow. That's good."

"Thanks!" Vicki beamed at him. "I'm glad you like it."

He took another sip. "I definitely needed this." He turned and walked off, taking quick sips of his coffee like he was afraid to swallow too much at once.

"What did you make him?" I asked.

"Secret recipe." She winked at me. "It was something I came up with back when I was in college and had to pull all-nighters studying. I don't think I would have made it through, otherwise." She tapped her chin. "I wonder if we should consider adding it to the menu." Her gaze drifted as she considered it.

I left her to it as the door opened and the one man I wanted to see—other than my dad, of course—entered.

"Krissy, are you okay?"

I came around the counter and fell into Will's arms. He looked especially good today, dressed for work. He was a doctor, and a sexy one at that. He had that creamer-rich coffee skin tone that made me want to lap him right up. I swear it felt like I was on one of those medical dramas where all of the doctors were drop-dead gorgeous and I was the not-quite-so-pretty girlfriend. I'm not sure how I ever got so lucky.

"As good as I can be under the circumstances," I said, stepping back. "What are you doing here? Don't you have to work?"

"I heard about what happened and wanted to make sure you're okay." He looked me up and down as if he thought discovering dead bodies could cause physical harm.

"I'm fine," I said. "I only found him." An involuntary shudder worked through me.

"That can't be easy. You knew the guy, right?"

"He was my dad's agent. I didn't really like him all that much." I wasn't sure why I added the last. It wasn't something you wanted to admit when the man in question was murdered, yet it kept popping out of my mouth, anyway.

"Still, it had to be hard." Will pulled me close and gave me the world's best hug. "I came as soon as I heard. It's all over town."

"You didn't have to come." Though I loved that he did. Will Foster was everything I could ever want, yet my stupid brain kept waffling between him and Paul Dalton. I knew what I *should* do, but for some reason, I couldn't seem to bring myself to take the plunge. Maybe I was afraid it would turn out that the perfect man didn't exist and if I were to give myself fully to him, he'd just vanish in a puff of smoke.

"I did," he said. "How's your dad handling it?" He glanced around the room, searching for the man in question.

"He's not here," I said, some of my melancholy coming back. "The police took him in for questioning."

Will's eyes narrowed. "Was it that Dalton guy? Do they think he did it?"

I shook my head, then started to nod, before finally shrugging. "I don't know what they think. Some woman said she saw my dad leave Rick's room last night, but I know that can't be true. Dad never would have hurt him." I paused, his first question finally registering. "And yes, Paul was the one who came to get him."

Will was silent for a really long time before he said, "I'm sure it will work out."

"Everyone keeps telling me that." I sighed. "Dad went in voluntarily to give his statement. I know I shouldn't worry, but I can't help it. He's my dad."

Will squeezed and then released me. "I completely understand. It's hard not to worry when someone you care about might be in trouble." He gave me a pointed look I chose to ignore.

"Exactly!"

"Excuse me, dear."

I turned to find Rita leaning forward, phone still in hand, with most of the other writers standing behind her. She was flush with excitement, which only served to anger me. I mean, a man was dead, and here she was, gossiping about it like he'd done it just to make her life more exciting.

"What do you want, Rita?" I tried hard to keep the exasperation out of my voice, but failed.

She didn't seem to notice, or care. "Well, I was just wondering if you know whether or not Mr. Hancock will still be holding his signing this weekend. There are some people who don't want to make the drive if he isn't." She held up the phone, as if those people were waiting on the other end of the line. Knowing her, they probably were.

I really tried to rein in my temper, but with everything that had happened, I just couldn't keep a handle on it, and I snapped.

"I don't know. Maybe you should ask the police about that. I know, maybe I can drive you down there right now and you can ask them yourself. Walk right in on an interrogation, perhaps? Because a book signing is *so* much more important than a man's death."

Rita jerked back from me as if she thought I might bite. "Well, I never!"

I started to say more, but Will pulled me back. "Krissy has had a very stressful day," he said. "She could use a little time alone."

Rita glared at me a moment longer before sniffing as if I were beneath her. "Well, I guess I'll have to talk to the man himself." Her eyes lit up, and she turned to the crowd of writers. "Maybe he'll pass on our novels to his next agent!"

"I . . ." Red dots flashed before my eyes. I was seconds away from exploding, and we're not talking just mentally or verbally. It felt like someone had put a volcano in my head and all my worry and stress was about to send it into a full-scale eruption. I knew I was overreacting, but I couldn't help myself. It was all just too much.

"I could look at them."

All eyes turned to the small man standing nearby. "I could look at your novels for you."

"You don't have to do that, Cameron," I said. He'd had just as hard of a day as I had, maybe more so since his job was as dead as, well, as Rick.

"No." He smiled. "I want to. I started working for Mr. Wiseman so I could eventually become a literary agent. Nothing says that just because he's gone, I have to give it up. In fact, it might be time for me to take that next step." He took a deep breath and held out a hand. "If you would leave your manuscripts with me, I'll happily take a look at them."

Rita, Joel, and the rest of the small gathering leapt upon him like a pack of ravenous lions. His heart was in the right place, but I had no doubt Cameron was going to regret his offer before the day was out.

"I should get back to work," Will said, now that the attention was off me. "You should go home and get some rest. You've had a stressful day."

"I'll be fine," I said, though I knew I wasn't. I'd snapped at Rita, and while I don't think I was wrong, I never should have said anything. Or, at least, been so mean about it. "I want to wait for my dad."

"No, he's right." Vicki came up to stand beside me. "I called Jeff in early. He'll be here soon. Go home and try to get some rest. You look as if you need it."

"But . . ." The protest died on my lips. I really didn't want to be there. Working and worrying didn't go well together. Dad would let me know when he was back, and then we could talk about why it took so long.

Until then, some R & R would do me some good—as would a tub of Rocky Road.

"Okay," I said, relenting without putting up much of a fight. "Thank you both."

"I can drive you home if you'd like," Will offered.

"That's okay. You go ahead and get back to work. I'll be fine." I smiled in the hopes of reassuring him.

He looked skeptical, but nodded. He leaned in and kissed me on the forehead, right where Paul Dalton had done the same a little over an hour before. "I'll talk to you later." And then, with a wave to Vicki, he was gone.

"Are you sure about this?" I asked her as I gathered up my things. "I could stick around until Jeff gets here. I don't want to leave you shorthanded."

"I'm sure." She practically pushed me toward the door. "Go home. Get your head on straight. I'll see you in a couple of days."

A part of me hated leaving, but leave I did. I got into my car, started it up, and then hesitated. Free from work, nothing was stopping me from going down to the police station to demand someone tell me why they had kept my dad so long.

Well, nothing but Paul's plea and everyone's advice. Maybe for once, I should listen.

"You're doing the right thing, Krissy," I told myself out loud, needing to hear it as much as say it. "Like everyone says, it'll all work out in the end."

And like a good girl, I listened to the reasonable part of my brain, and I headed straight for home.

8

"What am I going to do?"

Misfit stared at me from his perch on the island counter. He held my pen between his paws and regarded me a long moment before he leaned forward and resumed chewing on the cap. An open puzzle book lay next to him, though I hadn't been able to work on it. I was too distracted for anything but the simplest of tasks, and even that was stretching it.

Dad had yet to call even though the minutes kept ticking by. I couldn't imagine what was taking so long. Unless he saw the killer, there was very little he needed to tell the police. I doubted that was the case since he would have told me if he'd seen someone else there last night.

Wouldn't he have?

"I should go down there." I nodded to myself, but didn't make a move for the door. I paced back and forth in the kitchen, instead. Dad would have warned me about wearing a hole in the floor if he were here, though it was a habit I'd picked up from him. Anytime he was stuck on one of his novels, he'd pace in his office, sometimes for hours on end. And here I was, doing the exact same thing.

Misfit managed to work the cap from the pen. It dropped to the floor and bounced beneath my chair. Before he could stab himself in the roof of the mouth with the pen, I snatched it up, as well as the cap so he wouldn't decide to snack on it later. After recapping the pen, I shoved it into my purse and moved it out of reach of his prying paws. He glared at me before rising, taking two steps, and plopping down on my open book.

"Go ahead," I told him. "I can't work on it, anyway."

He closed his eyes and put his head down for a nap.

I sighed and rubbed at my temples. I was beside myself, and I knew of no way to make things better. Puzzles were my way of working through problems, of relaxing and getting my head on straight, yet I'd taken one look at the crossword and knew I wouldn't be able to do it. My brain was stuck on one track, and until I was certain my dad was safe and out of jail, it wouldn't unstick.

A knock at the door caused my heart to leap into my throat. "Dad?" I gasped, rushing over to the door. I hadn't heard a car, but I'd also been pretty distracted with my own worrying thoughts. I threw open the door and was about to launch myself into a hug, when I realized it wasn't my dad standing out there.

"Jules?" I blinked at him, startled. The little Asian man was holding his white Maltese, Maestro, under one arm. He was dressed for home in a white polo and khakis. When at work, Jules Phan was known to dress far more extravagantly. "What are you doing here?"

"I hope you don't mind me stopping by," he said. Maestro gave a little bark and tried to worm his way out from under Jules's arm to get to me. I rubbed him behind the ears, which only seemed to agitate him more. He was panting nonstop, eyes eager for freedom.

"No, it's no problem," I said. "I thought you'd be at work."

"I closed a little early today," he said. "Maestro had to pay a visit to the vet, didn't you, boy?"

The dog barked an affirmative.

"I hope he's okay."

"Just a checkup." Jules hugged the dog close to his chest. "Everything's fine."

"Good." I stepped back. "Do you want to come inside?"

"I'd better not. Maestro is excitable today. He always gets this way after a trip to the vet. Unlike most animals, he seems to actually enjoy it."

I couldn't say the same for Misfit. I had to dress in thick, padded clothing, and wear gloves, just to get him into his cat carrier. And then once we were there, he'd often refuse to come out, swiping at anyone who attempted to touch him.

"I'm sure he'll be fine," I said. "Please, come in."

Jules bowed his head in thanks and then stepped inside. He took a quick look around before following me into the living room. I was a little self-conscious about the state of my house, knowing how clean and orderly Jules kept his own place. He didn't seem to mind my mess, however. Or at least he was kind enough not to say anything.

Maestro was nothing but churning feet and a panting tongue by now. Jules was struggling to keep hold of his little dog, and in a way, it was cute.

"You can put him down," I said with a smile.

"I don't know." Jules was looking at Misfit, who was now standing on the island counter, hackles raised, but he hadn't hissed or made a sound as of yet. "I don't want him to mess with your cat."

"Don't worry about him," I said. "Misfit will stay up there as long as the dog is in the house. And if he feels the need to escape, he knows how to get around without touching the floor."

"Are you sure?"

"Positive."

Jules looked reluctant, but he lowered Maestro to the floor. As soon as his feet touched, the dog was off, rushing straight for the counter, barking up a storm. Misfit stood there, looking down at the invader, but made no move to attack or run. I think he was kind of curious about the strange animal, but he'd never admit that to me.

"I heard about what happened," Jules said, watching the Maltese. "It's absolutely terrible that horrible things keep happening to you. Are you holding up okay? I heard you found the body."

I sighed. "I'm fine." I had an inkling I knew where he'd heard about Rick's death. Rita and her gossip crew were probably working overtime on this one. "My dad's at the police station, giving a statement, so I'm a little frazzled at the moment."

Jules's eyes widened. "They don't think he did it, do they?"

"I don't know." No sense in lying. "A witness places him at the bed-and-breakfast near the time of Rick's death. I know he didn't do it, and I'm pretty sure Paul Dalton does as well, but I wouldn't put anything past Officer Buchannan." I refrained from calling him an unkind name, since he hadn't actually done anything to me yet this month.

A faint smile lit the corners of Jules's mouth. "Still having problems with the good officer?"

I shrugged. "I guess. He's been nicer to me lately, though that's not saying much. Ever since Halloween and . . ." I trailed off, not wanting to relive the last murder investigation I'd found myself right in the middle of. At least that time, the police had asked for my help, though Buchannan wasn't thrilled by my participation. In the end, I think he actually appreciated what I'd done to put the killer behind bars.

"That was a terrible business as well," Jules said.

"I think Buchannan's coming around and is starting to realize I'm not the bad guy. He hasn't come over for dinner or anything, but at least he doesn't come running at me with handcuffs at the ready every time something illegal happens."

"That's good. I've always felt he was too critical of you," Jules said, taking my hand and giving a squeeze before dropping it. "You're a good person."

"Thank you." I felt myself blush. "Where's Lance, by the way?" I asked, redirecting. "I haven't seen him in a few days." Lance Darby was Jules's live-in boyfriend. Or husband. I wasn't actually sure whether or not they'd ever tied the knot, and had never asked. Either way, they were perfect together.

"He's out of town on one of his trips," Jules said,

sounding a little sad. "He's not due back for another week."

"That has to be hard."

"It is sometimes. The house feels so empty when he's not around." His eyes strayed to where Maestro had given up barking and was now sitting down, staring up at Misfit, who stared right back. I think they were starting to like one another.

"You know, you could always stop by here if you ever feel lonely." I paused, realizing how that might get misconstrued, so I added, "Just for company. We could talk."

"I wouldn't want to intrude." Jules looked embarrassed, like he didn't want anyone to think he might actually get lonely sometimes. "I'm just being melodramatic. Time apart is nice. I can sit back and read or catch up on a few shows Lance doesn't especially care for. And it does make the time we have together that much more special." His eyes twinkled at that.

I gave a little wistful sigh. What I wouldn't give to have someone like that, a partner who could make my every day that much brighter. I guess it's true what they say about absence making the heart grow fonder. It was definitely working with Will, who I didn't get to see nearly as much as I'd like.

"Well, don't hesitate to stop by if you need to talk," I said. "I don't have many guests visiting, so I'd welcome the company." The last visitor I'd had was Vicki. She'd stopped by so we could binge watch *Making a Murderer* on Netflix, and that had been over two months ago.

"I'll keep that in mind." Jules took my hand again. "And if you start to feel overwhelmed about any of this, our door is always open."

"Thank you." I could hear the sincerity in his voice, and it made me want to cry. What did I do to deserve such a good neighbor and friend?

"I should get back to the house," he said, giving my hand one last squeeze. "Maestro is being good for the moment, but I can see the calculation in the tilt of his head." He clapped his hands together, causing the little dog's head to whip around. "You're thinking of jumping up there, aren't you?"

Maestro's tail wagged in what I assumed was a big fat "yes."

"Thanks for stopping by," I said as Jules gathered his dog. "I appreciate the concern."

"I do hope it all works out. You deserve some peace for once."

"Tell me about it," I muttered, but then plastered on a big smile. "Come in to Death by Coffee sometime. Tell whoever is working that I said it is on the house."

"You don't have to do that." But I could tell he was pleased.

"I'm happy to," I said. "You've made me feel a lot better."

And he had. It wasn't really anything he'd said or done, other than the fact he was willing to take the time to come over and make sure I was doing okay. That meant a lot to me. Ever since I'd moved in next door to him, Jules had been nothing but nice to me, and I hoped I could adequately repay him someday.

We said our good-byes, as did Maestro, who was barking his own farewell to Misfit, who was watching the display with trepidation. I walked Jules outside and waved as he cut across the yard to his own home. I waited until he entered his house before turning to go back inside. A curtain swished in the house on the other side of me, and I knew Eleanor Winthrow had been watching us.

"Great," I muttered. Rumors that I was sleeping with my gay neighbor would be all over town soon enough. I had half a mind to go over there to set her straight, but knew it wouldn't make much difference. She seemed to think that my life was a string of one lover after another, and nothing I could do or say would change her mind about it. The last time I'd tried to go over and talk to her, I'd ended up in jail, so it was probably better if I stayed in my own yard.

I went back inside and closed the door. Misfit was still sitting on the island counter, glaring at me, tail swishing back and forth so hard, he'd knocked my puzzle book to the edge. A few more angry swishes, and it would hit the floor.

"He didn't hurt you," I said. "In fact, I think he only wanted to play." I crossed the room and snatched up the puzzle book and dropped it into a drawer. "You could try to make friends, you know?"

Misfit's eyes narrowed before he jumped off the counter and started for the hall.

"I'm sure you'd like him if you gave him a chance!" I called after the annoyed feline.

All I got in return was a tail swish before he was gone, off to my bedroom, where he'd likely spend the next hour pouting before coming back out for dinner. No matter how mad at me he might be, as soon as it was time to eat, all would be forgiven.

Now that Jules was gone and Misfit was ignoring me, I felt alone. I looked at the clock, my trouble growing. Dad should have been back by now. And while he was under no obligation to call me or stop by to let me know he was okay, it was common courtesy to do so. He wouldn't leave me hanging like this.

But I wasn't going to go down to the police station, no matter how much I wanted to. If I got word they'd arrested him, then I'd make the trip to raise holy hell. But not before. I was going to be a good girl this time.

I swear I heard someone snicker on my left shoulder, because right about then, a new idea started to form in my head.

The police station was out. I couldn't go to Death by Coffee because Vicki would just send me home. And there was no way I could continue sitting around the house, doing nothing. I'd go insane.

But nothing said I couldn't go back to Ted and Bettfast and talk to the witness, right? The police had already talked to her and had taken her official statement, so it wouldn't be such a big deal if I showed up and asked her a few questions. Once I heard Iris McDonahue's story straight from her lips, I'd be able to figure out why she thought my dad could have killed Rick when I knew for a fact he hadn't. She had to have heard or seen something else, and I was determined to figure out what that might be.

Before I could truly think about what I was going to do and talk myself out of it, I grabbed my purse and keys, called good-bye to Misfit, and was on my way.

9

There were fewer cars in the Ted and Bettfast parking lot than when I was last there. No cruisers remained, either. After the excitement from earlier, the silence sat heavily in my ears. A part of me expected to show up to find half the town gathering to get a look at the murder scene, but instead, it looked like everyone had abandoned the place. Justin's truck was still there, at least, and I wondered if the police had taken Rick's car in, which would account for one of the missing vehicles.

I shut off the engine and sat back. Even though the sun still lounged in the sky, albeit on its descent, a gloom hung over the bed-and-breakfast, one I knew they would have a hard time dispelling. I knew what it was like to have someone die in your place of business. It wasn't pleasant, and it always left its mark.

I got out of my car and hesitated before closing the door. Getting involved in murders was usually how I ended up getting myself into trouble. How much easier would my life be if I'd simply stay home instead of poking my nose in other people's business?

Of course, my nose poking was precisely why a handful of cold-blooded killers were now behind bars.

And this was my dad. There was no way I was going to leave him hanging. I didn't trust Buchannan to do the right thing, especially since there was a witness. If anyone deserved my special brand of investigative genius, it was James Hancock, the man who not only raised me, but whose writing and life influenced most of my decisions, good or bad.

With head held high, and a mind full of questions, I marched straight for the front door, determined to get to the bottom of Rick's murder.

Justin was sitting just inside the door, looking dejected. He glanced up when I entered, gave me a limp wave, and then went back to contemplating his sneakers. He looked like he wanted to be anywhere but here, and it was no wonder; a murderer was on the loose, and there was no telling when he or she might come back.

I looked past Justin to where Ted and Bett Bunford were standing by the stairs, talking. They hadn't noticed me yet. Worry lined each of their faces, and they both looked at least a dozen years older. Ted's hair was quickly graying, something I hadn't noticed before, and Bett's black dye job had faded to steel gray. I wondered if their rapid aging had anything to do with the two men who'd stayed with them and were subsequently murdered. It would be hard not to blame yourself, even if you had nothing to do with it.

Bett's hands were worrying at one another. She said something to her husband that had him shaking his head. He paused midshake, eyes landing on me.

Bett turned to follow his gaze and immediately started scowling.

"Hi!" I said in a vain attempt to exude friendliness. I doubted either one of them wanted to see me right then, especially after my grisly discovery. "I'm Krissy Hancock. Do you remember me?"

"How could we forget," Bett said. "Every time you come around, someone ends up dead."

"Now, dear," Ted said, his voice much softer and kinder than his wife's. "She only shows up after the fact."

Not exactly a clanging endorsement, but I'd take what I could get.

"I knew the victim," I told them, playing the sympathy card. "He was my dad's literary agent." I pointed to where I'd left the flyers earlier. They were still sitting on the desk.

Bett's eyes narrowed. "You're the one who found him."

It was a statement, but I answered, anyway. "I did."

"What were you doing in his room, hmm?" Bett glared at me, her implication clear. "We don't condone that sort of behavior here, you know."

I suppressed a shudder. I didn't want to think about Rick that way when he was alive, let alone now. "No one had heard from him, so I stopped by to make sure he was okay. We didn't . . . do anything."

"Mm-hmm." She glanced at her husband and rolled her eyes.

"We're sorry for your loss," Ted said. At least one of them was pretending to be nice, though with the way he said it, I got the distinct impression he wanted me to leave.

It made me feel bad. The Bunfords didn't deserve

this. There were quite a few people who wouldn't want to spend the night in a room where someone had died. And since another murder victim had once stayed in the very same room, people might start to think it was cursed. It would be hard to attract customers when people started to believe that staying the night here was a death sentence.

But darn it, it wasn't my fault!

"I had nothing to do with his death," I said, planting a hand on my hip. "Neither did my dad, no matter what anyone says." I glanced up the stairs as if I thought Iris might be standing there, watching. "This is a tragedy and I'd like to find out who is responsible, just as much as you would."

Bett looked abashed as she scowled at her hands, while her husband looked embarrassed.

"It's hard," he said, rubbing at his Burt Reynolds–style mustache. "They've got the room taped off and guests are canceling reservations."

"It's unfair," Bett put in.

"Did either of you see anyone go in or out last night?" I asked. "Someone who might have killed Rick?"

Both Bunfords shook their heads, though it was Bett who spoke. "Mr. Wiseman knew, as do all of the guests, that the doors are locked at ten sharp. They aren't to have unpaying visitors anytime afterward. I'm not sure how someone got in that late."

"We were asleep," Ted said.

"What about an employee?" I asked. "Could one of them have seen someone? Let them in, perhaps?"

"This isn't a hotel." Bett sounded offended, though it hadn't been my intent to insinuate anything. "We don't have anyone on desk duty or anything like that."

"Our employees are here to help us make the stay pleasant for our guests," Ted said, taking over. "We used to handle it ourselves, but we can no longer manage it like we once did." He sighed, as if thinking about the old days.

"Does anyone work nights?" I asked.

"Yes."

"Who was working last night? Maybe they saw something that might help."

The Bunfords looked at one another, and for a second, I thought they might withhold the information. They were under no obligation to tell me anything, yet I could see the look of concern in their eyes. They wanted this case solved quickly so they could move on with their lives. They might not approve of me, but they knew what I could do.

"Kari Collins," Ted said after a moment. "She's our night lady. She cleans up downstairs and makes sure the doors get locked every night."

"Will she be in soon?" I asked, hoping to talk to her.

"Not tonight. We decided it might be best to take care of things ourselves for a few days. There is quite a mess to clean up." I don't think he was referring solely to the room.

I filed Kari's name away for later. "Do you think she would have let anyone in to see Mr. Wiseman after closing time?" I asked.

"I doubt it," Bett said. "She is a stickler for doing things right. She can be . . ." She glanced at her husband.

"Unpleasant."

"But she works hard."

"This has never happened before," Ted said. "I don't believe for one second Kari would have let anyone inside without informing us first. It was a busy night, so perhaps someone stuck around who wasn't supposed to be here."

I could have continued to grill them about last night, but there was no point. Neither had seen anything, and it was clear their night lady hadn't told them anything. I would just have to talk to Kari Collins on my own when I got the chance.

But for now, there was someone who *was* here I wanted to see.

"Is Iris McDonahue still here?" I asked.

"Why?" Bett's face contorted in suspicion.

"I'd like to ask her about what she saw last night. She claims she saw the murderer."

"She did," Ted said. "And she gave her statement to the police."

"I just want to hear her side of the story from her own lips," I said, smiling brightly. "I'm not going to accuse her of anything or upset her."

Bett sighed. "She's here, though I don't think she will be for long."

"She's leaving?"

"She says she can't take the stress," Ted said. "She comes here to relax and this tragedy is about as far from relaxing as you can get."

"I could talk to her for you," I said. "See if I can get her to stay."

Ted and Bett glanced at one another before he answered. "I suppose it couldn't hurt. If you can talk her into staying, it would help us out a lot."

I thanked both the Bunfords and then headed up the stairs. The door to Rick's room was closed, yellow police tape strung across it in a big X. I stopped and stared at it, thinking back to all the other times I'd been stuck in the middle of a police investigation. It was becoming a habit, one I was starting to think I might need to kick before it got me killed.

The door opened behind me, and I turned to find Iris coming out of her room, a pair of heavy-looking suitcases in hand. She jumped when she saw me standing there, and then scowled at me like I'd done it on purpose.

"Excuse me," I said before she could walk away. "My name is Krissy Hancock. Is it all right if I talk to you for a moment?"

Iris took a step back from me and looked me up and down. "You're that author's girl, aren't you?"

"I'm his daughter," I said, not sure if that's what she'd meant, or if she thought I was Dad's girlfriend.

"What do you want with me?" she asked. "I already talked to the police."

"I know," I said. "I'm hoping to help them find Rick's killer." I jerked a thumb toward the taped-up room.

Iris snorted in a very unladylike way. "Uh-huh." Sarcasm dripped from her words. "You're just looking to interfere."

My hackles rose, though I did a good job of not rising to the bait. "I just want to help." I glanced at her suitcases. "Are you sure you should be leaving? The police might want to talk to you again."

"They might," Iris said. "And if they do, they can find me at a nearby hotel where I feel safe. I'm not staying here."

She moved as if to push past me, but I stood steadfastly in her way.

"You said you saw my dad, James Hancock, leaving

Rick's room last night," I said. "How can you be sure it was him?"

"I know." She scanned me again. "Just like I could take one look at you and know you was his offspring. I read his books and saw his picture and I never forget a face."

"Was it dark in the hall?" I asked.

"The light was off, sure, but they have those night-lights down there." She pointed to a small light plugged into the outlet. "So guests don't trip over their own feet when they have to take a leak."

"What exactly happened last night?"

Iris clenched her fists on the handles of her suit-cases. "I don't have to tell you anything."

"No, you don't," I admitted. "But it will help me understand what happened. I knew Rick. And you said you saw my dad. It's kind of personal."

Iris huffed, but relented. "I was in bed when I heard an argument. These walls aren't nearly as thick as they look." She thumped one as if to prove her point. "The shouts got louder until I heard someone scream, 'You're fired!' I peeked out the door just as the author came storming out of the room, looking guilty as hell."

"Did he see you?"

"How stupid do you think I am?" Iris asked. "I closed my door right quick and locked it. He'd just killed one man. What was to stop him from killing me?"

"Are you sure he killed him?" I asked. "Did you see a body?"

"I didn't, but I know what I did see, and the look on your father's face was one of a killer. He tried to hide it with that hat, but I could see it."

"Have you ever met my dad before?" I asked.

"Well, no," Iris admitted. "Before last night, I'd only seen his picture on the backs of the books I've read."

"Do you have the books here with you?"

"I don't."

"So, how can you be sure it was my dad and not someone who looks like him?" I didn't even bring up the fact that those book jacket photos were older and didn't truly represent what my dad looked like. They'd all been staged with him dressed like a detective.

Iris narrowed her eyes at me. "Are you questioning my integrity?"

"No," I said. "I'm questioning whether or not you actually saw my dad, or if perhaps you might have been mistaken."

"I wasn't."

She sounded sincere. Dad had said he'd come to the bed-and-breakfast last night, so it was entirely possible she *had* seen him. But to say he'd killed Rick for certain was simply not true. By her own admission, she didn't see the body. Rick could have been sitting there, stewing in his room, making the vanilla latte that ended up spilled on the carpet, when the killer had snuck in.

"Did you see anyone else that night?" I asked.

"There were lots of people in and out. They made a hell of a racket, but it quieted down eventually." Iris snorted. "No respect for those of us trying to sleep."

"Did you see anyone else enter or leave Mr. Wiseman's room? Did you hear anything after my dad left?"

"Of course not," she said. "The man was already dead."

"Did you stay up long after he was gone?" I was getting annoyed by her certainty that my dad did it, and was struggling to keep from yelling at her.

Iris laughed. "I wasn't about to waste my night sitting by the door. I went to bed and fell asleep almost immediately."

Which meant she might have missed it if something else had happened.

"Now, if you'll excuse me, I'm leaving." Iris pushed forward, forcing me back a step.

"You should stay," I said. "The killer isn't going to come back."

She snorted and continued on down the hall. "Right. I'm not taking the chance." She started down the stairs, suitcases clumping heavily on each step.

I watched her go with a frown. I wasn't entirely buying her story. She might have seen my dad, but she hadn't seen him kill Rick. Nor had she seen a body. She admitted it was loud before the fight, but hadn't said whether or not anyone else had threatened the surly agent. And since she went to bed after it quieted down, she very well could have missed Rick's murder. It didn't look like he'd struggled enough to make much noise. Other than the coffee, nothing had been knocked over.

But who would have had a reason to kill him?

And why?

I turned, eyes falling on the X blocking the door to Rick's room. Any evidence of who might have been there the night of his death could very well be behind that door. The police had already looked around, but they might have missed something important. I was alone, with no one watching me, with nowhere else to be, so no one would miss me. What harm could a few minutes of poking around really do?

I glanced toward the stairs. Iris was gone. Ted and Bett were nowhere in sight. They were probably dealing with their fleeing guest, so they might not think to come looking for me.

With a quick prayer that I wouldn't get caught, I started for the door.

10

The door to Rick's room was unlocked, which I guessed meant the police were completely done with investigating the space. The police tape was likely still there to preserve the scene, though since I didn't know exact procedure, this was pure conjecture. For all I knew, they were monitoring the room, just in case the killer decided to come back.

The thought gave me pause, but only for an instant. If they were watching the place, I was already busted, so I might as well take a look before they arrested me. I slipped through the tape and into the room. I managed it without having to touch much of anything, and I mentally reminded myself to be careful about what I did touch. If the police *weren't* done and the door had been unlocked due to an oversight, I didn't want them finding my fingerprints all over the place.

The room looked pretty much the same, other than Rick's body being gone. Although I'll admit, I didn't look around too hard the first time I was there. I peeked on the far side of the bed and was relieved to see there was no body outline like you'd see in the movies—just the coffee stain and a darker stain near the bed that I didn't want to think about.

"Who would have wanted to hurt you, Rick?" A quick rush of sympathy washed through me as I looked at those stains. I mean, the guy wasn't the friendliest man around. In fact, he was a downright self-centered jerk who thought everyone should bow down to him and give him everything he demanded, simply because he'd represented an author who'd done pretty well for himself. His ego had to have been the size of Texas. Still, that was no reason for someone to want to kill him.

I tore my gaze away from the stains, and instead focused on the latte machine. It might have been the last thing he'd touched before he'd died. The machine was one of the expensive brands, rivaling what we had at Death by Coffee, but in no way would it make a superior coffee to what I made. Had he been preoccupied with making his latte, so that when the killer came in, he hadn't heard him? These machines didn't make *that* much noise, but I supposed it was possible.

Or had he known the killer? I didn't see another mug anywhere, though I doubted Rick would have offered anyone else a drink. Maybe he'd been standing here, drink in hand, when the killer came in.

Worry made my stomach clench. Rick would have let Dad in without too much complaint. The only other person in town who wouldn't have been thrown out on his ear was Cameron. I'd much rather think the killer had snuck in and done the deed than to think it had anything to do with Dad's writing life.

Glancing toward the door to make sure no one was

coming, I moved to the end table by the bed and
opened the single drawer there. A ratty Bible and a
capless pen lay inside. I picked up the Bible and
flipped through it to make sure nothing had been
hidden inside, before returning it to the drawer.
Turning, I started for the closet, but my foot collided
with something hidden just beneath the bed.

I screamed as I tripped, falling hard on the floor.
Thankfully, I was on the other side of the bed and
hadn't fallen where Rick had died. If that had been
the case, I probably would have passed out from the
horror of it, and someone would have found me
sprawled across his bloodstain. Not a pretty thought.

Still, I might not have tripped in the exact spot
where he'd been murdered, but it was close enough.
Heart thumping, I scuttled away from the bed, half
afraid I'd find an arm sticking out from beneath it.

Instead, the corner of what looked to be a stack of
papers poked out from beneath the comforter, which
hung nearly to the floor.

"What have we here?" I muttered, crawling over
to the pages. I carefully lifted the comforter, just in
case there *was* someone hiding beneath the bed—or
worse, another dead body—and peered into the
gloom.

There wasn't just one stack of pages, but many,
bound by rubber bands or large clips. It didn't
take a genius to figure out I was looking at novel
manuscripts—at least seven at first glance. I assumed
these were novels Rick had brought with him from
home to review while he waited for Dad's signing to
be finished, but when I glanced at the desk where I'd
seen the manuscripts before, they were gone.

"Huh." It was possible the police had taken the

manuscripts, but if that was the case, how did they miss these? The stacks were haphazard, as if shoved quickly beneath the bed. One of the manuscripts lay unbound, pages scattered and bent.

This wasn't Rick's style. He was a perfectionist, always needing everything to be in its place. There's no way he would have left such an untidy stack. It was highly unlikely he'd shoved them under the bed, not unless he was trying to hide something.

Nervously, I pulled the manuscripts out one by one, checking the top page for names. Joel Osborne. Rita Jablonski. Albert Elmore. All names I knew either from town or from the last writers' group meeting. I couldn't find the cover page for the one scattered all over the place, but the header atop the pages listed the author as Drummand, so it was safe to assume it was Theresa or Barrett's great American novel.

Sifting through the manuscripts, I did find one name I didn't recognize: Tony A. Marshall.

My eyes strayed to the desk again. Were these the same manuscripts that had been sitting beside the latte machine earlier? I hadn't looked for names there at the time, so it was possible. But why move them? Had the police done it? Someone else? It couldn't have been the killer because I'd seen them sitting on the desk after he was gone—not unless he'd come back.

Or perhaps I was making too much of it. Why would anyone kill over a stack of unpublished—and likely unpublishable—novels?

I considered trying to pack up all of the manuscripts to take them with me, but there had to be well over three thousand pages there, not exactly something I could sneak out without notice. I doubted I could even pick them up at the same time, let alone lug them down the stairs.

Instead, I grabbed one of the single sheets, as well as the pen from the nightstand. I scrawled all of the names on the back of the manuscript page. After a moment's hesitation, I went ahead and added the titles next to each name, just in case there was a plagiarism conspiracy that somehow led to Rick's death. Unlikely, yeah, but you never knew in this town. Once that was done, I dropped the pen back into the drawer and shoved the rest of the pages back beneath the bed.

Satisfied no one would realize I'd been poking around, I folded my page, which contained only the header of "Drummand—122" and the words "to the death!" and shoved it into my purse. From there, I made a quick check of the dresser and closet, finding nothing of interest, before heading out of the room. I closed the door behind me, checked to make sure the police tape looked secure, and then headed downstairs.

Iris was gone, having fled to a hotel where no one had died, leaving only the Bunfords and Justin inside the bed-and-breakfast. I headed straight for Ted and Bett, mind still on what I'd found in Rick's room. While I didn't want to tell them I'd been snooping around, I did have concerns about the door being unlocked and the manuscript pages beneath the bed. If I was lucky, they would go in and check and then contact the police without my having to admit anything.

"I saw the room upstairs was taped off," I said as I approached.

Bett glanced at me and sighed, clearly not happy

I'd come back to bother her. "The police don't want anyone inside." She narrowed her eyes at me as if she suspected I'd done just that, which, of course, I had.

"I wouldn't do such a thing!" I said, placing one hand on my heart, and the other behind my back so she couldn't see me cross my fingers. "But I think someone else did."

Both Ted and Bett looked startled.

"What do you mean?" Ted asked.

Time for a lie, something I was becoming alarmingly good at. "After I finished talking with Mrs. McDonahue, I noticed the door across the hall was open a crack and the tape was loose in one corner, like someone had pulled it free and then replaced it."

"The room was locked!" Bett said with a firm shake of her head. "No one could have gotten in."

Interesting. It sure hadn't been locked when I'd tried the door. "Well, I was worried when I saw it. No one was inside the room, and being the concerned citizen I am, I fixed the tape and closed the door." I forced myself to look suitably concerned. "But I'm pretty sure someone had been inside snooping around. Did the police come back sometime recently?"

Ted shook his head. "Once they left, the only people I've seen are here right now."

"Other than Iris," Bett muttered, obviously bitter about her guest's flight.

"Neither of us have gone inside the room," Ted went on. "And I can assure you no one else has either." His eyes flickered toward where Justin was slouched against the wall. He glanced at us, reddened, and looked away. "You must have been mistaken."

"I can only tell you what I saw," I said solemnly. "You can check the door if you'd like. It's still un-locked."

Bett immediately stormed for the stairs. Ted frowned at me a moment before following after. As soon as they were gone, I turned and made a beeline for Justin.

"Spill it." I could tell he had something to say. He was nervous by nature, but he became even more so when he knew something.

"I didn't go in there," he said. "I've been down here ever since the body was discovered."

"But someone else did, didn't they?"

He looked down at his feet, hair falling into his face, hiding his eyes. "I'm not sure."

"What do you mean, you're 'not sure'?"

A very loud, very blunt curse came from upstairs. Bett wasn't very happy about her unlocked door.

Justin cleared his throat, eyeing the stairs like he thought he would get into trouble if they came down-stairs and saw him talking to me. Knowing how the Bunfords felt about me lately, I wouldn't be surprised to learn he was right.

"Come on, Justin," I said, putting on my "we're best friends" voice. "You can tell me."

"I'm not sure I saw anyone," he said. "So much was going on, it could have easily been my imagination."

I could tell he didn't believe that any more than I did. "What did you see? And when was it? Before the police got here?"

He shook his head. "After. The Bunfords weren't out here. They were in the office, trying to convince Mrs. McDonahue to stay. I went out back for some fresh air, you know? It was crazy in here and well"—he shrugged a bony shoulder—"when I came back in, I thought I saw someone come down the stairs and hurry out the front door."

"Are you sure?" I asked, mind racing. It would almost have to have been the killer, wouldn't it? Who else would sneak into a place where a murder had just taken place?

Other than me, of course.

"I don't know. It was bright outside and when I came in, I had those dark spots you get when you look into the sun too long."

"Could you at least tell me if it was a man or a woman?"

Another shrug. "A man, I think. It's hard to tell. All I know for sure is he was pretty big."

"Big as in tall?"

"Big as in big." He held his hands out from his stomach by a good foot and a half.

The only fat man I knew that might have had any contact with Rick was Harland, though my dad wasn't on the light side these days, either. As scrawny as Justin was, anyone would look fat by comparison, so I could be looking for someone of average size.

"When was this?" I asked. If it happened while I was with my dad, then there was no way he could have been the one to sneak in and out of Rick's room, leaving Harland as my only suspect.

"An hour ago, maybe?"

My heart sank all the way to my toes. I hadn't heard from Dad for hours now. He'd gone to the police station to give his statement, sure, but it seemed like an awfully long time had passed, more than enough to give a statement and leave.

He wouldn't have come here. I refused to believe it. It had to have been someone else. Harland was a big man, though why he'd kill Rick, I had no idea.

"The door was unlocked," I said. "Could someone who works here have gone in?"

Another shrug. "I don't know. I doubt it. When I'd gone outside, I'd left my keys on the counter. They were there when I got back, but I'm pretty sure they'd been moved."

I thanked Justin and wandered out the front door in something of a daze. I needed to call Paul and find out how long they'd kept my dad. Maybe he was still there. For the first time, I hoped they were holding him for some reason. If he had come to Ted and Bett-fast after giving his statement, I'm sure he would have had a good reason, but would the police accept it if they found out? Maybe he'd simply come to apologize to Ted and Bett about the argument last night.

But that wouldn't explain why he would have gone upstairs, into Rick's room, and shoved those manuscripts under the bed. I couldn't imagine why *anyone* would do something like that.

I got into my car, stomach twisted in knots. I knew deep in my heart that Dad had nothing to do with Rick's murder, but that knowledge wouldn't keep him out of jail if Buchannan were to catch wind of what Justin had told me. He'd twist it around until he could pin everything on Dad, just to spite me. He might not treat me as badly as he used to, but Buchannan and I weren't exactly best buddies, either.

I dreaded it, but I picked up my phone and prepared to call Paul. If anyone could tell me where my dad was right now, it was him.

Just as I unlocked my screen, the phone vibrated

to life, causing me to scream and nearly drop it onto the floor. I checked the ID and saw the call was coming from Death by Coffee. *Maybe Dad just got in and is calling to let me know everything went okay.*

I swiped across the screen and answered. "Dad?"

"Hey, it's Lena." She sounded strangely out of breath.

Great, what else has gone wrong? "Is everything okay?" I asked, voice hitching on the word. Right then, I wouldn't have been surprised to learn the shop was on fire.

"I don't know." There was a slight pause where I noted loud voices in the background, though I couldn't tell what they were saying. "Your dad's here."

I breathed a sigh of relief. "Is he doing okay?"

"I'm not sure." I didn't like the sound of that. "I think you'd better get down here," Lena said. "Something's happening, and I'm pretty sure you're not going to like it."

11

Tires screeched as I slammed to a stop in front of Death by Coffee. I fully expected to see smoke rolling from the front door or possibly a riot taking place inside, glass strewn across the sidewalk, bodies lying in pools of blood. My mind has a tendency to go to the worst places when I don't know what to expect, so I very nearly broke down and cried when I saw nothing wrong with the place. There were no cop cars or ambulances nearby. People strolled up and down the street like nothing was happening at all.

I sucked in a deep breath. I should have demanded Lena tell me what she'd meant when she'd called, but after my trip to Ted and Bettfast, I wasn't thinking straight. She'd hung up, and I'd raced here, thinking my entire life was going up in smoke.

I took a moment to park properly, not half in the road like I had been, and then got out of my car, heart still pounding. Nothing might appear out of place from the outside, but that didn't mean something horrible wasn't going on *inside*.

I sprinted the short distance to the door and threw

it open, eyes immediately scouring the store. No fire. No bodies. No overturned table or hostage situations. Lena was standing behind the counter, serving a guest, so whatever she'd wanted me here for wasn't bad enough she felt she had to monitor it.

Rita's voice broke through then. I tracked the sound of it to find her upstairs, just barely in view. She was standing next to Dad. A crowd was huddled around them, listening to whatever she had to say. From my place by the door, I couldn't quite make it out.

Slowly, almost fearfully, I made my way across the store, up the short flight of stairs, and stood at the back of the small crowd to listen.

"We cannot let it stand!" Rita proclaimed, stomping a foot and wagging a finger. "A man has been murdered. The police here in Pine Hills don't know who did it."

A grumbling rippled through the crowd. A man beside me said, "They're imbeciles." It appeared the town had about as much faith in the local police department as I did. Though, to be fair, I'd been told numerous times they'd never had to deal with murders in Pine Hills, not until I arrived, so I supposed they could be forgiven for not being the best when it came to murder investigations.

"I think it is time some of us take matters into our own hands," Rita went on. "We now have an expert in our midst. He can solve this case and put Pine Hills on the map!"

Dad looked embarrassed as he smiled. The crowd nodded, and a few started clapping.

A sinking feeling started in my stomach. No wonder Lena had called me in and sounded so worried. Rita was going to drag my dad into this, and I knew it would somehow end in disaster. I had to put a stop to it long before that happened.

I pushed through the crowd as Rita started to speak again. She saw me and immediately latched on to Dad's arm, like she feared I might grab him and drag him away from her. I had to admit, it wasn't such a bad idea.

"Dad," I said, cutting her off. "Why didn't you call me? When did they let you go?"

Rita huffed, but didn't argue when Dad turned to me.

"Hey, Buttercup." He sounded almost relieved. "Officer Dalton dropped me off just a little while ago. I was going to call, but kind of got swept up in the moment."

Rita beamed. "I've had a brilliant idea!" she said.

The small crowd was watching us. I gave them a good glare until they started to disperse, then turned back to Dad.

"I was worried," I said. "When you didn't call, I thought they'd arrested you!"

"I'm fine." Dad pulled from Rita's grip to give me a quick hug. "I appreciate the concern, but there was no reason to worry. I had nothing to do with Rick's death, and I'm pretty sure they know that."

"Still . . ." I took a deep breath and stepped back. "I didn't know what to think. I sat around the house, worrying, and then when Lena called, I was afraid something had happened to you."

"I wouldn't have let anything happen to him," Rita said. "In fact, I believe James here can solve Mr. Wiseman's murder in no time! It's what I was telling everyone else when you showed up. It's not often we have a brilliant mind working local crimes."

"Hey!" I said, mildly offended.

Rita flapped a hand at me. "I don't mean just you. I'm talking about the Pine Hills Police Department! They leave a lot to be desired when it comes to brainpower, if you know what I mean?" She winked at Dad.

Okay, so I might have thought the local police were a little slow on the draw sometimes, but they *had* come to my rescue more than once when I'd gotten in over my head. And just because I tended to get involved in their murder cases didn't mean they wouldn't have figured out the correct culprit on their own eventually. I just sped things along, usually by getting myself attacked by the murderer.

"Dad's not working on the case," I said, crossing my arms. "None of us are going to get involved." I pointedly ignored the nagging voice in the back of my mind reminding me about my recent visit to Ted and Bettfast.

"Nonsense," Rita said. "You've done an adequate job making Pine Hills a safer place, but we have a professional here now. We can't let this opportunity pass."

I ground my teeth together. "He's not a professional," I said. "He's an author."

"Same thing," Rita said, rolling her eyes.

"While I'm flattered that you think I could be of help, my daughter is right." Dad rested a hand on Rita's shoulder. She practically melted at his touch. "I've never worked an actual murder investigation before and I'm afraid I'd only get in the way if I tried."

"Pah!" Another patented Rita hand wave. "Your

books speak of your intelligence and capabilities. You know what you're doing." Her eyes lit up. "Maybe you could both work together! Father and daughter, solving crimes in our little town!" She clapped her hands together. "You could solve the murder, and we could pitch it to someone in Hollywood. It would make a great movie." Her eyes glazed over as she thought about it. Chances were good she was picturing herself in a starring role.

"We're not going to get involved," I said, and right then, I was pretty sure I meant it. Normally, I'd have been all over the case, poking into everyone's business like it was my own.

But my dad was here. I couldn't put him at risk by sticking my nose where it didn't belong. And there was no way I was going to let him wander around town, acting the part of an amateur sleuth, all because Rita thought he was some sort of brilliant detective. He'd only get himself hurt, much like I did every time I started snooping around.

"I could be your sidekick," Rita said, clearly not listening to a word I was saying. "I could ask the hard questions of people in town and bring you whatever I found out." She rubbed her hands together in a way that made her look more like an evil mastermind than a detective on the side of good.

Dad looked amused as we watched Rita plot what would inevitably be our downfall. She was lost in her own world, and nothing I said would drag her back to reality. I glanced back behind the counter to where Vicki stood, watching us, smiling in a way that told me she knew exactly what was going on. I had no idea how long Rita had been babbling about solving the case, before I'd gotten there.

"Can I have a moment alone with my dad?" I asked, cutting Rita off, midfantasy.

She looked startled, like she'd forgotten we were even there. "I suppose so."

"Thanks." I grabbed him by the arm and all but dragged him across the room and in between a pair of shelves, where Trouble was sprawled out on the floor, head resting on a book that had fallen. It was likely he'd pawed it down on his own. Normally, I would have taken the book, but he looked so peaceful, I let him lie.

"You can't be seriously considering this," I said in a harsh whisper as we came to a stop.

"No, not seriously," Dad said. "But it's nice to be appreciated. She's rather nice, isn't she?" He glanced back to where Rita was still standing, talking to herself.

"What happened at the police station that took so long?" I asked, changing the subject in the hopes he'd forget all about Rita and her mad schemes.

"Not much. I gave my statement, answered a few questions, and that was it. The police were pretty friendly overall. I signed a few autographs on my way out."

Of course he had. "You didn't go back to Ted and Bettfast afterward, did you?"

He shook his head. "No. Officer Dalton drove me directly here from the station. I haven't left since. Why?"

A knot in my chest eased. "Well, I might have stopped there after I went home." When my dad started to frown, I added, "I only went to check on a friend who works there." I wondered how many white lies it took before they turned black.

"Did you see someone who looked like me?" he asked.

"No, but Justin—the worker I was telling you about—said he saw a fat man leave the bed-and-breakfast a few hours ago. The door upstairs was unlocked and it looked like things had been moved around."

"A fat man?" Dad sounded wounded as he touched his gut.

"I don't mean you're fat!" I said. "Justin said he didn't get a good look, and I was worried that perhaps . . ." I trailed off, unsure how to fix my gaff.

Dad smiled. "It's all right, I know what you mean. I've put on a few pounds these last few years, haven't I?" He chuckled and patted his belly.

I flushed. "It's not that bad."

"Did you go into Rick's room?" Dad asked, face going somber. "You weren't investigating, were you?"

"Not really," I lied. I was really going to have to stop doing that. "I sort of noticed the door and peeked inside out of curiosity. I found something . . . strange." I reached into my purse and removed the folded manuscript page. I handed it to him.

Dad scanned the names. "What is this?" he asked, handing the page back.

"A list of manuscripts I found beneath Rick's bed. They looked as if they'd been tossed there, as if whoever put them there had been in a hurry."

"Why would someone hide a bunch of manuscripts?"

"I don't know," I said. "I asked myself the same question. I *do* know that when I found Rick, there were manuscripts on the desk. They aren't there now."

"Maybe the police took them."

"That's what I thought," I said. "But how did they miss these other ones?" I tapped the paper before shoving it back into my purse. "I think someone moved them for some reason. Bett Bunford swears the door to Rick's room was locked, but when I checked, it most certainly was not. Someone went in there after the murder and I think they hid the manuscripts under the bed after the police left."

"But why, I wonder?" Dad got a faraway look in his eye, and I immediately regretted telling him anything. I didn't want him involved, and here I was, giving him fuel for an investigation.

"I'll let the police know what I found," I said. "We can let them handle it. Neither of us needs to get involved." It pained me to say it, but I felt I had to. I mean, I'd had a hand in every murder investigation since I arrived in Pine Hills, yet here was one far closer to me than the others and I was thinking of keeping out of it, all because of my dad.

He smiled and nodded. "I know, Buttercup. I was just fantasizing a bit about playing the part of the hero. I've written so many of them, it would be nice to be one for a change."

"You are a hero to me." Even as it came out of my mouth, I realized how cheesy it sounded.

Dad only laughed. "Thank you." He sighed. "I guess my part is done. I gave my statement and that's all I need to do." A look of sadness passed over him. "Rick and I might have had our differences as of late, but he didn't deserve this. I should be focusing on whether or not to continue with the signing, or if I should call it off in his name."

"Don't let Rita talk you into doing something you

don't want to do," I said, not just meaning about the signing.

He smiled. "I won't, Buttercup. I promise."

He started to walk away, but I stopped him as a new thought came to mind. "Hey, Dad, why don't you get your things and stay with me instead of that hotel?" I wasn't even sure why he hadn't asked me before.

"I don't want to intrude," he said.

"You wouldn't be," I said. "It would be nice having you around, kind of like old times."

He smiled wistfully. "I guess it would be nice." He still didn't sound convinced, so I pressed.

"Besides, we don't know if Rick was the killer's real target, or if he or she was after something else, like your unpublished novel." Rita's name flashed through my mind, but I quickly dismissed it. She might be obsessed with Dad, but not so much that she would kill just to read his novel early. "I'd feel better having you close."

Dad sighed and nodded. "I suppose you're right. It's better to circle the wagons and all that." He put an arm around me and hugged me, shoulder to shoulder. "And this way, we'll be able to keep an eye on each other and make sure we both stay out of trouble."

"Yeah, great." I forced a smile. Maybe this wasn't such a good idea, after all. I mean, I didn't want Dad investigating Rick's murder, and I might have said I wouldn't get involved either, but that didn't mean I wouldn't end up in the middle of it somehow. I had a tendency to find myself exactly where I didn't belong, and I didn't want to drag Dad along with me.

But it was too late now. I'd just have to try harder.

"Let me get my things from the hotel," he said. "I'll be over afterward."

"Sounds good."

"See you in an hour or two, then." He kissed the top of my head and left. Rita was still standing where we left her, muttering to herself. I had a feeling she wasn't going to be easy to dissuade, and I, for one, didn't feel like trying—at least not yet.

I stood in the stacks a moment longer, wondering if I was doing the right thing. I looked to Trouble for help, but he was still off in dreamland. He'd probably stay that way until Vicki came to gather him up for the night, which was going to be soon.

"What am I getting myself into?" I asked the snoozing cat. A whisker twitch was all the response I got.

With a quick wave good-bye to Vicki and Lena, I put Death by Coffee behind me and headed for home.

12

I snatched a pair of dirty socks off the floor and tossed them into the clothes hamper. My house wasn't a total disaster, but it could use a real cleaning, something I'd been meaning to do for the last week or three. Okay, the last month or more. I ran the vacuum and did the laundry regularly, but simple stuff like dusting and picking up old discarded newspapers and the like wasn't a high priority since I lived alone and rarely had guests.

Now that my dad was coming to stay with me for a few days, I was in full-on cleaning mode. Every surface needed to be scrubbed, every piece of trash found and discarded. I wanted the house to look pristine and smell of pine and bleach. I didn't want him thinking I was a slob, even if it was kind of true.

Of course, not everyone shared the same enthusiasm for cleaning as I did.

"Put that down!" I shouted as Misfit snatched up a tissue that had fallen from the bathroom trash can. He ran out of the room, through the bedroom, and down the hall, where he vanished in the living room, likely behind the couch, where I'd struggle to get to him. He'd have the flimsy tissue torn to shreds in seconds, and I knew he'd find a way to spread it all over the house, just to watch me panic trying to pick it up.

I gave chase, sweat beading my brow. Cleaning is already a workout, so I didn't need to add to it by chasing after a misbehaving cat. To his credit, Misfit dropped the tissue when he heard me thundering behind him. It could have been an accident, but a part of me hoped he was taking pity on me.

"Bad kitty," I scolded him. He glared at me from his perch on the armrest of the recliner. I ruffled his fur, picked up the tissue, and then carried it to the trash can in the kitchen. I couldn't be mad at my big fluffball for long. Normally, when I cleaned, I didn't mind what he did, be it stealing stray trash or batting around bra straps. But tonight was different, and I hoped he understood that.

I filled his bowl and turned to call for him, only to find he'd magically appeared at my side and was scarfing down his dinner like he hadn't been fed for weeks.

"You're hardly starving," I told him as I scanned the living room for anything else I needed to pick up.

My house was thankfully of the smaller variety, so cleaning hadn't taken as long as it could have. The spare bedroom took the longest because I never set foot in there. Dust had coated practically everything, and at some point, I must have decided it was the perfect room to toss spare boxes, because there had been ten of them strewn about. They were now broken down and tucked next to the trash can, and the dust had been knocked free and swept up, though it still smelled like a dusty, unused room.

At least Dad wouldn't have to worry about it. I'd decided I'd take the room, old bed and all. Dad could have my newer, more comfortable bed, as well as the privacy my bedroom provided. The spare bath was small and contained only a stand-up shower, sink, and toilet. I'd have to make due with no long soaks in the tub for the few days he'd be here, but thought I could manage.

Satisfied I'd gotten everything picked up, I moved to the closet for the vacuum just as there was a knock at the door. My eyes darted toward the clock, afraid I'd run out of time. I'd been cleaning for well over an hour now, and while Dad had said he'd get his things and be over, I'd kind of hoped it would take him longer.

Misfit's back was arched as he stared at the door. I could practically read his mind.

"The dog isn't coming back," I assured him. I swear I saw him narrow his eyes at me in suspicion as I headed for the door.

The knock came again, this time more insistent. A brief flare of worry worked through me, but I suppressed it. Dad was probably weighed down by his laptop, and quite possibly half a dozen books. He was never one to travel light, and I doubted this time would be any different.

I plastered on a nervous smile, gave the house one last scan, and then turned to open the door.

"Are you okay? I heard all about it."

Someone who was most definitely not my dad barged past me, into my house, uninvited. He looked around, appraising the place, before turning back to face me. He held out his arms like he expected me to rush into them.

That was so not going to happen.

"What are you doing here, Robert?" I asked, not hiding my irritation. Robert Dunhill was my ex, had been for a while now, a fact that seemed to have escaped his attention. He was a no-good cheat who'd followed me to Pine Hills, choosing to live close to me when I wanted nothing to do with him. Somehow, no matter how many times I told him to go away, he never quite got it.

He gave me a concerned look I wasn't buying for one second, before dropping his arms. "I heard about the man's death. You knew him, didn't you? To find the body like that . . ." He shook his head and tsked, like it was the worst thing he could think of happening to anyone.

At least there, I could sort of agree.

"Yes, I knew him. I'm fine. Now leave." I held the door open for him.

"Don't be like that, babe," he said, not moving. "I'm only concerned about you."

"Yeah, right," I said. "I'm surprised you didn't show up with some girl draped over your arm just in case you didn't get what you wanted out of me."

He had the decency to look somewhat chagrined at that. "I'm better than that now," he said. "I've learned my lesson. I swear you're going to see how much I've changed. Just give me a chance to prove it to you."

"No, Robert. We're done. You ran out of chances a

long time ago." It felt like I'd been saying that for half my life now. "Please leave. I have company coming."

His concern for me vanished like smoke, proving it had all been a put-on. "Is it that man?" he asked.

It took me a moment to realize who he was talking about. "Will?" I asked. "No, it's not," I said when he nodded. "And even if it was, it's no business of yours who comes over to see me."

"He's no good for you," Robert said, crossing his arms. "I would treat you far better than he ever could."

"Robert, you . . ." I shook my head, unable to continue. I couldn't believe he was standing there, acting like I'd just up and forgive him for what he did to me. How many ways could I tell him that he screwed up and I was done with him before he'd finally get it?

"I'm really hurt here," he said, adopting his poor-me pose, with shoulders slumped, eyes downcast. "I came here only to make sure you were okay, and you treat me like this. It's not right. In fact, it's indecent."

"The only thing indecent here is your insistence on injecting yourself into my life. It's late. I have things to do. I want you to leave."

"You might want to do what the lady says."

I just about jumped out of my socks when my dad spoke behind me. I'd been so focused on getting Robert out of my house, I hadn't even heard him drive up.

Robert paled. "I was just checking up on her."

"Sounds to me like you were harassing her." Dad stepped past me and leveled hard eyes at Robert. I'd been a victim of his angry glare before, and let me tell you, it's not something you ever want to repeat.

My dad wasn't a violent man, but, boy, could he stare when he wanted to.

Robert wilted beneath those intense eyes, nodded, and then scurried past me without another word. I slammed the door right behind him for good measure.

"Thanks," I said. "I can't believe he came over."

"Don't mention it," Dad said. "I always thought you could do better than him, Buttercup. I don't know what you saw in him in the first place."

"Me either," I muttered, before perking up. "Do you have everything?"

Dad held up a pair of heavy-looking suitcases. "All accounted for. Where should I drop them?"

I led him into my bedroom, where he deposited his suitcases by the bed.

"You don't have to give up your space for me," he said, looking around the room. "I can take the couch or a spare room if you have one."

"No, you're staying here, and that's final."

He smiled and nodded. "If you say so."

"I do." I took a deep breath to settle my nerves. Now that he was here and hadn't run shrieking into the night after seeing how I lived, I was feeling better. I led him out of the bedroom, to the kitchen, where I put on some coffee. "You remember Misfit, don't you?"

"I do." He scratched the orange furball behind the ears. "He always allowed on the counter?"

"I don't think he'd forgive me if I didn't allow it," I said. Misfit had claimed the island counter as his main perch from the moment we'd moved in. Displacing him was completely out of the question.

"So, I thought I heard you mention something

about a guy named Will?" Dad asked, nonchalant as could be, not looking up from Misfit.

I reddened. "Yeah. Him."

Dad chuckled. "New boyfriend, I take it?"

I suddenly felt fifteen again. "I guess."

"He nice?"

"Very." I melted as I said it.

"Good." Dad sighed and sat down on one of the counter stools. "I know how hard it can be to date again after a long time with someone else." He glanced toward the door as if he could still see Robert there.

I filled two mugs with coffee, dropping a cookie into mine. I carried both mugs to the counter, grabbed some cream and sugar for Dad, and then took a seat next to him. "After Robert, I wasn't sure I'd ever want to date again."

He nodded and stared down into the black depths of his coffee. "It's been a long time since your mother died." He cleared his throat, scratched at the back of his neck. "I was thinking that maybe it was time I got back into, well"—he glanced up at me to see how I was taking it before continuing—"I was thinking of trying to date again."

"Oh." I didn't know what else to say. It had always been Mom and Dad, even after she'd died. He didn't even have a female friend that helped him through the tough times. A part of me always thought that now that she was gone, he would continue on, just the same as always.

"I knew you wouldn't approve."

"Oh no!" I reached out and took his hand. "I think it might actually be a good idea." And oddly, I wasn't lying. Now that I was confronted with the possibility of my dad dating someone else, I realized it was probably a good idea. He shouldn't have to spend his life alone.

"I don't know." He shrugged, looking embarrassed. "I feel like I'm going to hurt you, or mar her memory somehow if I went out with another woman."

"Don't," I said. "You aren't forgetting about Mom. She wouldn't want you to remain alone for the rest of your life. I'm no longer there to help you if something were to happen to you." A fact that hadn't dawned on me until that very moment. "If you meet someone, I say go for it. You deserve to be happy."

"I am happy, Buttercup." He squeezed my hand, and I swear I saw a tear in his eye before he looked away. "But I also get lonely sometimes."

"Then do it," I said.

He nodded and went about doctoring his coffee. He paused halfway to pouring his creamer and touched the chip in the mug. He glanced at me and smiled. I could only shrug. I'd started chipping my coffee mugs because of him. It was just one of those things that helped me feel at home, even when I was so far away.

He chuckled and continued pouring his creamer. I took a sip of my own coffee and considered how I'd feel in a few months when I saw Dad with someone else. Would I still approve then? Or would I feel like it was a betrayal, even though I knew Dad wasn't trampling on Mom's memory?

It was hard to tell. But I was willing to see how things panned out.

"I didn't do it, you know?" Dad said suddenly, drawing me out of my contemplations.

"Do what?"

"Kill Rick."

I was taken aback that he actually felt the need to tell me that. "I know! You never could have hurt him."

He shifted uncomfortably in his seat. "But I did."

"Did what?" There was that dread again, creeping its way into my gut.

"Hurt him." Dad sighed and scrubbed at his face with both hands. He looked exhausted. "When I went over to confront him about what had happened outside the church, I lost my temper. He was so damn smug about it." He glanced up at me. "Excuse the language."

"It's fine," I said. "I've heard far worse."

"I don't know." Dad shrugged. "When he said he didn't know what I was so upset about and that you could make up your own mind about him, I lost it. I punched him right in the nose, fired him on the spot, and stormed out."

"You punched him?" I gaped at him, in complete shock. I'd never seen Dad so much as squish a fly, let alone hit someone.

"I did. It was the first time I think I really saw Rick for the bastard he was." Pause. "Excuse the language."

I couldn't believe it. Well, I could see Dad standing up for me, but to hit a man he'd worked with for decades and to fire him, all because of me? It made me feel all warm and fuzzy inside.

And then the reality set in.

"Did you tell the police you punched him?"

"I did." Dad took a sip of his coffee and frowned. "They would have figured it out on their own, I'm sure." He showed me the back of his right hand, where a small scab decorated one knuckle. "I got blood on him, not to mention busting his nose.

They'd eventually find that and would have put two and two together."

I wasn't so sure about that. This wasn't like a bigger city where they'd do DNA tests or anything. And unless he pointed it out, the scab on his knuckle was so small, there was a chance no one would have noticed it. Heck, I hadn't, and I'd been around him for a while now.

"I'm sure they understood," I said, thinking of Paul. He had to know my dad would never kill anyone.

"Maybe." Dad yawned, took a final sip from his mostly full mug of coffee, and stood. "I should hit the hay. It's been a hard, long day, and I could use some rest."

"Do you need me to get you anything?" I asked. "I don't have a lot of spare blankets or pillows, but I'm sure I could scrounge some up somewhere if you think you'll need them." Even if I had to go next door and beg Jules Phan for them.

"No, I'll be fine. Thanks, Buttercup." He started for the hallway.

"By the way, Dad," I said.

He stopped and turned. "Yeah?"

"Make sure you keep the blinds closed."

He gave me a curious look, but nodded. "Will do."

I watched him go, worried. I couldn't imagine what I would do if the police decided to arrest him for Rick's murder. I'd probably end up going on a punching spree myself, landing my own butt in jail, right next to him.

My cell rang, and I pulled it from my purse, still contemplative. "Hello?" I asked, not bothering to check the ID.

"Hi, Krissy. It's Will."

Suddenly, I was all ears. "Hi, Will!" I checked the hall to make sure Dad was truly gone, and then walked to the farthest corner of the living room, just in case. "I was just thinking of you."

"I'm flattered."

"My dad is staying with me now and I had an unpleasant run-in with my ex, Robert." I gave him a quick rundown of what happened. "I wish you could have been here."

"I can't believe that guy," he said. I could imagine him shaking his head in disbelief, sexy dark eyes boring into my own, lips forming whispered words . . .

I cleared my throat, feeling myself warm. Those were definitely not thoughts I wanted to have with my dad in the next room.

"Anyway, I wanted to call and make sure you're doing okay," he said.

"As good as can be, I suppose." I would have been better if he'd stopped by instead of called, but this would have to do.

"Well . . ." With the way he drew out the word, I knew he had something important to say, which only served to make my belly fill with butterflies.

"Yes?"

"The real reason I'm calling is that my parents found out your dad is in town."

The butterflies decided to start moshing around. "Oh?" It came out a croak.

"They'd like you and your father to accompany me to dinner at their place tomorrow night."

"Dinner?"

"Uh-huh."

"With your parents?"

"With my parents."

"And my dad?"

"That's right."

I swallowed a dry lump that had risen in my throat. "Sounds great." *What are you thinking?!*

"Okay, great." Will sounded relieved, like he'd been worried I might decline. "I can pick you up, if you'd like. Or I can give you the address. It's totally up to you. I won't pressure you either way." He coughed, obviously realizing he'd started to babble.

"The address is fine," I said. I wasn't sure I could handle the ride with both of them in the car together. The same house was going to be bad enough. I'd never been comfortable bringing boys around Dad. He never threatened them or anything, but I always feared he'd think I was making a mistake, especially after how my last relationship had turned out.

Will gave me his parents' address, and after a few quick good-byes, we hung up, the date planned.

I returned my phone to my purse and slumped down onto the couch. What had I just gotten myself into?

13

"I'm surprised you haven't taken off already."

I glanced over at Vicki, who was smiling mischievously. The morning coffee rush was over, and I was doing my best to relax behind the counter, cleaning up a few spills and trying hard not to think about Rick's murder. Vicki had told me I didn't need to come in, but I decided I'd feel better with something to do. Leave me at home, and I'd end up poking my nose where it didn't belong.

"Why's that?" I asked, all innocence.

"I'd think you'd be all over this one," she said. Despite the early rush, not a hair was out of place on her head, but she checked it, anyway. "Since it is someone you knew who died, and the police have yet to arrest anyone, it seemed like the sort of thing that would be right up your alley."

"I'm going to stay out of it." Which was true, to a point. Sure, I might have already gone snooping around the crime scene, and I'd talked to the witness without police knowledge, but when I woke up this morning, I'd decided it would end there. With Dad in town, I needed to be on my best behavior.

A chair clanked against the wall as Jeff moved it back to pick up trash that had been discarded under the table. I swear, people get messier and messier each day. The trash can was all of two feet away, yet the customer had chosen to drop his trash on the floor before leaving.

"Uh-huh," Vicki winked at me. "So, your dad is staying with you now?"

"He is." I was thankful for the change in subject. If Vicki kept asking about the case, I'd start thinking about it, and nothing good could come of it. "He promised he'd stay at the house today and deal with work instead of coming here. He's going to have to figure out what he's going to do now that Rick's dead. He didn't belong to an agency with a lot of agents who could fill in until something more permanent could be arranged. He's going to have to find someone else."

"What about Cameron?" Vicki motioned toward the freshly minted agent, who was talking with Rita, a thick manuscript on the table between them.

"I don't know," I said. "He seems nice enough, I guess, but I bet Dad will want someone with more experience. He's not producing books like he used to, and at this point in his career, he needs someone who knows what he's doing." I frowned at Rita's manuscript a moment before I realized something I'd forgotten. "Crap!"

Vicki jumped at my sudden outburst. "What happened? You okay?" She glanced at my hands as if to make sure I hadn't cut myself on something.

"I'm fine," I said. "But I forgot to call Paul and tell

him about what I saw at Ted and Bettfast." I paused at her knowing grin. "What?"

"I knew you couldn't stay out of it."

"This was before I'd decided not to get involved," I said, sullenly. "And I doubt there's anything to what I found."

"Spill," she said, leaning on the counter beside me.

I glanced around to make sure no one was listening, especially the prospective authors in the room. Rita wasn't the only one hanging around now. Both the Drummands were here, as was Andi Caldwell, and Harland. If I were still investigating the case, I'd end up asking the big man about why he was at Ted and Bettfast, or, at least, if he was the fat man Justin had seen. As it was, I could only watch him and wonder.

The door opened, and Joel Osborne came in, joining the others. Apparently, Death by Coffee had become the de facto hangout for the literary types while they were in town. I couldn't say I disapproved.

"I found manuscripts inside Rick's room," I whispered once I was sure no one was eavesdropping on us.

Vicki frowned. "That doesn't sound too strange. He was an agent, so I would expect there to be a few novels lying around."

I shook my head. "These weren't normal manuscripts." I paused, frowned. "Well, they were, but I remember Rick refusing to look at any of them, yet there they were, hidden under his bed. All of them were written by . . ." I jerked a thumb toward the dining area.

Vicki's eyes widened as she took in the small gathering. "You think one of them killed him?"

I shrugged. "I don't know what to think yet. He

had them in his room, so maybe Rick changed his mind and took the manuscripts in. But why shove them under his bed? It doesn't make sense."

"Maybe he took them and put them there to forget about them."

"But why not dump them into the trash?"

"Perhaps so he could give them back after pretending to read them?" Vicki spread her hands. "Or maybe he was planning to do something with them later."

"Maybe." I sighed. "When I first was there, I saw manuscripts on the desk, but when I went back later, they were gone."

"Do you think the ones under the bed are the same ones?"

"I don't know. They could be." I stepped closer to her and lowered my voice. "I was told someone came downstairs after the police left, and it is likely they had gone into the crime scene. Bett swears the door was locked, yet when I checked, it wasn't."

"So, what? You think the killer came back for something?"

"Could be," I said. "Though I have no idea what he could have wanted. The police had already been through the room, so any evidence would have already been collected."

"Huh." Vicki grinned. "It doesn't sound like you're staying out of things, you know?"

I stuck my tongue out at her. "You started it."

She laughed. "And I don't think you'll have to worry about calling Paul to tell him about what you found."

"Why's that?" I followed her gaze to the door. "Oh."

Officer Paul Dalton stepped inside, removing his hat as he did so. He took a moment to pat his head to smooth down a few wild strands of hair that refused to be tamed. He took a quick look around and then leveled his gaze at me.

"Have fun," Vicki whispered before gliding up to the bookstore.

"Thanks," I grumbled, heart hammering. Was he here because he'd learned something? Or was there a more sinister reason for his visit? I *had* gone against his wishes and talked to Iris, but that had been well after he'd gotten her statement, so he couldn't hold it against me, could he?

I didn't have long to wait to find out.

"Krissy," he said, coming over to where I stood. "Is there someplace private we could talk for a few minutes?"

I nodded, heart sinking to my toes. If he wanted to talk privately, then what he had to say wasn't going to make me happy. "Jeff," I called. "Take over back here for me, would you?"

"Sure, Ms. Hancock."

I led Paul back to the small office behind the counter. Memories flooded in as I took a seat in one of the two chairs back there. When I'd first met Paul, it had been on my first day of work, and I'd taken him back here under similar circumstances.

"Brings back memories, doesn't it?" he asked, echoing my thoughts.

"Sure does," I said. "But I hope this time the news isn't so grave." By the look on his face, I knew it was going to be.

Paul heaved a sigh as he sat down to face me. "I need to ask you a few questions about your relationship with Mr. Wiseman."

"He was my dad's agent," I said. "You know that."

"I do." A smile flittered across his face and then vanished. "How long did you know him?"

I shrugged. "Most of my life, I guess. We didn't live in the same state, so I only ever saw him when my dad had a big book release or event of some kind. Rick liked to fly in and take part."

"Would you describe your relationship as close?"

I didn't like where this conversation was heading, especially since we'd already talked about Rick and how I felt about him when we were at Ted and Bettfast. "No, not particularly. We weren't friends or anything, if that's what you are asking."

"You didn't like him, did you?"

"No," I said. "I already told you that. He was rude and often quite crude." Though I hadn't realized until the night of his death how rude he really was.

Paul nodded as if I were following his script perfectly. "Would you say you were nervous around him? Did you actively dislike spending time with him?"

"I guess." I frowned. The questions felt leading, something I didn't think the police were supposed to do. "Why are you asking me these things?" I asked. "You don't think I killed him, do you?"

"I don't," Paul said. "But there is some evidence I've uncovered that I think you need to be aware of. I wanted to make sure you heard it from me, not someone else."

A cold chill washed through me. "What evidence?"

He reached into his jacket pocket and removed a couple of folded pages. Silently, he handed them to me.

I took a deep breath before unfolding them, thinking I'd find some sort of love letter or incriminating block of text. What met my eyes was far worse.

"Where did you get these?" I asked.

"From Rick Wiseman's phone and computer."

I flipped through the pages slowly, looking down at my own smiling face. All of the photographs came from when I was young. There was a picture of me standing next to my dad when I was about eight, wearing a ratty skirt and knee-high socks. Another of me at twelve. Another at about the same age, clearly taken while I was unaware that anyone was taking my photo.

"Why would he have these?" I asked, handing the stack back to Paul.

"I'm not positive, since there was nothing but the photographs in the folder. Everything else on the laptop related to his work."

"Were there others?"

"No, just these."

"I mean, other girls? Were there more?"

"No. I believe Rick Wiseman was infatuated with you."

"But I was just a kid!" My mind went back to all those times I'd been near him, how he'd look at me, smile at me. I'd never noticed it before, but he had always treated me better than he did everyone else. He never took advantage of me or anything. I'd been alone with him in rooms before, and he'd never tried to touch me or said anything to me that was out of line—at least until the other night, that is.

"I feel sick," I said, sitting back. "I had no idea he had any of those."

"Do you think your father knew?"

I shook my head. "He would have fired him a long time ago if he had."

"Do you believe he could have found out?" Paul

asked. "Our witness claims she heard your father fire Mr. Wiseman before his death."

"If he fired him, then why bother killing him?" I asked, annoyed that Paul was back to suspecting my dad. "I doubt he saw the pictures. He went over there that night because he saw Rick hit on me and he wanted to confront him about it."

Paul shifted in his seat, eyes going hard. "Mr. Wiseman hit on you?"

"Came right up and asked me to come back to his room at the bed-and-breakfast. He said he wanted to see if I had any novels he could look at, but I knew he meant something else."

"I see."

"I didn't kill him, and neither did my dad." I crossed my arms over my chest and glared. "He would have been angry, sure, but James Hancock isn't someone who goes and kills people he's unhappy with."

I vaguely wondered what Dad *had* said when he'd given his statement. He'd told them he hit Rick, but did he say why? From what I could tell, Paul hadn't known about Rick's come-on, which meant Dad had left something out, or had lied. I was really hoping for the former.

"I believe you," Paul said. "But it is important you keep me in the loop."

I sucked in a deep breath and let it out in a relieved sigh. "I'm glad," I said. "I don't think I could stand it if you came after my dad."

Paul reached out and put a hand on my knee. Warmth spread throughout my entire body, all from his comforting squeeze. "We'll find out who did this," he said. "I promise."

"Thank you." I cleared my throat and stood. It was

getting quite hot in there. "Is there anything else you wanted to talk to me about?" I asked. "I really should get back to work."

Paul followed my lead and stood. "Not at this time. If you know anyone who might have wanted to hurt Mr. Wiseman, please let me know." In his tone, I detected a warning not to go asking around.

Which reminded me . . .

"There was something odd I noticed when I was in Rick's room earlier."

"Okay?" Paul frowned, but he removed a notebook from his front pocket and flipped it open.

"There were manuscripts written by local authors under the bed."

"Under the bed?"

"I accidentally tripped over one."

He tapped his pen on the pad of paper, a slow frown forming. "I remember a stack of pages sitting on the desk," he said, thoughtfully. "I don't recall seeing anything under the bed, and I looked." His eyes narrowed at me. "When did you see them?"

Uh-oh. "I might have gone back and taken a quick peek," I admitted. "The door was unlocked and Bett said it wasn't supposed to be."

Paul's frown deepened. "So, someone unlocked the door and shoved a bunch of manuscripts under the bed? Why would anyone do that?"

"Maybe they were looking for something else and accidentally knocked them off the desk. Instead of stacking them up again, they kicked them under the bed, out of the way." I still wasn't sure it made sense, but it was all I had. "Justin said he saw a fat man leaving the bed-and-breakfast after you left."

"He never said anything to me."

"You were gone," I said, wishing I'd left Justin's name out of it. "He didn't think anything of it until I mentioned that the door was unlocked."

Paul scribbled something down on his notepad. "Did he say what this man looked like, other than fat?"

"No. He'd just come inside and didn't get a good look at him. It might not mean anything."

Paul sighed and shoved the notepad back into his pocket. "Looks like I'm going to have to talk to this employee again. Is there anything else you need to tell me?"

"That's it," I said. I actually felt proud of myself. I'd told the police everything I knew, and I'd done it before it could get me into trouble.

"All right." Paul put his hat back on. "Stay safe, Krissy. This one is hitting a little close to home and I don't want you to get hurt."

"I will." I made an X over my heart. "I swear."

He nodded, though he looked resigned. I didn't think he believed me.

And then we both just stood there, looking at one another. A trickle of sweat ran down my back as the temperature seemed to rise, yet again. Paul opened his mouth and then snapped it closed before saying anything.

"Well, I . . ." I coughed and looked at my feet.

"I should get going," Paul said. He cleared his throat and then spun on his heel so fast, he very nearly fell.

I followed after him, trying hard not to think about those pictures he'd shown me or the way just looking at Paul Dalton caused me to break out in a sweat. Everything about that encounter had been uncomfortable in ways I couldn't quite explain. I was supposed to be over him, yet moments like that reinforced how wrong I was.

"Ah, there you are!"

I jerked to a stop at the sound of Dad's voice.

"Officer Dalton," he went on. "Is everything all right?"

"Mr. Hancock." Paul tipped his hat. "I was just checking in with Krissy. Everything is fine." He glanced back at me, and I saw a hint of panic in his eye before he turned away. "I'll see you later." And then he was gone, practically running out the door.

"They went on a date once," Rita said, coming up behind my dad. "It wouldn't surprise me in the slightest if they were trying to reignite that old flame." She giggled.

"Rita!" I just about died. "It wasn't like that at all." I stared daggers at her, which only seemed to tickle her funny bone that much more.

"I never accused you of anything," Dad said, though he was grinning like a fool. Ha, ha. Everyone laugh at my obvious embarrassment. "I hope everything is okay."

"It is." Not content to be the only one interrogated, I narrowed my eyes at him. "What are you doing here? I thought you were going to stay at the house and get work done?"

He shrugged. "I got bored. Thought I'd come in and see how you were doing. I didn't realize you had company."

Rita snickered, and I thought I heard a snort of a laugh coming from where Vicki stood upstairs.

I could argue that nothing happened until I was blue in the face, but I was pretty sure it would get me nowhere. Once the ribbing started, it wasn't going to stop until I acted like it didn't bother me anymore.

"Can I get you anything?" I asked, sweet as could be.

"A coffee would be fine," Dad said, doing little to hide his grin. "And maybe a cookie."

I quickly threw together his order and then handed it to him. "I'll take care of it," I said when he tried to hand me money. "You go ahead and eat so you can get back to the house and do some real work."

Dad chuckled as he took his food back to the table. Rita followed him over, talking a million miles a minute. I knew she had to be relaying every detail of Paul's and my failed relationship, what little of it there was.

I groaned and slouched against the counter as I watched them. Why did this kind of thing always happen to me?

"It's okay, Ms. Hancock," Jeff said, coming around the counter, rag in hand, goofy smile on his lips. "I won't tell anyone."

And then, with a wink and a smile, he turned and walked away.

14

"They're talking about me; I know it!" Even as I spoke, Rita glanced my way, leaned forward, and whispered something to my dad with her hand covering her mouth.

It had been like that ever since Dad sat down with his coffee and cookie, and showed no signs of stopping anytime soon. I don't think Rita even asked him if it was okay for her to join him. She just kept on talking like the world was on fire and she had to tell him about my entire life in Pine Hills before everything went up in flames. I tried to ignore it, but it was hard. They were *right there*.

What would Dad think of me once he heard how I'd made such a mess out of my relationship with Paul? It was my fault that everything had fallen apart before it could really even get started. If I hadn't been so nosy, perhaps things would have been different, but as they were, I was with Will now, Paul a not-so-distant memory. And it wasn't like the two men had fought over me. By the time I'd met Will in that bowling alley, Paul and I were kaput.

But somehow, I knew Rita would twist it all around and make it seem like I'd led Paul on while flirting with Will. It was the way she was. I mean, it was laughable to think any man would fight for me, let alone two of them. Dad had to know that.

"She's probably making things up," I grumbled. "She'd do anything to get him to pay more attention to her, even if it makes my life that much harder. I should go over there and set them straight."

"Could you do it after you get my coffee?"

I started, having completely forgotten who I'd been talking to. "Sure. One sec."

I hurried back and threw together the coffee, mind still on Rita and Dad. I supposed it was better than dwelling on Rick's murder or the photos he'd had of me on his phone and computer. If Rita's gossip was doing anything positive, it was keeping me from thinking too much about things I'd sworn to keep out of.

Still, it didn't mean I had to like it.

I carried the coffee back to the counter. "Here you are." I forced myself to tear my eyes from Rita and focus on the man in front of me. He was wearing a paper mask over his nose and mouth, yet his eyes were still watering like fountains. I didn't realize anyone could produce so many tears.

"Thanks." He handed over exact change and made straight for the door. Todd Melville, despite his apparent allergy to cats, had become a regular. He came in almost every day, wearing that silly mask and acting like every second in Death by Coffee might be his last. I mean, Trouble hardly ever came downstairs, and when he did, he was usually chased right back up into the bookstore by Vicki or me. I had yet to see the feline today at all, but I guess if you have really bad allergies, even a little dander in the air is enough to set them off.

I watched as Todd stepped outside the shop, removed his mask, and then strolled down the sidewalk, sipping his coffee as if nothing in the world could bother him. Either he was quick to recover, or he was something of a hypochondriac. Maybe it was a combination of both, though I don't think he was doing it in order to scam us somehow. I'm not even sure how he'd do such a thing.

Now that Todd was gone, I was left alone downstairs. Jeff was on break and had gone down the street to grab something to eat. Vicki was upstairs, working her magic with the books. Many of the prospective authors were nowhere in sight, leaving when Cameron had left, a stack of manuscripts in his arms. He was taking his new role seriously, though I feared he was going to struggle finding a gem here in Pine Hills. I'd heard readings from many of the locals, and to be honest, none of them seemed ready for the big time.

With nothing else to do but scrub down a counter I'd already cleaned twice, I found my gaze lingering back on my Dad and Rita. They were both looking at me now. Rita was smiling, while Dad had a contemplative look on his face. He nodded once, smiled at me, and then turned back to whatever Rita was saying.

I spun on my heel and went to the back, thinking I'd do some dishes, but after only a minute or two, I realized I wasn't going to be able to focus on the job. For one, it left no one out front to keep an eye on the counter. And secondly, I couldn't let them continue gossiping about me. Who knew how it would escalate? I should have put an end to it a long time ago.

Determined, I left the back room, and once certain no one was about to order anything, I headed straight for the table where they sat. Rita patted Dad's hand as I approached, and they both instantly clammed up, confirming my belief that I'd been the prime topic of conversation.

"Is there anything I need to know?" I asked.

"What do you mean, Buttercup?" Dad extracted his hand from Rita's own. I'd been so focused on their faces, I hadn't noticed she hadn't removed it until that very moment.

It doesn't mean anything.

Or, at least, I sure hoped it didn't.

"You two have been sitting here all day, gabbing away about me. I want to know exactly what was said, and I want to know it now!" I focused the last on Rita.

"We weren't talking about you, dear," Rita said. "Well, not directly about you, anyway."

"We were just socializing," Dad said, drawing my eye. "Nothing is wrong with that, is there?" He smiled sweetly at me, and I knew he wasn't telling the full truth.

I crossed my arms and glared at them both. Rita continued to smile at me, not a care in the world. Dad lasted all of fifteen seconds under my intense scrutiny before he broke.

"We were talking about Rick's murder," he said.

"Really?" I asked, not sure if I was relieved they hadn't been talking about my dating life or not. "What about it?"

Dad and Rita shared a look before they made room for me at the table. I glanced back at the counter, saw no one waiting, and sat down, positioning myself so I could keep an eye on the door, just in case someone came in. It was our usual slow hour, so I was hoping the customers would hold off until I got the whole story.

"Okay. Spill."

Rita was all too happy to. "I was telling James here that I'd gone to see Mr. Wiseman after the meeting. He wouldn't even open the door, the louse!" She sniffed disdainfully. "I have no idea why anyone would ever want to deal with that man." She aimed the last at my dad.

"Loyalty, in my case," he said. "It's the only thing that makes sense. I didn't really like him." He shook his head sadly, as if his dislike was shameful because the man in question had so recently died. "I stayed with him because I was afraid of moving on. I guess I thought of him as something of a good luck charm. He was the one who gave me my start. Before Rick, all I had to show for my writing was a pile of rejections." He paused, shrugged. "And I guess I'm afraid of change."

That sounded like Dad. Back when I was eight, he used to take me to the same sandwich shop a block from our house every day for lunch. Neither of us much cared for the place, but the owner was nice and always gave me a sucker afterward.

"Who else went with you when you went to see Rick?" I asked Rita.

"A few of us went," she said. "I don't remember who exactly. Andi came along, of course. As did Albert and a few others. I was elected spokeswoman, so none of the others came upstairs right away."

"And you said he wouldn't open the door?"

"Not even a crack!" She huffed. "He shouted at me to go away and then fell completely silent like he thought that if he ignored me, I'd comply. That nice man Cameron was in the room with him at the time and apologized to me as best as he could through the door. I think he got yelled at for it, too."

"So, Cameron was in Rick's room with him?" I hadn't known that, though I wasn't sure if it was important or not. All of this happened before Dad got there, and Rick was still alive then.

"He was," Rita confirmed.

"Was he there when you went to see him?" I asked Dad. If Cameron had been hanging around, then he could verify that Rick was alive when Dad left his room.

"I never saw him," Dad said. "Though I suppose he could have been in the bathroom at the time. If he was, he was pretty quiet about it."

"So, if Rick wouldn't open the door, how did he get your manuscript?" I asked, turning back to Rita.

She straightened her back, a smug look spread across her face. "Well, I wasn't about to leave without doing what I set out to do. I decided to leave my book outside his door, figuring he'd have to take it in eventually. I told everyone what I did, and many of them followed suit."

"Were the manuscripts still outside the door when you got there?" I asked Dad.

He shook his head. "I didn't see them. But I wasn't exactly looking for them, either. I wasn't quite thinking straight by the time I went to talk to him." He reddened.

So, Rita had gone to the bed-and-breakfast soon after the meeting had ended that night and left her manuscript behind, as did a few other authors. I would imagine that anyone else who might have come along would have seen the stack and added theirs to the pile, though I found it hard to believe there'd been a steady stream of writers hoping to annoy an agent into looking at their work. Cameron was with Rick at the time, and Rick was quite clearly alive while all of this was going on.

At some point between the time Rita and her crew had left their manuscripts and when Dad got there, someone had collected them. Since I'd seen some of them in Rick's room, that meant either Cameron carried them inside for him or Rick relented and took them in on his own.

The big question was, how did it relate to Rick's murder? And of the ones I'd seen hidden under the bed, how many of them had been on the desk when I'd found his body? All of them? None of them? Did it even matter?

"Do you know someone named Tony A. Marshall?" I asked, thinking back to the names I'd seen. "I found one of his manuscripts with the others from Pine Hills. It was the only name in the stack I didn't recognize."

Rita tapped her finger on her chin and then shook her head. "Not that I recall," she said. "I know for a fact there was no one named Tony with us when we delivered our books. And he certainly hadn't come to that night's meeting. I would have known."

Now that I thought about it, Tony could very well be another of Rick's out-of-town clients, much like my Dad. Why his manuscript was mixed with those from Pine Hills, I didn't know. Maybe Rick had simply added it to the pile accidentally. Or perhaps it was the only one he'd brought from home. Maybe it was all some big coincidence, and it didn't matter where it had come from.

But still, none of it explained how they'd all ended up under the bed after the police had left. There had to be something to that.

"After you left, Rita, did you go home right away?" I asked, trying to solidify the time line in my head. "Did anyone stay behind, someone who insisted on talking to Rick?"

"I can't speak for anyone else, but I went straight home and typed out an angry e-mail to him. It was rude how Mr. Wiseman treated us, and I wanted him to know what I thought about it."

"You sent him an angry e-mail?"

Rita nodded, satisfaction pouring from her. "He deserved to get a little piece of my mind after what he'd done."

I groaned. How she thought that would help her case when it came to landing Rick as an agent, I'd never know. Add to the fact the man was murdered and had an angry e-mail sitting in his in-box, it couldn't look good for her. I had no doubts the police would find the e-mail and ask her about it. I didn't think they'd ever consider her a real suspect, but it wouldn't make her life any easier.

"What about Harland . . ." I frowned. I didn't think I'd ever heard Harland's last name.

"Harland Pennywinkle?" Rita asked. "What about him?"

"Was he with you that night?"

She nodded, and then her eyes widened. "Is he a suspect?"

I didn't think before I answered. "Someone saw

a man matching Harland's description leaving the bed-and-breakfast after the police had left. Someone snuck into Rick's room, stealing Justin's keys and snooping around, and I'm thinking it might have been him."

Rita got a faraway look in her eye, and I quickly realized my mistake.

"Don't go spreading rumors," I warned her.

She nodded absently, wheels still churning away.

I sighed. Great, now everyone in town was going to know Harland might have been snooping where he shouldn't. Somehow, I knew it would come back and bite me on the butt.

Dad was watching me in a way I didn't quite like, either. All this talk of Rick's murder had gotten the inquisitive juices flowing. I couldn't let that stand, not if I wanted to keep him out of it, as well as keep myself from investigating, so I changed the subject.

"We have a date," I blurted.

"A date?" Dad asked, confused for obvious reasons.

"Will," I said. "You remember me telling you about Will, right? He's invited us over tonight for dinner with his parents. It's not a real date. I mean, you aren't going to be dating his mom or anything. And I'm not on a real date, though I guess he's kind of my date. It's just food. We're going to eat." I dropped my head into my hands and stopped babbling before I made an even bigger fool of myself.

"Dinner sounds good," Dad said. He sounded amused, though he was being nice and not calling me on my embarrassing ramble.

"You haven't met Will Foster yet?" Rita was practically bubbling with excitement.

"I haven't," Dad said, sounding interested.

"No!" I looked up just as the door opened and about a dozen people strolled in, ready for lunch. "Rita, please!"

"You'd better take care of that," she said, waving a hand toward the unmanned register. She had that look in her eye that told me she was going to spend the next hour talking about nothing other than Will, no matter how much I begged and pleaded for her not to.

"We'll be okay, Buttercup," Dad said, a crooked grin on his face. "I don't want to keep you from work."

I wanted to stay and argue. Actually, I wanted to grab Rita by the arm and drag her away from Dad so she couldn't tell him every dirty little secret she knew. I mean, I didn't even know everything there was to know about Will. I was afraid Dad would learn something I had yet to find out and it would end up causing some sort of awkward situation where I looked like the clueless girlfriend while everyone stood around snickering at me.

But I couldn't abandon my job, no matter how mortified I might be later. Vicki was upstairs, dealing with customers of her own, and Jeff wasn't back from break yet, so it was all up to me.

Shoulders slumped, I rose from my seat and gave Rita one last pleading look I was sure she'd ignore. And then I slunk my way back behind the counter, just catching the start of Rita's spiel, "Now let me tell you something about Will Foster . . ."

15

"So . . ." I glanced at my dad out of the corner of my eye. "What'd ya talk about?"

Dad chuckled. "Don't worry about it, Buttercup. I didn't let her say anything that would upset you."

I bit my lip and focused on my driving. I really wanted to know what Rita had told Dad once I'd been dragged back to work, but he was being tight-lipped about it. I'd asked him at least a dozen times already, and had gotten the same answer just as many times. He claimed he'd stopped her from gossiping, but they *had* sat there for a good hour more, talking. I found it hard to believe conversation had moved on to something innocent, like the weather.

I swallowed back my frustration and turned my mind to what was to come. I'd never been to Will's parents' house before. It wasn't like I was heading down the street to a place similar to mine. They, unlike me, had money. Once Will had given me their address, I'd looked it up online and found they lived in the hills that gave Pine Hills its name. There were no cheap houses there, no quaint little cottages or cabins in the woods. We were likely about to walk into a mansion, or something darn near close to it.

I guess I shouldn't have been so surprised. Will was a doctor, and he himself was loaded. His parents had shown up at a pretty exclusive party last Halloween, which told me they had some decent money and influence. I wasn't sure what either of them did for a living—or used to do, since they could very well be retired—but knowing they often took regular vacations out of the country, I guessed they'd made a pretty penny in their time.

And here I was, a little nobody coffee shop girl, dating their doctor son, and feeling way in over her head. *Overwhelmed* would be an understatement.

"You okay?" Dad asked, cutting into my worry.

"I suppose." I forced my fingers to relax on the steering wheel. If I kept it up, there'd be permanent impressions left behind. "I'm just nervous."

"Your relationship with this man serious?" It was asked in a way that told me he was just as uncomfortable with the topic of conversation as I was. Relationships have never been our strong suits.

I started to answer, but paused. Was it? What constituted *serious*? Will had an important job that often had him working late nights, sometimes for days at a time. There were times I wouldn't see him for two weeks straight, or if I did, he'd look so exhausted, I felt like I was intruding.

But whenever we did get a few quiet moments alone, I felt safe. Secure. Just thinking about him made me smile.

"I don't know," I admitted. "I really like him and I think he likes me, but we're taking it slow."

"There's nothing wrong with that."

I sure hoped he was right. A part of me was afraid Will was taking it slow with me not because he wanted to savor every last moment of our relationship, but, rather, because he was afraid I was a looney snooper who couldn't keep her nose out of other people's business, and he wanted to make sure I wouldn't go completely crazy on him. Could my fascination with catching murderers be driving him away?

Thankfully, we arrived, so conversation ceased, allowing me to worry in peace. I was relieved to see the Foster house wasn't as large as some of the other homes I'd seen along the way. It was still a lot bigger than my dinky little place, but I didn't feel as over-whelmed by it as I had before. Even in the falling dark, the grass was a vibrant green that told me they had someone who took care of their yard for them—if they didn't do it themselves. The driveway was paved and led to a garage that was big enough for at least four vehicles. Five, if you squeezed them in. The doors were closed, so I didn't know if there were actually that many cars inside, or if part of the garage was a workshop or storage area.

Two cars were parked in front of the garage. I chose to park beside Will's Lexus, noting that the other car was an Audi that looked just as expensive. I could practically hear my poor little Ford whimper in embarrassment as I shut off the engine.

"Here we are," I said, speaking more to myself than to Dad.

"We are." He winked at me, unbuckled, and got out of the car.

Would it be bad form for me to turn around and drive away? When I'd gotten dressed, I'd put extra

care in looking nice, something I rarely did. I'd opted
for a thin white blouse, dark skirt, and flats. It wasn't
cocktail-dress quality, but it was a far cry nicer than
anything else I'd worn in the last year or two. Dad
had elected a pair of black slacks and a button-up
shirt that was starting to show its age. We looked quite
the pair, and I hoped we wouldn't stand out too
much.

Heart hammering, I shoved my keys into my purse
and forced myself to get out of the car. Will wouldn't
care what I wore, and from what I knew of his parents, they wouldn't, either. We weren't going out, so
I didn't have to worry about public appearances.

So, why was I so nervous?

One look at the man next to me, and I knew. This
was the first time my dad was going to meet any of
them. He wouldn't disapprove, I was sure, and I
doubted the Fosters would turn their noses up at us.

The front door opened, and Will stepped outside
in all his sumptuous glory. He was wearing what I
took to be causal for him—a pair of khakis and a
button-up shirt that put my dad's to shame. His
sleeves were pushed up to midforearm, yet he made
it look relaxed and formal at the same time.

"Krissy." He sounded genuinely glad to see me.
"Mr. Hancock." He shook Dad's hand. "Please,
come in."

"Thank you." Dad stepped past him, into the
house.

"Hey." Will stopped me before I could follow.

Something in my stomach clenched. *Here we go: the
bad news.* "Is there something wrong?"

"Oh no!" He smiled. "I just wanted to warn you
that there are more people here than anticipated."

My eyes widened in alarm, imagining a house full of his relatives. "How many are we talking about?"

"It's just my sister," Will said. "She got a babysitter for Gemma so she could come. She really wanted to meet you." Gemma was Will's six-year-old niece.

I wasn't sure how to take it. On one hand, I was glad his entire extended family hadn't decided to come. On the other, even one more might be too much for my frazzled nerves to handle. Not only was I going to have to sit there with Will's parents, hoping they weren't judging me and my choices, but now I'd have to impress Will's sister as well.

"Don't worry yourself over it," Will said, clearly noting my distress. "This isn't a big deal. Relax. Have fun."

Have fun. Right. "Sure thing." I beamed a smile at him, while, at the same time, my knees knocked together. This was going to be cake. *I'm so going to screw this up.*

Will held out his arm, and I laced my own through it. He led me into the foyer, and I tried not to squeeze his arm off as fear clutched at me. Dad was already talking to the Fosters in a large dining room dominated by a gigantic table with places for ten. Plates had been laid out for six, which gave me hope there'd be no more surprise visitors that night.

Keneche—Ken—Foster was a tall man, skin and eyes both dark. He had a heavy African accent that hadn't been softened in the time he'd spent in the US. When he laughed, the whole room seemed to shake with it.

His wife, Maire, was his polar opposite. Short, red-headed, and pale as a ghost. Freckles dotted her aged face, accentuating an already exuberant personality.

Her Irish roots definitely showed through, and not just in her accent. When she started talking, it was hard to make her stop.

They both turned to face me as I entered, smiles as wide as the horizon stretched across their features.

"Kristina," Maire said, clutching at my forearm. "I'm so glad you could come on such short notice."

"Thank you for inviting me." I blushed.

"It's good to get friends and family together often," Ken said. He put a special emphasis on *family*, which more than one of us noticed. My blush deepened, and Will started coughing, his own face reddening.

"Is this her?"

I turned to find a beautiful woman coming down the stairs. Her skin wasn't as dark as Will's, and her hair had definitely come from her mother, though it was a darker, deeper red. She was fit, and I didn't mean skinny, but fit as if she'd spent her life exercising. Bright green eyes looked me up and down, and a crooked smile flashed across her face.

"It is," Will said, letting my arm fall away. "Krissy, meet my sister, Jade."

Before I could say anything, she crossed the room and enveloped me in a hug. When she squeezed, all the air was crushed from my chest.

"I've heard so much about you," she said, releasing me.

"It's nice to meet you," I said, wishing Will had told me more about her at some point. I hated that the only thing I knew about her was that she was Will's sister and had a daughter.

Jade's gaze moved to Dad. "Is this your father?"

"It is."

She wrapped him in a hug that caught him by

surprise. Apparently, Jade had no problem with physical contact with people she'd just met.

"Dinner is almost ready," Maire said, cutting into the greetings. "I'd better go check on the turkey." She hurried off before anyone could offer to help.

"Mom loves to cook," Will said. "She wanted to do something a bit more traditional, but I wasn't sure if you'd like it. I talked her into turkey and potatoes. I hope that's okay?"

"I'm sure it's fine," I said.

"Maire makes a mean shepherd's pie," Ken said with a smile. "You would have loved it."

"Maybe next time," I said, though I honestly wasn't sure what a shepherd's pie might contain. I'd be willing to find out if it meant I got to spend more time with the Fosters. I might have been nervous coming over, but now that I was here, I was starting to feel more comfortable. Their big smiles and friendly demeanors had a lot to do with that.

"I'll be back in a few," Ken said. "I'd better make sure Maire doesn't overdo it." He chuckled and hurried out of the room.

I turned to Jade. "I've met your daughter, Gemma," I said. "She's beautiful."

"Thank you." There was definitely pride in her voice. "If only I could say the same about her father."

"I told you he wasn't right for you," Will said. "But you've never been good at choosing men for yourself, have you?"

"As if you knew what constituted a good man," she said, rolling her eyes. "He just couldn't handle the fact I was better than he was."

I looked questioningly at Will.

"Soccer," he said. "Jade should be on the Olympic team."

She snorted. "I'm not *that* good." Though I could tell she was pleased by the compliment.

"She's just being modest."

"Well, hopefully, I'll get to see you play someday," I said.

"Dinner is served!" Ken called, carrying in the turkey, Maire behind him with a tray of sides.

The next half hour was a flurry of food and conversation. Maire had outdone herself, but all of it was spectacular.

A large portion of the conversation was focused on Dad and his books. Neither of the elder Fosters had read his work, though Jade said she thought she'd read one back in her college days. Dad tried to deflect conversation to me, but they were having none of it. I was glad I wasn't the focus; it gave me a chance to sit back and actually enjoy myself without worrying I might say the wrong thing.

Dinner wound down, and I sat back, feeling stuffed. Will was to my left, smiling and looking as content as a man could be. I'd probably eaten double of what he'd had, but I didn't care. Dad was to my right and had eaten at least as much as I did. He looked ready for a nice long nap, and I couldn't say I disagreed.

"It was wonderful," I told Maire.

"Thank you," she said, beaming. "I'm so glad you enjoyed it."

"So, what are you going to do now?" Ken asked, tossing his napkin—cloth, of course—down onto his plate. He directed the question to my dad. "I heard about what happened. It's terrible."

"It is," Dad said. "I'm not sure what I'm going to do yet, about the signing or my career."

"I can't believe someone would do such a thing in Pine Hills of all places," Maire said. "It's a good thing Kristina here is on the case."

I started, surprised. "I'm not working the case," I said. "I'm going to let the police handle it."

"Why?" Maire asked, sounding truly perplexed. "You've done such a great job helping them since you've arrived in town. Will has told us all about your exploits, and I do say, I'm quite impressed."

My face flamed red, and I was unable to answer.

Will did it for me. "She's too close to this one, Mom," he said. "She knew the victim. It's probably better if she steps back and lets the police handle it this time."

"They don't view you as a suspect, do they?" Ken asked my dad.

"I don't know. But even if they do, I'm not upset by it. I'd rather them do what they can to catch the killer, even if it means taking a closer look at me to eliminate me as a suspect."

I wasn't sure that would actually help anything, since they'd be spending time looking into the wrong man. And if they looked too long, there was always a chance they'd find something they could use to pin it on him. And that's not to mention the fact that the real killer could sneak out of town, or worse, strike again in the interim.

"I've heard about those murders you've solved," Jade said from across the table. "It's actually quite fascinating. How did you ever get into doing such a thing?"

I shrugged. "It's nothing really," I said, unable to stop blushing. "It just sort of happens."

"It's definitely not nothing," Maire said. "You've done a lot for this town. Think of all those bad people that might still be on the loose if it weren't for your intervention."

"I'm proud of her," Dad said.

"As am I," Will added.

I wanted to crawl away somewhere and bury my head in the sand until the compliments stopped coming. All I'd really done was stick my nose in other people's business, usually where it didn't belong, and nearly got it shot off or bashed off in the process. It was by pure luck that I'd solved any of the cases, and honestly, I'm not sure I would have managed any of it without Paul Dalton's help.

I shifted uncomfortably in my seat, wishing someone would change the subject. I was glad I'd helped out all those times, but I was never good at taking compliments, especially when I hadn't done it for the accolades.

"I think you should march right down to the police station tomorrow and make them deputize you," Maire said with a sharp nod.

"It doesn't work that way, Mom," Will said. "Besides, she'll be busy tomorrow."

"I will?" I asked, genuinely perplexed.

"Your appointment," Will said. "With Paige."

In the excitement, I'd completely forgotten I'd set one up with her. I had yet to get a doctor since I'd moved to Pine Hills, and with the way I kept getting knocked around, I figured it would be a wise move to have one. Choosing someone from Will's practice only made sense.

At least for now. If something happened, and we broke up, it might end up being a bit awkward. I'd have to cross that bridge if and when I came to it.

"I'm sure that won't take all day," Maire said, stubbornness spread across her features. "You need to figure this out before someone else gets hurt."

I looked at Dad, but he only shrugged. No help there. How was I supposed to stay out of the way when people kept telling me to get involved? It was like a conspiracy to get me into trouble. First Rita, now Maire!

Thankfully, my cell phone rang just then. I leapt from my chair and grabbed at it like it was a lifeline. I glanced at the caller ID and groaned when I saw it was Paul, no longer sure it was a blessing. "One sec," I said, carrying it into the next room, hoping no one would consider it rude. If he was calling me now, it couldn't be good. "Hello?"

"I'm sorry to bother you so late," he said. "But something's come up and I need you to come down to the police station."

"Can it wait?" I asked, glancing back into the dining room. Maire was still talking, and I was pretty sure she was still pushing the issue. Hopefully, either Dad or Will would talk her out of pressuring me anymore, because quite frankly, she wouldn't have to push too hard to get me to cave.

"It can't," Paul said. He sounded grave. "It's about the murder investigation. I think we need to have a talk."

16

"I could come with you," Dad said from the passenger seat. We were idling in front of my house twenty minutes after I'd received Paul's call. Eleanor was peering out her window at us, making no move to hide her spying. She probably couldn't see us well enough from behind slightly parted curtains, so she'd pulled them open and was leaning forward, binoculars gleaming in the evening light.

"No, I'd better do this alone." I had no idea why Paul wanted me to come down to the police station, but I was darn sure I didn't want Dad there when I found out. If they were going to accuse Dad of killing Rick, I wanted him as far away from the station as possible. California would be best, but I doubted he'd jump on a plane, even if I asked. My house would have to do.

"You sure? Why does he want you?"

"I'm sure. And I don't know. He didn't say."

Dad frowned. "I don't like this."

"Neither do I, but I've got to do it." A part of me wondered if Paul had called simply to break up my dinner date with Will. I knew it was a ludicrous thought, yet I couldn't help myself. It would be a far cry better than anything else I could come up with.

"Okay, Buttercup. You know best." Dad kissed me on the cheek, sighed, and then slipped out of the car. "Let me know when you get home."

"Will do." I waved as he closed the car door, and then I backed out.

I should have demanded Paul tell me exactly why he wanted me to come down to the station, but our conversation had been cut short when something had happened on his end. He'd told me once more to get there as soon as I could and hung up before I could even tell him whether or not I was coming. It would serve him right if I didn't show.

But both he and I knew I wouldn't be able to resist showing. My curiosity always won out. It was probably why he didn't take my calls or return them after he hung up on me. And believe me, I'd tried four times on the way home, hoping he would explain himself. He was either ignoring me, or something big was happening that had captured his full attention.

There were only a few things Paul could want with me at this late an hour. Either he'd had a break in the case, one that needed my input, be it about my dad, Rick and his presumed fascination with me—or it was something completely different. Perhaps he simply needed my insight on the case, realizing how important I was not just to him, but to the police force.

"Maybe he *will* deputize me." Now that would be a riot.

Other than discussing Rick's murder, I couldn't think of a single reason for Paul to call me downtown. As much as I wanted to make it about me, I knew he wouldn't have called just to tell me he'd made a mistake and wanted to get back together. I'd tell him no, of course. But it would be a nice gesture.

I pulled into the police lot and parked out front. No one else was outside as I got out of my car and headed for the door. It wasn't like on TV, where the cops were always dragging felons in, usually against their will. In fact, the Pine Hills police station was pretty sedate almost every time I'd been here. The town simply didn't have that much crime.

Other than the murders that have sprung up since I moved in.

Not exactly a comforting thought, but it was true.

I headed inside, nervously chewing on my thumbnail. There were only a couple of cops in view as I made my way to the counter. The officer there, Officer Garrison, looked up and frowned when she saw me.

"Down the hall," she said with a jerk of her thumb. "Interrogation room."

"Thank you." Apparently, Officer Garrison still wasn't my biggest fan. We'd only ever met one time, and that was when she'd driven me home after a night's stay in one of the downstairs cells. I'd never seen her smile, and was starting to wonder if she knew how.

I hurried down the hall to the indicated room and peeked inside. Paul was sitting at the table, rubbing his forehead. His hat lay next to him. Even from the back, I could tell he was exhausted.

"Paul?" I asked, stepping inside. "You wanted to see me?"

He looked up at me, and any hope I might have had about him wanting to see me for a more pleasant reason than murder fled. "Krissy," he said, standing. "Come in. Take a seat."

I hesitated before crossing the room and sitting on the couch. There was no way I was going to sit on one of those uncomfortable plastic chairs like a common criminal. I was here because he'd asked me to come, not because I'd done anything wrong.

Paul picked up his hat, put it on his head, and then closed the door. He stood there a moment, facing away from me, before turning. His eyes looked sunken in, and a light stubble coated his chin and cheeks. He scrubbed at it with his hand before he moved to sit on the edge of the table.

When he didn't speak right away, I did. "Why am I here?"

"I thought I asked you to keep out of Mr. Wiseman's murder investigation." It was a statement, one spoken with a resigned exasperation only someone who knew me could muster.

"What do you mean?" I asked. "I haven't done anything since the last time we talked!" Was that really only earlier that day?

Paul studied me a long moment before speaking. "Earlier tonight, we got a call about a disturbance. Apparently, a woman took it upon herself to question Harland Pennywinkle about Rick Wiseman's murder, and when he didn't cooperate, she forced her way into his home and started going through his things."

I stared at him, wide-eyed. "I did no such a thing!"

"*You* didn't," he said. "But someone claiming you put them up to it did."

"What?!" I crossed my arms over my chest. "I didn't put anyone up to anything. Someone has been telling bald-faced lies."

Paul sighed, closed his eyes. "Krissy, I want to believe you . . ."

"I'm not lying!" You'd think after all this time, he'd have learned to trust me. "I have no idea what you are talking about. The only people who know anything about my suspicions of Harland are you, my dad, and . . . Oh no."

"Rita Jablonski," Paul finished the thought for me.

I'd almost forgotten how gung ho she'd been about working the case with my dad and me, whether we wanted to or not. I guess I figured she'd drop it once we stopped talking about it.

But then she'd spent those hours talking to my dad. And I just had to bring up Harland while we'd sat there. I should have known Rita wouldn't be content with spreading rumors, not when Dad was there for her to impress.

"It's not my fault," I said, slouching. "I might have mentioned Harland's name to her earlier today, but I never told her to go talk to him."

"Why were you even discussing the case with her?" Paul asked.

"You know Rita. You can't stop her once she starts talking about something. She got on a roll and it sort of slipped out. I didn't realize she'd go so far. I swear!"

"She claims you put her up to it. Said you told her what to do in case he didn't cooperate, that she was only following your lead."

"You know I wouldn't do such a thing. I try not to confront suspects directly if I can help it."

Paul gave me a flat look. "Have you forgotten Heidi Lawyer and her mother, Regina Harper?"

I blushed. "Well, that was different. I was just

wanting to talk to Heidi." Besides, I was new in town then. How was I to know Regina was such a grouch?

"And what about at the Halloween party?"

"You told me to keep an eye out!" My shoulders slumped. "But I get your point."

"Mrs. Jablonski swears she only did what she did because of you."

"I didn't tell her to do a single thing, other than to stay out of it. She did this of her own volition."

Paul eyed me a moment before sighing. "I figured as much, but wanted to talk to you first before I released her to you."

"Wait, she's still here?"

He flashed a mischievous smile that quickly faded. "She's with Buchannan. He's keeping her company while she waits in a cell. Mr. Pennywinkle decided not to press charges, so she'll be free to go."

"And what does that have to do with me?"

Another smile. "She needs a ride home."

Paul rose and started for the door. I stood and made to follow after him, but he stopped and turned.

"Please tell me you're going to stay out of this," he said. "It's already complicated enough without you getting involved."

I crossed my heart. "I have no intention of getting in your way." Though after what Maire had said, I was finding it harder not to want to at least poke around a little.

He didn't look convinced, but nodded, anyway. "You can wait out front. I'll go get her for you."

Paul walked me to the doors and then continued on to get Rita. I noted he didn't go downstairs, to the dank, unused cells Buchannan had shoved me in during my brief incarceration a few months back. I watched him go and then turned to find Officer Garrison watching me.

"I had nothing to do with it," I told her.

She snorted and walked away.

Buchannan stalked by a moment later, looking monumentally annoyed. He glared at me, but refrained from accusing me of anything. Rita had probably talked his ear off, and, knowing her, had found a way to embarrass him in front of his colleagues. I remembered her saying something about him frequenting a less than respectable establishment, and wondered if she'd asked him about it.

"There you are! Lordy Lou, can you believe they would do this to me?"

Rita came storming over, practically dragging Paul along behind her. He had a hand on her arm, presumably to help escort her to the front, but she was having none of it. She marched straight for me, mouth running nonstop.

"It's downright unthinkable that they would put me in a cell of all places! I did nothing wrong! It was all a misunderstanding." She glanced back and glared at Paul. "You should be ashamed of yourself."

"She's all yours," he told me. He was practically laughing.

"Thanks," I told him. "Let's go, Rita."

She harrumphed and followed after me as I made my way to my car. It was a wonder she didn't jabber the entire way. I unlocked the car and slid into the driver's seat. She flopped down beside me and immediately started in.

"I went to Harland's, just like you implied I should."

"I never did such a thing," I told her.

She waved a hand at me. "They already know you're involved, so no sense denying it."

I opened my mouth to protest, but snapped it closed again. Arguing with Rita was like arguing with a cat. Neither listened to a word you said and both did whatever they wanted, when they wanted, regardless of the consequences. I started the car and backed out.

"Anyway," she went on. "I went over there and tried to get him to talk. When he wouldn't, I took it upon myself to have a look around."

"While he was there," I said. "Watching you. What do you think would have happened if you'd found something?"

"Well, I would have called the police, of course."

"And if he stopped you? Rita, he could very well be a murderer. Don't you think you should have been more careful?" I tried not to think about how many times someone had said that to me.

"I know how to take care of myself, dear," Rita said. "I'm not an idiot."

An involuntary tic made my cheek jump, but I held my tongue.

"I didn't get a real chance to look around, anyway," she said. "His place was an absolute mess! I swear, Harland Pennywinkle needs to find someone who can clean up after him. His house was a pigsty! It's a wonder he could find anything in that mess. I know I couldn't." She leaned toward me. "Can you believe he doesn't even own a computer? He types all of his stories up on an old typewriter!" She said it like it was the oddest thing she'd ever heard.

"So, you found nothing that would implicate him in Rick's murder?"

She shook her head. "Not a thing."

Did that mean Harland had nothing to do with Rick's death? Or could it be there was nothing to find in his house? Rick *had* died at the bed-and-breakfast, and the murder weapon had been left behind, so it wasn't like there was much that *could* be found, other than some bloody clothes, I supposed.

"I was thinking I could try again tomorrow," Rita said. "Maybe you could come along! Oh! Or James. He would know what to say."

"No. Absolutely not."

"But . . ."

"No *but*s," I said. "Dad and I are going to stay out of this one. And you need to as well."

She huffed and crossed her arms over her chest. "Well, I don't think it is wise to give up so easily."

"No one is giving up." A headache started to form behind my eyes. "The police are on the case. If you go back to Harland's, they're going to arrest you, and this time, they might not let you go after a few minutes in a cell."

She glowered at me, but surprisingly didn't speak.

"Promise me," I said. "Tell me you'll stop trying to investigate." And in turn, I hoped she'd stop implicating me in her actions.

"Fine," she said, sinking down into her seat. "I suppose I should leave it to the professionals."

Somehow, I didn't quite believe her, but it was all I was going to get. I just had to hope that the next time she decided to get involved, she did it in a way that wouldn't get me into trouble. I managed to do that fine and dandy on my own, thank you very much.

"Good," I said, sighing. "Let's get you home."

17

Dad was already in bed by the time I got home, leaving the house blessedly quiet. I headed straight for the living room and dropped down onto the couch with a sigh. Misfit was curled up next to me, and he glanced up and sniffed before putting his head back down. My laptop lay on the coffee table in front of me. I scooped it up, set it on my lap, and then stared at it.

This was all Maire's fault. I thought I'd been doing a pretty good job keeping my involvement in Rick Wiseman's murder investigation to a minimum, but after our dinner, I was starting to feel that all-too-familiar itch. And thanks to Rita, I wanted to learn more about the authors who'd left their manuscripts, as well as those who hadn't. What did I know about Harland or Joel or any of the others? Nothing—that's what.

"I don't know if I should do this," I said.

Misfit looked up again, yawned, and then went right back to sleep. I stroked him a few times, earning me a stretch and a soft purr. Normally, that would have been enough to get me to relax and put the laptop away, but not tonight. Tonight, every ounce of my inquisitive nature was rearing its ugly head, and I felt powerless to resist.

I snatched up my phone and dialed without thinking. It was only a little past nine, so surely Vicki would still be up. If anyone could talk me out of doing something stupid, she could.

"Krissy?" she asked, sounding out of breath, as if she'd run to the phone. "Is something wrong?"

"No, not really," I said with a sigh. "I'm just sitting here, trying my darndest not to start prying into Rick's death. I thought you might be able to set me straight."

There was a moment of muffled silence, as if she'd pressed the phone to her chest. And then there was a giggle, followed by what sounded like a light smack. "Sorry," she said. "What was that?"

"I . . ." Then it dawned on me. "I'm so sorry."

"For what?" And then a whispered, "Stop it!"

"I didn't mean to interrupt anything."

"You didn't." I could tell by the sound of her voice, I had. And while she might not come out and say she minded, she definitely had better things to do than talk to me.

"I'll go," I said. "Tell Mason I said hi."

There was a moment of silence before she whispered, "You can tell?"

"I can." And honestly, despite my embarrassment, I was glad for her. Vicki deserved to be happy. Her love life was apparently firing on all cylinders, and I counted that as a good thing.

Of course, it did make me realize how mediocre my own was. Sure, I'd just gone to dinner with Will and his parents, but instead of retiring to his room or sitting on the back deck watching the stars, I'd ended up having to pick up Rita at the police station. Instead of a romantic ending to my evening, I was sitting on my couch, with my cat, interrupting my best friend and her boyfriend.

"Hi, Krissy," Mason called from somewhere in the room.

"I'll talk to you tomorrow."

"It's okay if you want to talk now," Vicki said. "Especially if something is wrong."

"It's nothing," I said. "I was just bored."

"You sure?"

"Positive."

We hung up after a quick good-bye, which included a few more giggles and a yelp from Mason.

"Well, crap." I sighed and opened my laptop. At this point, I'd much rather look into the suspects, just to get my mind off Vicki and Mason.

My purse was on the floor next to me. I bent over and snagged the strap, pulling it up far enough so I could grab the page I'd taken from Rick's room, before dropping it back to the floor. I spread the page out next to me so I could use it as a checklist. Misfit eyed it, and I knew he was considering whether or not it would be worth the effort to get up, move a foot, and then lie down on it. I didn't give him the chance, choosing instead to move the page to my other side. He huffed and closed his eyes, the matter settled.

I already knew a few of the names on the list, but Googled them, anyway. There was nothing on Albert Elmore or Vivian Flowers. Neither even had a Facebook page—at least, none that I could find. There was one newsletter item from the Cherry Valley library Web site, saying their writing group was holding meetings there, but otherwise, there wasn't anything on either of them on the Internet.

I skipped over Rita's name, figuring I'd end up finding a gossip blog or something similar. While it might be interesting to see if she said anything about me, I was worried there'd be something on there about my dad, something I wouldn't want to read. Knowing she had a cardboard cutout of him in her bedroom was enough information for me.

That left the names of people I wasn't so familiar with. Any one of them could be the killer.

I started with Joel Osborne and found he maintained a Bobby Drake fan page, dedicated to my dad's most popular recurring detective—the source of the smudged fedora. I skimmed the page, looking for some insights to the man behind it, but the site was almost entirely about Bobby Drake, with very little about Joel anywhere. Checking the message boards, I found there to be only a handful of posts, mostly arguing about the various story lines and hidden meanings behind each scene of the books.

While the names were all just screen names, I wondered if Harland Pennywinkle was one of the posters. Some of the threads were pretty nasty and sounded a lot like the argument Joel and Harland had at the meeting. Then again, Rita had said he didn't have a computer. Unless he posted from his phone, or went somewhere else to rant online, it was unlikely he was one of the posters. Since I couldn't tell for sure, I decided Harland should be next on my list, despite the fact his novel wasn't with the ones I'd discovered under Rick's bed.

Unfortunately, all I found was an infrequently updated Facebook page, telling me he got online somehow every now and again. I'd hoped to find some indication of what his screen name might be, if he in fact was posting on Joel's site, but there was nothing anywhere. Not many people posted using their real names, which made sorting through them that much harder.

"This could be going better," I muttered to Misfit. So far, I'd found a whole lot of nothing, and I feared it would continue that way.

I moved on to the Drummands. They were a little more connected than the last couple of people I'd checked. Both Theresa and Barrett had Twitter and Facebook accounts, as well as a joint Web site where they blogged about their fledgling writing careers. Neither had been published anywhere, but judging by Theresa's posts, she thought her husband was very close.

I skimmed through all their posts, but found nothing that would implicate them in Rick's death. Theresa seemed to be the most active online, though she was just as timid on the Web as she was in person. More often than not, she downplayed her own skill, while talking up Barrett's. Something in the way she wrote, however, told me their relationship wasn't in the best place it could be. She didn't come out and say it outright, but the undertones were there.

I sat back and sighed. As interesting as all of it was, it brought me no closer to finding out who would have wanted Rick dead. I feared I was barking up the wrong tree, because why would the authors want to hurt what could very well be their only chance at their big break? You didn't kill the man who could help you achieve your dream. He might have been a jerk, and might have said he wouldn't look at the manuscripts, but he *had* caved and brought them into his room. Who knew what the next step would have been?

With little hope I'd find anything, I typed in the one name I didn't know: Tony A. Marshall. A few names popped up, but none of them seemed right. Everyone I found was from well outside of town, not someone who would have traveled to Pine Hills to meet with Rick. Maybe it really was a manuscript he'd brought with him, and not one he'd gotten while here.

"Huh," I said, sitting back, frustrated. Maybe I should ask Cameron about him. Since he worked with Rick, he might know where the manuscript had come from.

"What you doing, Buttercup?"

I slammed the laptop closed and just about tossed it from my lap. "Nothing!" I sounded as guilty as a teenage boy caught by his mom trying to browse the Internet for porn. Misfit glared at me, annoyed by my frantic movements, and jumped from the couch, going into the kitchen to check to see if I'd bothered to feed him yet.

Dad smiled and made his way over to where I sat. "It didn't look like nothing."

"I thought you went to bed," I said, tucking the page with all the names on it under my leg.

"I couldn't sleep." He paused and gave me a concerned look. "Is everything okay?"

It took me a moment to realize what he was referring to. "Yeah," I said. "Rita got herself into a little trouble poking around. They let her go. I had to drive her home."

Dad didn't comment. Instead, he nodded toward my laptop. "What were you working on? Did it have anything to do with what she found?"

I considered lying and saying I was updating my mostly neglected Facebook page, but decided that would only make me feel worse than if I told the truth. I hated lying to my dad, and it wasn't like what I was doing was illegal. If I found something, I could simply call Paul in the morning and tell him about it. Just because I was looking didn't mean I had to actually do anything about it myself.

"I was looking up some names," I admitted, picking up the manuscript page and handing it to him. "They all had novels waiting to be read in Rick's room. I thought maybe I'd find something on one of them that might help me figure out who could have killed him." I shrugged. "It was something to do."

Dad scanned the page and then handed it back to me. "Come up with anything?"

I shook my head and sighed. "Not really. I can't find anything on this guy." I pointed to Tony's name. "And I know almost all of the others personally. None of them have a motive as far as I can tell."

"Rejection can be hard," Dad said. "Maybe one of them snapped when he told them he wasn't interested. It's easy to take something like that personally."

"Maybe." I could see Harland getting angry enough to resort to violence if he didn't get his way. He'd looked like he'd wanted to bash Joel's face in when they'd argued about their favorite Drake book.

"Who do you think would have had motive, then?" Dad asked. "I did, obviously, having fought with him that night." He didn't sound proud of the fact. "But since I didn't do it, someone else has to have had a reason, right?"

"I'm not sure." I thought about it, and then opened my laptop. "What was Cameron's last name again?" I asked, bringing up the browser.

"Little," Dad supplied.

And there it was, the very first link. I read it out loud, not quite sure I believed it. "Cameron Little Literary Agency." I glanced at Dad, who was frowning. "Seems awfully suspicious for him to have a Web site up already."

"It does."

I opened the link and was surprised to see how professional his site looked. You didn't throw something like this together overnight, maybe not even in a day or two.

"Does Cameron do Web design?" I asked, skimming the page. It was the only thing I could think of that would explain why he had such a professional-looking page up so quickly. Then again, when would he have found time to do it, considering he was supposed to be reviewing the local authors' manuscripts?

"I don't think so," Dad said. "I'm pretty sure Rick always hired out of the office, so he didn't do the Wiseman Lit site. I suppose Cameron could have done it in his spare time, a sort of pet project or hobby."

I clicked the "About Me" tab on the site and read through it. The photo was definitely professionally done, not something he could have had taken while in Pine Hills. He must have had it done before, though I'd have to check Rick's agency site to see if maybe he'd lifted it from there.

"What's a Brony?" I asked, spotting the odd term in the middle of the bio. Apparently, Cameron was a proud one, whatever it was.

"Isn't that adult male *My Little Pony* fans?"

I shrugged. "Is it? Huh." Who would have figured?

I continued on down the page and noticed that Cameron mentioned working with a literary agent, but didn't call him by name. I pointed it out to Dad.

"Do you think he's trying to separate himself from Rick?" I asked.

"It's likely," Dad said. "Rick wasn't very popular among his peers."

Or anyone else for that matter.

I glanced at Dad, mind whirring. Was Cameron distancing himself from Rick because his former boss wasn't a very nice man, or could it be because he'd had a hand in his untimely demise?

"Cameron does have the most to gain by Rick's death," I said, thinking out loud. "He is hoping to take on his former clients, as well as pick up new ones here, all of which wouldn't be possible if Rick was still around."

"But why kill him?" Dad asked. "He could have simply walked away and started his own agency. That sort of thing happens all the time. No one has to die for it."

I thought about it. Killing someone for their job did seem a bit drastic, but not completely unheard of. It was unlikely Dad would have left Rick for Cameron; at least, he wouldn't have before their argument that night. Maybe Cameron had killed Rick, not realizing he had a golden opportunity sitting right there in front of him. A day more, and it would have all worked out, and Rick would still be alive.

"Maybe Rick had something against him," I said, still trying to think it through. There were so many reasons why Cameron could have wanted Rick dead, it was almost funny. He wasn't just the best suspect, he was practically the *only* one with a rock-solid motive—outside my dad, of course.

"Like what?" Dad asked, eyeing the screen.

"Like some deep dark secret no one else knew." Of course, his proclamation on his site about being a proud Brony shot that down. I didn't think many people would openly admit such a thing, especially on a professional Web site, unless they were completely at ease with who they were. "Maybe Cameron has a dark side and is interested in something illegal, something he wouldn't want anyone else to know about." That made more sense.

"Like what?" Dad asked again.

Like what indeed. "I'm not sure." I closed the browser and shut my laptop lid.

"Why'd you do that?"

I turned on the couch so I could face Dad better. "Should we be doing this?" I asked him.

"Doing what?"

"Poking around. Getting involved."

"Isn't that what you do?"

"Well, yeah. But it feels wrong somehow. It's Rick we're talking about here. We knew him."

"All the more reason to make sure his killer is found."

It was then I could see it. It was more than just catching Rick's killer that had my dad interested in personally solving the case; he wanted to work with me, see how I did what I did. All that time sitting alone in California, hearing about the cases I was solving, had to have been killing him. He'd never investigated anything on his own, though he'd often said if he could live life again, he might choose to become a detective instead of a writer.

And this was his chance to see what it was like, even if only for a few days.

How could I take that away from him?

And more personally, could I really pass up yet another opportunity to do what I myself loved?

"We should call it a night," I said.

Dad's shoulders slumped, and he nodded. "I guess you're right."

"We can talk about this some more tomorrow." A mischievous grin spread across my face. "See what we can dig up."

Dad's eyes lit up. "Tomorrow, then."

"I have a doctor's appointment early, but afterward, I'll come home and we can discuss our next move."

He stood, grinning ear to ear. He looked at least ten years younger. "I can't wait."

I rose and gave him a quick hug. "Thank you," I whispered in his ear.

"For what?" he asked.

"For believing in me."

"Always, Buttercup. Always."

And with that, we both headed to our respective bedrooms to get a good night's sleep—for tomorrow, we would be investigating.

18

I woke up bright and early the next morning, feeling refreshed despite my stressful evening. I showered, got dressed, and got my morning coffee started, mind sorting through what I should do next now that I'd decided to look into Rick's murder more closely.

There were a few options that were immediately evident. I could talk to Harland Pennywinkle and see if I had any better luck getting him to crack than Rita had. I could also pay a visit to Cameron and ask him about his agency, and why it appeared he'd been planning to start it long before Rick died.

And then there was what very well might be the only person who could have seen something that night: Kari Collins. She was working the night of Rick's murder, and if she was as much of a stickler for the rules as the Bunfords said she was, it was unlikely she would have let someone in without questioning them first.

It was as good a place to start as any.

I crept down the hall and peeked into my bedroom. Dad was still sound asleep, Misfit curled up next to him. From the sound of his snores, it didn't appear as if he was going to get up anytime soon. I considered waiting for him, but decided that if I got a head start on the day, he couldn't fault me for it. I'd fill him in later.

I went back into the kitchen, grabbed my phone, and looked up a number. I dialed quickly, before I could change my mind.

"Ted and Bettfast, this is Jo. How may I help you?"

I breathed a sigh of relief. "Hi, Jo. It's Krissy Hancock. Do you remember me?"

"I do." She didn't sound as thrilled by it as I was hoping. The last time I'd talked to her, she'd been practically giddy with the idea of me investigating a murder. I guess having yet another dead body affect her workplace had soured her on me like it had with everyone else at the bed-and-breakfast. Hopefully, finding whoever killed Rick would put me back into their good graces.

"I won't take up much of your time," I said. "I'm calling because I'm looking for someone who works there. Her name is Kari Collins, I believe. I think she works nights most of the time."

"She does," Jo said. "Is she in trouble?" The first hint of interest crept into her voice.

"No trouble. I just want to talk to her and ask her a few questions. What time does she come in?"

"She won't be coming in tonight," she said. "It's her night off and with everything that's happened . . ."

"Okay, thank you." I paused, hoping I wasn't over-reaching by asking more questions, but if I was going to talk to this woman, I wanted to know as much about her as I could ahead of time. "What can you tell me about Kari?"

Jo was silent for a long moment before she said, "She works here. That's all I have to say."

"Do you like her? Is she a good worker? Anything at all you can tell me about her would help me prepare."

"I really need to get back to work."

"Jo . . ." But she was already gone.

I hung up and frowned at the phone. Either Jo was brushing me off, or there was something about Kari Collins that got under her skin. It could be she was annoying, a gossip who couldn't stop talking. Or perhaps there was more to what was going on than anyone was letting on. I could wait until Kari came in to work next to find out.

Or I could look her up and pay her a surprise visit.

I downed my coffee and quickly scooped out the cookie and ate it as I flipped through the white pages. I had a doctor's appointment in a few hours, but that still left me with enough time to pay Kari a visit before I had to head to the doctor's office. There were quite a few Collinses in the book, but only one Kari. I scribbled down her address, finished off the last of the cookie, and then with a silent apology to Dad for leaving him behind, I headed out the door.

Kari didn't live too far from me, which made my decision to stop by that much easier. Her house was a small ranch that could use a fresh coat of paint. The shutters were once black, but were now streaked with white spots that hinted that someone had tried to do just that, but had stopped somewhere short of actually painting them. Near the foundation, the white siding had turned shades of brown and green. A pair of ugly faded pink flamingos stood on either side of the cracked brick walk that led to the front door.

Somewhere out back, a dog barked in a decidedly unfriendly way.

I made my way carefully up the walk, wondering if I'd made the right decision coming here alone. Most of the houses down the lane looked better than Kari's, but all were modest in size. Many driveways held pickups with prominent gun racks attached to the back, Kari's included.

Swallowing hard, I knocked on the door. I was here, so I might as well get it over with now. I definitely didn't want to come back here anytime soon. Who knew if someone would decide to train one of those guns on me for prying?

"What?" The shout came from somewhere inside the house and held a similarly unfriendly tone as the maniacally barking dog.

"Ms. Collins?" I said, raising my voice to be heard over the racket. "My name is Krissy Hancock. I'd like to talk to you for a minute, if that's okay?"

Silence from the other side of the door.

"Ms. Collins?"

"Hold on to your jockstrap." Chains clinked. Many chains. As in, paranoid-that-someone-is-going-to-try-to-break-in-and-kill-you chains. The latch clicked a moment later, and the door opened. A woman who looked to be about forty, going on eighty, peered out. Her hair was a fuzzy mess atop her head. A cigarette jutted from her lower lip, burning slowly and fouling up the air. Her eyes were yellowed, as were her teeth. I wondered if I'd catch something by standing next to her, but there was no help for it, not if I wanted to ask her about that night.

"I'm Krissy," I said, reaching out a hand and mentally hoping she wouldn't take it.

She didn't. "You said. What you want?"

"I heard you were working at Ted and Bettfast the night of the murder."

Not so much as a blink. "Yeah? So?"

"So, I was wondering what you could tell me about that night."

"What's it to you?"

I cleared my throat and rapidly blinked my stinging eyes. "I knew the victim," I said. "I'm trying to figure out what exactly happened to him."

She studied me a moment, sucking hard on her cigarette. The thing burned almost all the way down to the filter before she blew out a bellow's worth of smoke, right into my face. I immediately started coughing, eyes burning from the poison being blown into them. I staggered back and tried to find breathable air, but it seemed to be saturated with smoke.

Kari laughed as if it was the funniest thing she'd seen. "Ain't much to tell you, honestly. The guy died. Probably happened while I wasn't inside."

"Smoke break?" I hazarded a guess when I could breathe again.

"'Course." She winked, snorted, and spat in the grass. "Was late is all I can tell ya. Didn't go looking at no clock. No one was supposed to be inside at the time, and I sure didn't let anyone in, so if somebody did the deed while I was there, they did so without my knowledge."

"Could they have slipped past you while you were outside smoking?"

"'Suppose." She shrugged as if she didn't care one way or the other. "But if they did, they were real quiet about it." She paused and removed what was left of her cigarette from her mouth. She pointed it at me.

"I did hear something while I was outside, though. When I went to check on it, there wasn't nothing there."

"What did it sound like?" I asked, ignoring her less-than-stellar grammar.

She studied her cigarette before snuffing it out on the side of the house. She dropped the crushed butt into what might have once been a flower bed, but was now little more than an ashtray.

"Something heavy hitting the ground somewhere outside. There was a thud and a flutter."

"A flutter."

"Yeah, a flutter."

"Like the sound a bird makes when it takes off?" I asked, imagining a giant parakeet landing somewhere outside Ted and Bettfast.

"Like a flutter."

Gee thanks, I thought bitterly. *That's such a help.* "And you said nothing was there when you checked?"

"Not a damn thing as far as I could tell. Was dark. It happened around the side of the place, where I couldn't see, and I wasn't about to go looking all over the property for something that probably didn't mean anything."

I thought about it a moment before asking, "Which side did the sound come from?"

"The right side."

Knowing it would be pointless to ask for clarification, I tried to envision it myself. If Kari had been facing Ted and Bettfast on her smoke break, the right side would have taken her to the same side Rick's room was on. Could someone have leapt from the window? But if so, what had fluttered? And why not leave the way they came in if they'd already managed to sneak inside? Unless whoever had snuck in had used the window to get in in the first place.

"Were any of the windows open that night?" I asked, trying to remember if Rick's was or not when I'd found him, and failing.

"Don't know. Didn't check."

I had to remember that she wouldn't have suspected anything to be amiss at that point. As far as anyone knew, Rick was still alive in his room. I was sure strange sounds happened around old mansions all the time. It wasn't like she would have automatically assumed a thump and flutter meant a killer was trying to escape.

Even I wasn't sure that's what had happened.

Kari fished out another cigarette, and I decided it was time for me to go. One cloud of smoke in my face was enough for a morning.

"Thank you for your time," I said. "You've been a great help."

"Whatever." She lit up, stepped back inside, and slammed the door in my face.

"That went well," I muttered, happy I'd managed to get anything out of her at all. I couldn't imagine that woman working someplace where she'd have to deal with people on a regular basis. Then again, she *did* work nights, where it was unlikely she would have to interact with anyone. It was probably the only time anyone would put up with her.

Knowing I was being a little too judgmental, especially since I'd only talked to Kari once, I got into my car and checked the time. I still had a good hour before my doctor's appointment. Ted and Bettfast might not be on the way, but I thought I could get there, have a look at the spot Kari indicated, and get to the office in time to meet with Paige.

Without giving it much thought, I started up the car and was on my way.

I wasn't sure if what Kari had told me meant anything or not, but I was hoping that if it did, there'd still be some indication of what had happened. It had been days since Rick's death, so there was a chance any evidence could be long gone by now. At least it hadn't rained, so maybe I'd get lucky.

The parking lot to Ted and Bettfast was depressingly empty as I pulled into an open spot. Only two cars were present, my own making three. I assumed one belonged to Jo and the other to the Bunfords. Murder was definitely hurting their business. If it kept up, maybe they could start advertising it as a murder house. There are actually people out there who would love to stay in a place where someone else had died, strange as it seems.

I got out of my car, but didn't head for the front doors. Instead, I walked around the side of the building, toward the right. I kept my eyes up toward the windows, but was disappointed to see they were all closed. I counted down to where I thought Rick's room would be and then lowered my gaze to the ground below.

It took all of two seconds to note the pair of side-by-side indentations in the grass. I moved to stand behind them, careful not to step on anything, and then bent my knees to hover over them to measure their size. Sure enough, the marks could have easily been made by someone falling hard and landing on their knees here, though by the size of the marks, it was someone larger than myself. I glanced back up and cringed at the height. Landing hard enough to leave a mark would have had to hurt. Chances were good that whoever jumped had spent the rest of the night tending sore knees, and might be limping even now.

So, I now had what I thought might be the killer's escape route. But what good did that do me since it wasn't like I could go around measuring people's knees. No other houses had sight lines to this location, and the only possible witness had been out front, smoking at the time. Looking at the side of the bed-and-breakfast, there didn't appear to be a way up to the windows, so it was unlikely the killer would have gotten in that way unless they'd brought a ladder. But if that was the case, why jump when they could have simply climbed back down once the deed was done?

I scratched the back of my neck and frowned. If the killer couldn't climb in through the window, then they would have had to take the stairs. I found it hard to believe that no one saw them. Then again, everyone but Kari was in bed. All the killer had to do was wait for her to go outside to smoke, and then sneak inside, kill Rick, and jump out the window.

Or the killer could have been hiding in one of the other rooms the entire time.

It made sense. Anyone could have stuck around after all the authors left their manuscripts. It wasn't like the bed-and-breakfast was locked up during the day. The killer might even have entered with Rita's crew and slipped away when no one was looking. All he or she had to do was wait until everyone was asleep, break into Rick's room, and kill him.

My mind went back to the fat man Justin had seen the next day. Had the killer hid afterward and snuck out once everything calmed down? Seemed strange, especially since someone *had* leapt from the window. Could the killer have left something behind and returned to retrieve it?

And what was that flutter Kari said she'd heard?

I returned my gaze to the ground. The grass hadn't been mowed in a few days, so it was a tad long, but not so much that I couldn't see. It took only a few moments for me to spot a faint tan blemish amid the green of the grass. I picked up the thin piece and held it up so I could see it better.

The tan object was a rubber band that had long since passed its prime. Little cracks spider-webbed along its faded surface. Had it belonged to the killer? Or had it lain out here, exposed beneath the sun, for months, dropped by an unsuspecting gardener? From the look of the thing, both were just as likely.

I pocketed the evidence, trying to remember if the manuscript that lay loose beneath Rick's bed had a broken rubber band nearby, or if this could have belonged to it. But if so, why take the rubber band and not the actual pages? It didn't make any sense.

I pulled out my cell phone, intending to call Paul and let him know what I'd found. He'd know better than I.

My eyes landed on the time, and panic shot through me. I was going to be late for my appointment.

Promising myself I'd make the call later, I stuffed my phone back into my pocket, hurried back to my car, and raced out of the parking lot.

19

"I'm sorry I'm late!" I hurried to the window and wrote my name down on the sign-in sheet there. "I'm here to see Doctor Paige."

"Doctor Lipmon?" the nurse at the window asked, looking over the top of her bifocals at me. She was at least eighty if she was a day. Her name tag read BEA.

I winced, still out of breath from the mad dash from my car to the office. I was late, but not nearly as late as I'd feared I would be. "Doc Lipmon, sorry."

Bea gave me an "are you a complete moron?" look before nodding toward the plastic waiting room chairs. "Take a seat. Someone will be with you shortly."

I started toward one of the chairs, but stopped. I turned back to the window and lowered my voice. "Could you let Doctor Foster know I'm here?"

Bea leaned toward me, arms crossed on the counter in front of her. "Are you here to see Doctor Lipmon or Doctor Foster? Can't be both."

"I'm here to see Doc Lipmon for a checkup, but I'd also like to talk to Doctor Foster. He knows me. We're sort of dating."

Bea looked me up and down. "Mm-hmm. Take a seat." She closed the window.

I sat down, feeling like a fool. Here I was, my first visit with Paige, and I'd already screwed it up. Thankfully, I'd already done the paperwork a few days ago when Will had brought it to me, thinking it would save me time. Little did he know how much I would need it.

There was only one other person in the waiting room with me—an older man who kept nodding off to sleep, only to jerk awake a few minutes later to look around like he had no idea where he was. The usual outdated magazines sat on a rack by the front door. A pretty nice flat-screen TV hung on the wall, tuned to *Ellen*, but was turned down so low, only the faintest murmur could be heard. At least the closed-captioning was turned on, so I could follow along without too much trouble.

"Krissy? You wanted to see me?"

I turned away from *Ellen* and rose. "Will." I went over to him for a hug, but he stepped back and shook his head.

"Working," he said with an apologetic smile. He glanced at the old man, who'd nodded off again. "I'll be with you in just a minute, Mr. Karmack." He just about shouted it, though it did little good. The old man didn't budge. "Is everything okay?" he asked me, looking me up and down as if he expected to find bullet holes.

Knowing my track record, it wasn't too far of a stretch.

"I guess," I said with a sigh. "I'm late for my appointment."

He winced. "Paige won't like that."

"I have a good reason." I lowered my voice even though no one else was listening. "I've learned a few things about the murder, possible suspects and what-not. Apparently, someone jumped from Rick's window the night he died. I'm guessing that someone was his murderer."

"Krissy . . ." Will gave me one of those looks usually reserved for a child who couldn't keep her hand out of the cookie jar. "You know you shouldn't be doing this." He sighed. "Mom put this idea into your head, didn't she?"

I blushed, thinking about last night's dinner. "Not really. You know me. I can't leave a good mystery alone, especially when I have a stake in the outcome."

"Even if it gets you into trouble." It wasn't a question, which I found pretty telling.

"Even if it does. Will, my dad is a suspect. They might not think he had anything to do with it now, but what happens in a few days when they can't pin it on someone else? I can't leave it be, not when Buchannan can come knocking on my door at any moment, handcuffs at the ready."

Another long-suffering sigh. "I know you can't. It's just, I worry. I have no idea what happened last night when you took off. You never called, never let me know you were okay."

It was my turn to wince. "I'm sorry about that. I had to take Rita home." I held up a hand when he started to ask a question. "I'll have to tell you later. It's a long story."

He smiled, glanced at Mr. Karmack to make sure he was still asleep, and then kissed the top of my head. "Just be careful, okay? I don't want anything to happen to you."

I made a cross over my heart. "I promise."

He didn't look convinced as he turned to face the napping old man. "Mr. Karmack," he called, raising his voice. "I'll take you back now."

"Me?" The old man blinked rapidly awake, eyes watering. "Where's my wife? Where's Tiffany?"

Will walked over and knelt by Mr. Karmack's chair. "Tiffany passed away five years ago." He sounded like this was something he'd had to say more than once.

"Did she, now?" Mr. Karmack looked close to crying before he frowned. "Where's my glasses? I think I left them at home."

"That's all right. We won't need you to look at anything today." Will helped him stand. "Do you have a ride home?"

"My car is in the lot, so I'd darned well better."

Will gave me a "what can you do?" look before he led Mr. Karmack into the back, holding on to his elbow so the old man wouldn't fall.

I was about to sit back down, when a good-looking male nurse poked his head into the room. "Kristina Hancock?" He looked right at me when he said it. Considering I was the only one there, it was no surprise.

"That's me."

"This way." He held the door open with a smile. As I passed, he pointed toward a scale at the far end of the hall. "Right down there. I'll need to take your measurements."

I refused to look as I stepped onto the scale. He wrote something down, a number I was sure was bigger than when I'd last weighed myself a year ago, and then he checked my height. After writing that down, he led me into a small exam room that held all the trappings of your usual doctor's office. The padded exam table was covered in white roll-on paper. Various health posters hung on the walls, warning of bad diets and early warning signs of disease. The computer looked new, though it was about as basic a machine as you could get. Cotton swabs and a box of disposable gloves sat on the counter by the sink.

"You're here for a standard checkup, right?" the nurse asked, moving to the computer.

"I am."

"First time here?"

"It is."

He flipped through the paperwork, and then typed a few things on the computer—likely the measurements he'd just taken. He then proceeded to ask me the basics: Do I smoke? Do I have any known diseases? Does my family have any history of various other diseases? All of these things had been answered before, filled out in the earlier paperwork, but answer them I did. After that came checking my blood pressure, which was higher than I'd like, though with everything going on lately, it was a wonder it wasn't much higher.

He opened a drawer beneath the exam table. "Go ahead and strip down to your underwear and put this on." He set an ugly blue gown down next to me. "Take off your shoes, but you can leave your socks on for now. It can get cold in here." He gave me a sympathetic smile.

"Sure thing."

"Doctor Lipmon will be with you shortly." And then he was gone.

I quickly got changed, shivering as the layers fell

away. The thin gown did little to warm me as I slid it on. I climbed back onto the table and swung my feet as I awaited the doctor's arrival. I wondered if Will's friends, Carl and Darrin, were in today, or if one of them was working at the hospital in Levington. I hadn't seen their names on the sign-in sheet, but that didn't mean much since I hadn't really been paying attention.

I was perusing a chart about diabetes in women my age when there was a quick knock at the door. A heartbeat later, it opened and the most beautiful woman I'd ever seen walked in. Dark flawless skin. Hair black as night. I sucked in a breath, thinking I'd somehow been transported into one of those medical dramas where all of the doctors and nurses were drop-dead gorgeous. Even Bea had looked pretty good for an elderly woman.

"Ms. Hancock, I'm Doctor Paige Lipmon. Your appointment was scheduled to start over thirty minutes ago."

"I know, I'm sorry," I said, forcing myself to stop staring. "Something came up at the last minute and I thought I could get it done before I needed to be here." I smiled weakly and shrugged. "I was wrong."

She eyed me, dark eyes searching, before she gave me a strained smile, exposing brilliantly white teeth. She moved to the computer and scanned my file before glancing at me again.

"My time is valuable, Ms. Hancock. I expect you to be on time for our next visit. You're lucky today. The person after you canceled, so you aren't holding anything up. If one person is late, it sets everyone else back, something I do not approve of."

"I understand." I lowered my head. I felt like a

middle schooler getting lectured by her teacher for being tardy.

Paige stepped around the computer to stand in front of me. "Will vouched for you," she said, voice softening. "So, I'll let it slide this time."

Something about the way she said his name caused something primal and quite jealous to stir inside me. "Do you know Will well?" I asked, which was a dumb question, considering this was a small practice and they were near the same age, but I couldn't help myself.

"We came out of college together."

My eyes instinctively went to her finger, which was surprisingly bare of rings. I'd have thought someone that gorgeous would have men falling all over themselves to marry her. Was she truly unmarried? Or was she simply cautious? It had to be risky wearing jewelry in a place like this.

"Were you close?" I was trying hard to not sound like a jealous girlfriend, but was failing miserably. "In college."

Paige smiled knowingly. "We are good friends, nothing more. You have nothing to worry about."

I flushed, knowing how silly I was being, yet this was a new experience for me. My last real boyfriend wasn't what anyone would consider a winner, so now that I was dating a real hunk, I didn't know quite how to handle myself.

"Will is a good man," Paige went on. "You're lucky. They're hard to come by." There was a faint sense of longing in her tone, but I don't think it was directed toward mention of Will, but, rather, at something else in her own life.

Even though prying is what I was used to doing, I

managed to keep from asking her questions about her love life. I mean, for one, it wasn't any of my business. And secondly, she was likely going to be my doctor for as long as I lived in Pine Hills. I didn't need to start poking around in her life, no matter how interesting it may be.

"I really like him," I said.

Paige nodded and then gave me a serious look. "He told me a little about you. I don't much care for how you keep putting your life at risk. From what I've heard, you sometimes get yourself hurt doing things you probably shouldn't. Is this an accurate statement?"

"Sometimes," I admitted. "But bad people get put away when I do, so it's worth it."

"I see." She jotted something down on a notepad she'd pulled from her pocket, and then she glanced at the computer screen. "You've been treated for a broken toe and a few scrapes and cuts over the last year or so, but not by this office."

"Nothing major so far," I said, crossing the fingers of both hands in front of me, and giving her my best innocent smile.

Paige sighed. "Are you planning on getting involved in this recent tragedy?"

My smile froze on my face while I tried to come up with something to say that would set her mind at ease. Paige might be beautiful, but I was quickly learning I shouldn't take it for a sign of weakness. Many people think that a pretty woman doesn't have a brain cell in her head, thanks to the way most women are shown on television and the movies. Paige was smart. Real smart. She was also very observant. I had a feeling there were quite a lot of men—and women—who were intimidated by that. She wasn't to be trifled with.

"I may be looking into it," I said, slowly. "I knew the victim. He was close to my dad. I can't just let it slide, not when there might be something I could do to make sure his killer is put behind bars."

She eyed me a moment and then nodded as if she completely understood. "I heard he wasn't a very nice man."

"Who? Mr. Wiseman?"

Paige tapped her pen against the edge of the counter. "My friend went to see him at a meeting of some kind. She came back upset, saying he wouldn't give anyone, let alone her, the time of day. She'd worked hard on her novel, and yet he acted like she was just some leech, trying to take advantage of him."

Interest piqued, I sat forward on the table, careful to keep my gown closed. "Your friend is a writer?"

"She is. This was the first time she's ever gone to the group, however. She doesn't really like the woman running it."

"Rita," I said. "I know how she feels sometimes."

"When she heard the agent was murdered, Amy was beside herself. She'd given him her manuscript just that night, left it outside his room, I think she said. I wasn't clear on what happened exactly."

"Amy is your friend?" I asked, thinking back to the manuscripts I'd seen under the bed. I did remember Rita mentioning someone named Amy at the meeting, but I don't recall seeing her name.

"Amy Goldstein," Paige said. "But she doesn't use her real name when she's writing." A wry smile crossed her lips. "She writes detective novels, the kind with the hard-boiled cops and what have you. Male protagonists, dames, and so on."

I nodded. Dad had written a few of those in his time.

"Well, when she first started writing and submitting them, they were all rejected. She kept getting told that no one wanted to read a detective novel written by a woman."

A lightbulb went on in my head.

"So, instead of taking one man's suggestion and writing romance, she changed her name."

Before Paige could say it, I did: "Tony A. Marshall."

She looked surprised. "That's right. She used her dad's first name, her mom's maiden name, and then slapped her initial in the middle."

No wonder I hadn't been able to find anything on Tony Marshall. He wasn't a *he* after all, but rather, a *she* pretending to be a *he*, just so she could find a home for her novel. I'd heard about that sort of thing before. Even popular authors often wrote under a pseudonym in order to have success in a genre that might not be their norm. It helped avoid confusion.

I had a million questions I wanted to ask Paige about her friend. Could she have seen something the night of Rick's death? What was her temperament like? Was she the type of person who acted before she thought?

But before I could even think to start asking questions, Paige's face went serious. She glanced at her watch, straightened, and removed a pair of gloves from the box beside the sink.

"Now," she said. "Sit up straight. It's time I had a look at you."

20

Embarrassed, but with a seemingly clean bill of health, I left the doctor's office feeling pretty good. Not only had I gotten to see Will and meet one of his colleagues, I'd also landed myself another lead, albeit a small one. But I'd take anything that would help me find Rick's killer before Buchannan found a way to pin it on my dad, even if it might be a long shot.

I got into my car and considered driving home to tell Dad what I'd learned. I quickly nixed the idea, however, realizing that if I went home, he'd want to come along. While I *had* told him we'd investigate together, I was thinking he might be better suited to research on the couch, rather than fieldwork. I would never forgive myself if I took him somewhere and he got hurt.

I fished out my phone and brought up Chrome. A quick Google took me to Amy Goldstein's Facebook page, but it was set to private, so I couldn't see anything other than her profile picture, which was of a flower—not exactly helpful. I tried a few more links, hoping I could figure out where I could find her, but came up empty. Finally, I went to the white pages online and found her phone number. Calling her sounded much more appealing than a face-to-face meeting, especially after my encounter with Kari Collins, so that's exactly what I did.

"Hello?" The voice on the other end was male.

"Hi, can I speak to Amy Goldstein, please?"

"Who's calling?" While there was an overtone of curiosity to the man's voice, he sounded friendly enough.

"Krissy Hancock," I provided, before prepping myself for yet another little white lie. "I'm calling on behalf of the Wiseman Literary Agency in regard to her recently submitted novel."

A pause. "I thought the agent was dead?"

"He did pass." I put as much solemnity into my voice as I could manage. "But his assistant is attempting to take on his clients, as well as any prospective ones who have recently approached him. I'd like to discuss her novel with her before she makes any sort of decision as to what her next step might be."

There was a scratchy sound, like the man on the other end of the line was rubbing his hand over stubble. "Amy's not here right now."

"Is there somewhere I could reach her? It's important I talk to her as soon as possible, Mr. . . . ?"

"Goldstein." Married, then. "She works at Flower Power on Oak Street. You should be able to reach her there."

"I know the place." In fact, it was only one street away from Death by Coffee.

"Have you read her novel?" Mr. Goldstein asked. He sounded hopeful, which made me feel bad.

"I haven't," I said. "I don't work with the books directly."

"Oh." Slight pause. "What did you say your name was again?"

Uh-oh. "Thank you for your time." I hung up before he could ask any more questions. It was likely only a matter of time before he realized who I was and put two and two together. I'd been all over the news during the last year or so, meaning it was likely he'd heard my name more than once before now. If his wife was somehow involved in Rick's death, I was hoping he wouldn't figure out where he'd heard of me until after I'd talked to her.

Putting the car in gear, I headed for Oak Street. My usual method of investigation was to walk up to someone and bluntly ask them whatever I wanted to know. It worked more often than you'd think, but didn't make me very many friends. I remembered seeing Amy at the writers' group meeting, but only a glimpse. I didn't know if she was a nice person or not, but I didn't want to make her hate me on sight, so I thought trying a little more tact in my questioning might be in order.

Of course, tact and I aren't the closest of friends, either. By the time I pulled up in front of Flower Power—a one-floor square building decorated in flower art done by local art students, if the sign out front was to be believed—I was at a total loss as to how to attack the conversation without simply walking up to her and blurting out whatever popped into my head. How did regular detectives do it?

I mentally prayed my good luck would hold out as I got out of my car. Not only were the walls of Flower Power painted in flowery designs, but the bricks near the base had flowers carved into them. Arrangements sat in the windows, though I couldn't tell one flower from the next. I didn't have a green thumb, and gave up trying to keep live plants long ago. Everything either died from inattention, or Misfit ate it. And while I wasn't exactly allergic, anytime I'd tried to grow flowers, the smell would overwhelm my senses to the point where I didn't want to bother.

An electronic bell chimed as I opened the door and stepped inside. It was like walking into a wall of aromas that, while not unpleasant in smell, had an adverse effect on me. My eyes instantly started to water, and I felt a nearly uncontrollable urge to sneeze, which I somehow managed to sniff back.

Okay, so forget about not being allergic. One step inside, and my throat was starting to feel scratchy.

Through my tears, I was able to make out three people in the room with me. Two were obviously employees, dressed in flowery aprons and gardener's gloves. The other was a man who looked as if he was looking for a way to dig himself out of the doghouse. He looked to be at a total loss as they showed him from one bouquet to the next. The middle-aged woman with curly red hair smiled, even as he shook his head at an arrangement of tulips, and then she led him to the next arrangement—this time roses.

The woman who followed behind them was Amy Goldstein.

I hadn't gotten a good look at her back at the group meeting, but that fleeting glimpse was all I'd needed to know it was her. She kept her hair short, cut to her chin, bangs just above her eyebrows. She looked light as a feather, but didn't look unhealthily skinny like so many young women these days. I placed her age at just under thirty, but then again, I was never great at guessing people's ages, especially when they took care of themselves, and from the look of things, she did.

I walked slowly into the room and pretended to look at a few of the displays without actually getting too close to them. I was sniffing incessantly by now and was beginning to wonder if this was what Todd Melville felt like every time he stepped into Death by Coffee when Trouble was around. I was going to have to start serving him his coffee outside to spare him the itchy, watery eyes, because no one should have to suffer this.

Doghouse settled on a pretty collection of flowers that ran the gamut of colors. He was led to the counter by the redhead. Amy turned my way, and her eyes widened in recognition before she heaved a sigh and headed my way.

"You're Krissy Hancock, aren't you?" she asked, coming to a stop in front of me.

"I am," I admitted, glancing around the room. "I, um, thought I'd have a look at a few flowers for the store." I wanted to slap myself upside the head for my lame excuse.

Amy snorted a laugh. "Damon called and told me you were coming."

I winced. I assumed Damon was her husband, and that meant she'd already gotten wind of my little white lie.

She crossed her arms and shifted all her weight to her right foot. "I remember you from the meeting the other night. You're the daughter of the writer." A coy smile lit the corners of her mouth. "And you have a tendency to investigate local murders. Or am I mistaken?"

"You're not," I said, guiltily.

"You're here about that agent's death, then?"

So much for me trying to not be blunt. It was a relief, actually, because I'd had no idea how I was going to go from flowers to dead guy without sounding like I was fishing for information. I'd have to leave the subtle snooping to someone else.

"I am," I said. "You write under a pseudonym, correct?"

Amy looked impressed. "I'm surprised you figured it out. Most people don't even consider that the name on the book might not be the author's actual name. And when I submitted my novel, I didn't put my real name on it anywhere, just to see if he responded to it differently than others."

I didn't want to get Paige into trouble by tattling on her, so I simply tapped the side of my nose and winked, like I'd figured out her secret identity all on my own.

"Well, I'm not sure what I can tell you," Amy said, fishing into her apron. She removed a tissue and handed it to me. "You look like you could use it."

I sniffed, wiped my eyes, and then my nose. "Thanks."

"We could step outside for a few minutes if you want?"

"Thank you."

I followed Amy out of Flower Power with a sigh of relief. As soon as the door closed behind us, I sucked in heaping lungfuls of air untainted by pollen. It was better, but I was still suffering.

"Allergies can be a pain," she said. "I'm allergic to

shellfish. Can hardly smell it without breaking out into hives."

"Sounds horrible."

"I don't like the taste of fish, so I don't mind." She shrugged. "I'm not sure what I can tell you about Mr. Wiseman. I barely talked to the guy."

"Seems like a lot of people are saying that."

Amy produced a toothpick from her pocket and started chewing on it. "Habit," she explained. "Terrible for my teeth, but it's better than chewing gum." She shuddered. "I tried to talk to Mr. Wiseman at the meeting, but he refused to listen to a word I said. He blew me off, just like he did everyone else."

"That had to make you mad."

She rolled her eyes and smiled. "I didn't kill him, if that's what you're implying."

"It's not." I reddened slightly. It had just sort of slipped from my mouth, having heard it from nearly every detective on television. I hadn't even considered how she might take it.

"Well, just to be safe, I'm telling you now: I didn't kill him. I was mad, sure. Everyone was. The guy flat-out ignored us like we weren't worth his time. I get it. He probably thought we were all just a bunch of hacks trying to capitalize on his presence. Admittedly, some of us were. But I worked hard at my craft, spent hours editing the damn thing. It's frustrating when someone who is supposed to be interested in literature blows you off without so much as a glance. It's rude."

"Rick did rub a lot of people the wrong way." Which was making narrowing down the suspects harder than it should have been.

"When I heard that Jablonski woman and some of

the other authors were going to drop manuscripts off at the bed-and-breakfast where the agent was staying, I decided to join them. I printed the stupid thing off just like she'd told me to, even though I knew for a fact Mr. Wiseman preferred his queries sent by e-mail. I should have known better than to listen to anything she said." Amy laughed, and then shrugged. "The others left before me, which was fine. I figured I'd be the last one there and wouldn't have to deal with any of them."

"But you weren't?"

"Nope."

The door opened, and Doghouse stepped outside, whistling and carrying his bouquet. He nodded to each of us in turn, winked at Amy, and then got into a Beemer. He revved the engine twice before speed-ing off.

I turned my attention back to Amy as she flipped the toothpick over in her mouth. One end was chewed to splinters. Nerves? Or did she simply like the sensation?

"Who else did you see when you went to see Rick?"

"I don't know his name offhand. Wore a sweater and a hat."

"A fedora?"

"Yeah, like in the detective novels I read."

"Joel Osborne?"

She shrugged. "Could be. He was at the meeting. Wore the same thing then. Got into a fight with a big guy."

That was Joel all right. "Was he alone?"

"He was when I saw him. He was leaving in a hurry. Don't think he even saw me."

Interesting. So, Joel was there *after* everyone else

had gone. If it weren't for the fact Dad had gone to see Rick later that night, I'd consider Joel a good suspect for having done the deed right then and there. But the timing was off. If he was our killer, then he'd done it some other time. He could have always come back later, still angry about something Rick had said, and finished the job when no one was around.

Of course, it was all still pure speculation. As far as I knew, Joel was in a hurry because he didn't want to miss his favorite show.

"Did you talk to Rick when you got there?" I asked, thinking that if he was agitated, then perhaps there *had* been an altercation. Then again, Rick was always agitated, so I wasn't so sure it would help.

She laughed. "I didn't even try. With how the man was acting, and seeing the pile of manuscripts outside the door, I got the point. He didn't want to talk to us, and nothing good could come of me trying. I figured it couldn't hurt to leave my work there on the off chance he read it. It wasn't like I couldn't print off another copy if he threw it away."

A knock on the glass behind us brought her head around. The middle-aged woman spread her hands, eyebrows raised, in the universal "what are you doing?" gesture, before walking deeper into the store.

"Look, I've got to go," Amy said, shoving the remains of her toothpick back into her pocket. "I wish I could tell you more because, quite frankly, I was hoping this agent was going to be my big break. Now that he's dead, I'm not sure what I'm going to do."

"I hear his assistant, Cameron Little, is looking to take on clients," I provided. "I'm sure he'd be willing to take a look."

Amy got a faraway look in her eye before snapping back to the present. "I might check him out." She started for the door.

"He's usually at Death by Coffee," I called after her. Not only was it true, but it would put her around the other authors. If one of them *had* killed Rick and had seen her that night, maybe they'd show some sign of being nervous. Another long shot, but hey, long shots sometimes worked out.

Amy nodded and waved before she stepped back inside Flower Power. I wiped at my nose and eyes one last time, still feeling the effects of the flowers inside, and then headed back to my car.

I sat back and considered my next move. Amy might have seen Joel at Rick's that night, but many of the authors had gone there then. I couldn't put too much stock in it, especially when I had a far better suspect in mind, one who, as proven by my referral, was benefiting from Rick's death.

And, like I'd told Amy, I knew exactly where to find him.

21

Cameron Little sat at one of the corner tables with just about every author in town clustered around him. He was talking, hands in constant motion, as he presumably explained the intricacies of the publishing world and how the small group could best accomplish their goals. Rita was just about leaning into his lap, her recent run-in with the law apparently forgotten. Georgina and Andi sat next to her, nodding along to Cameron's words, with Andi supplying the occasional gasp when he said something especially interesting.

Theresa and Barrett Drummand sat off to one side, Joel Osborne to their left. He was still wearing the battered fedora, but at least his sweater was different.

While Rita might have forgotten about her transgression from the night before, Harland Pennywinkle hadn't. He sat across from her, arms crossed, and glared. I eyed him, wondering if he could have killed Rick in a fit of rage, and whether or not he'd worked alone. He wasn't sitting with Joel, but the mousy man would glance up at him occasionally. Was it out of fear of another argument? Or had they put their differences aside in order to put Rick Wiseman in his place? They might not agree on a favorite Drake novel, but that didn't mean they couldn't work together if they thought it necessary.

It sounded so good in my head, I very nearly marched over there and accused them of it, but managed to hold myself back. The last time I accused someone of murder in front of a room full of people, it didn't go so well. In fact, every time I did it, something went wrong, and it usually ended up with me getting hurt. I wanted to talk to both Joel and Harland, but I thought it best to wait until I got them alone, or, at least, had police backup.

My interest moved from the two authors to Cameron. He hadn't noticed me yet, so it gave me a chance to watch him. He was smiling, energetic, and he spoke with such conviction, with such a love for what he did, it was hard to believe he might have had anything to do with someone's murder. He sure didn't look the part.

But the facts were the facts. He'd had the most to gain by Rick's death. And here he was now, reaping those benefits.

I crossed the room, eyes on Cameron. I couldn't quite hear what he was saying and wanted to listen in. I stopped just outside the ring of authors, hoping he'd somehow overlook me, but I had no such luck.

He turned a smile on me. "Ms. Hancock," he said. "Please, pull up a chair. I'd love for you to join us. I was just about to discuss the common mistakes I've found in many of their manuscripts in the hopes I can guide them to become even better writers."

"It's very enlightening," Rita said. "You really should join us, Krissy. You could use the help."

Ignoring the unwarranted barb, I kept my focus on Cameron. "Not right now. I'm not a serious writer." Or a writer at all, really. I might go to the meetings, but I never have anything to share.

My proclamation was met with the usual disbelief. They acted like they couldn't believe an author's child didn't inherit the same skill set and interests. It seemed like a completely foreign idea to them, as if they thought that simply because Dad knew how to string words together in a coherent manner, I could do the same.

"You sure?" Cameron asked, sounding mildly disappointed. A cynical part of me wondered if the only reason he'd offered was because he thought that if he managed to impress me, it would also impress my dad.

"I'm sure." I put on my cheery, happy face. "Actually, Cameron, I was hoping I could borrow you for a few minutes."

He looked surprised. "Me? Why?"

"I have a couple of questions I'd like to ask you. It's nothing major. I'd like to clear a few things up."

Rita's hand went to her mouth. "You don't suspect him of killing that agent man, do you?"

All eyes jerked my way. Harland's glower was enough to make me take a step back out of fear he might launch himself out of his seat at me. With Rick out of the way, Cameron was all these people had when it came to realizing their literary dreams. And here I was, about to mess that up. None of them looked happy.

"I'm not accusing anyone of anything," I said.

I was met with a round of "Mm-hmms" and "Yeah, rights."

Cameron stood, eyes concerned. "If there's any way I can help, I'll certainly do it. What do you want to know?"

"I think we should go upstairs and talk privately," I said, glancing around the group. If I started asking questions in front of them, not only would it be all over town in seconds, but I'd probably end up drawn and quartered for my trouble.

Rita jumped to her feet and grabbed me by the arm. She marched me a few steps away and lowered her voice. "Don't ruin this for us!" she hissed. "He didn't do anything wrong."

"I'm just asking him a few questions," I said, pulling my arm from her grip. "I'm not going to ruin anything."

She glared at me.

"It's all right, Ms. Jablonski," Cameron said, coming to our side. "I want to do this."

Rita glared at me a moment longer before turning to Cameron. "Please, call me Rita."

He smiled and nodded. "Rita, then." And then, to me, "Where do you want to do this?"

"This way." I led him up the stairs, into the bookstore portion of Death by Coffee. Rita looked like she wanted to follow, but she held her ground, arms crossed, foot tapping. I put a bookshelf between us and found a spot where I could still be seen, just in case Cameron tried anything. Vicki was at the counter, talking to both Cindy and Jimmy Carlton. A small box of books sat between them. We'd decided to donate a small collection to the library, and they were apparently there to pick it up.

"Okay," Cameron said, running a hand down Trouble, who was snoozing on the shelf next to him. "What did you want to ask me? I have nothing to hide." His eyes darted around the room, contradicting his words.

"I was curious about what exactly happened the night Rick died," I said. "I've talked to a few people who said they saw you in Rick's room and I was wondering if you saw or heard anything while you were there that would make you think someone had it out for him."

Cameron shrugged. "I told the police everything."

"I'm not the police," I said. "And I'm not here to accuse you of murder." Although I still wasn't sure he *didn't* do it. I wasn't ready to take that step, not until I had more facts. "I only want to know what happened so I can establish a time line of sorts."

He sighed. "There isn't much to tell. I drove him back to that bed-and-breakfast after the meeting. While he ranted and raved about how no one in town respects him, I made him his latte, like I always did."

I refrained from saying anything. I hoped someone dropped that darned machine out a window. Better yet, maybe they'd let me do it.

"Some of the authors started showing up a short time later," Cameron went on. "Rick refused to talk to anyone, other than to scream at them. When I tried to let some of them down softly, he turned on me. I backed off because I knew what he was like and didn't feel like spending my entire time here listening to it." He looked down at his feet as if he was ashamed.

"Do you remember who all he yelled at?" I asked.

"I don't know who was out there exactly. He wouldn't let me open the door, and I never looked out the peephole. He was in a mood, so all I wanted to do was gather my things and get back to my hotel room to take a hot shower. I figured he'd be calmer in the morning."

"Did you see anyone when you left?"

"Not a soul." He paused. "Well, I did see one of the women who worked there. She was working on something at the desk. She didn't even look up when I passed by."

"What time was this?" I asked.

Cameron frowned, and then shrugged. "I'm not sure. I didn't look at a clock."

So, the woman could have been Bett Bunford. Or Jo. Or even Kari. None of them had said anything about Cameron leaving that night, but why would they? He'd dropped Rick off and then left. There was nothing sinister in that.

I decided to go with a different tactic and hope it didn't rub Cameron the wrong way, though if it did, maybe he'd let something slip.

"It seems like Rick's death has paid off for you." I said it casually, looking across the room, rather than at him.

A smile flickered across his features, and he actually blushed. "It has. I hate to say it, but his murder is probably the best thing that has happened to me in a long time." He blinked a few times, and then the smile faded as if he just realized how that sounded. "It's a tragedy, for sure. And while my career has advanced since, I'm scared I'll mess it up without his guidance."

"Have you signed anyone yet?"

He shook his head. "I've read through a few of the manuscripts, but haven't found anything publishable as of yet. I'm hopeful though. They aren't all terrible."

"What about through your Web site?" I asked, watching him closely this time. "Anyone contact you through there?"

Cameron hesitated before saying, "You saw my Web site?"

"I came across it," I said, trying to make it sound like it was an accident, not that I'd been actively looking into him.

He took a step closer to me. "I know it looks fishy," he said, voice low and pleading. "But I've been planning to start my own agency for a while now. I had the Web site made up a few months back, but haven't advertised it anywhere. When Rick died, and I decided to work with some of the authors here, I figured it was time, so I published it."

It sounded plausible enough, but it was pretty crappy timing. I decided there wasn't much more I could ask him, not without accusing him of anything. I still had questions, but wasn't sure how to broach them quite yet.

"Well, I hope you have good luck finding authors for your agency. Starting up can be hard." And I knew that from experience. There were times when I thought Death by Coffee would be the death of me, no pun intended.

Cameron smiled. "Thank you. It's been a journey. I was shocked to learn one of the local authors had only one copy of his manuscript." He shook his head in wonder. "I mean, I can't even imagine not saving it somewhere, just in case. What if I were to lose it?"

"Doesn't seem very smart," I allowed.

"No, it doesn't." He sighed and pushed his glasses back up onto his nose. "It's why we usually only accept digital copies, so something like this never happens. But what can you do?" He glanced at his watch. "I should probably go. There's a lot of work left to do, and I'd like to get through the rest of the manuscripts and talk to each of the authors about their work before I head back home."

"You've been a great help," I said.

Cameron turned and hurried away.

"What do you think?" I asked Trouble, gently stroking him. He was being irregularly docile. I wondered if he'd spent some extra time being a terror today, or if he only did that when I was working.

I wasn't sure what I thought about Cameron now. He seemed genuine, yet I couldn't shake the thought that he almost had to have had something to do with Rick's death. Who else benefited? You didn't kill someone simply because he was jerk, or, at least, no sane person did. But who, other than Cameron, had a solid reason to be angry at Rick?

Other than Dad, of course. I absolutely refused to follow that line of thinking.

"Can you believe what she's done?" Rita's voice pierced through my thoughts. I followed the sound of her wail to find her clutching at Dad, who'd apparently just walked through the door. "He left! I didn't even get a chance to tell him about the changes I'm going to make to my story, and she went and scared him off!"

Groaning inwardly, I hurried down the stairs. "What are you doing here?" I asked Dad.

"I came looking for you," he said. "What is she talking about?"

"Nothing." I glared at Rita, silently warning her not to contradict me. Dad didn't need to know I'd been investigating without him. "Cameron had to go. I had nothing to do with it."

"She took him aside and accused him of killing your agent!" Rita said it loud enough that the entire store stopped to stare.

"I did no such thing!"

"What else could have happened?" she asked. "It's just the sort of thing you do all the time." She huffed. "You never care how your actions hurt others."

I rolled my eyes. "Like you're one to talk," I muttered.

"Ladies," Dad said, grinning. "There's no need to argue. I'm sure Kristina has a perfectly good explanation as to why she wanted to talk to Cameron with no one else present." He looked at me expectantly.

There was no way of talking myself out of this one. I felt ashamed, and it wasn't because of my encounter with Cameron. I'd told Dad we could look into Rick's murder together, and here I was, running off and doing it on my own. I might have felt like I'd had a good reason at the time, but now, I was wishing I would have waited for him.

I grabbed him by the elbow and led him away from Rita, who gasped as if I'd just stolen her most prized possession. Thankfully, she took the hint and didn't follow us over.

"I might have done some snooping while I was out today," I admitted, guilt causing my ears to burn.

"Oh?" He sounded as disappointed as I feared he would be. "Did you learn anything?"

"I'm not sure. It appears someone jumped out of Rick's window the night of his murder. I'm guessing it was the killer, but I can't be sure." I fingered the rubber band in my pocket, but didn't remove it.

"Do you think Cameron could have done it?" He sounded skeptical.

"He gained quite a lot from Rick's death," I said. "But while he has a pretty good motive, I'm just not sure he could pull it off. Everyone knew he was Rick's assistant and had access to his room. Why kill him there and then jump out the window? Why not lure him somewhere else?"

"Rick was pretty stubborn. No one lures him anywhere he doesn't want to be."

"Okay, fine, but why jump out the window? Why not just walk away? I don't think anyone would have thought it strange for him to be there. He was Rick's assistant, so people would expect him to be hovering around."

"Maybe he got blood on him."

I paused. Why hadn't I thought about that?

Dad looked contemplative. "Whoever stabbed Rick would likely have had to change afterward, right?"

"Right."

"Even a little blood would stain. Black and red clothing might hide it, but it couldn't erase the evidence entirely." He shook himself. "But we shouldn't be talking about these things right now."

"We shouldn't?"

Dad put his arm around me. "I'm thinking we find somewhere to sit down and grab a late lunch. We can discuss the details of the case over a hamburger." His stomach growled, as if on cue.

I glanced around Death by Coffee and realized I had no reason to be here any longer. All of the suspects were gone. Only Rita and her gossip pals, Georgina and Andi, were still here. Apparently, the rest of the authors had left when Cameron had gone, leaving me with no one to interrogate.

"You're right," I said, my own stomach giving a small growl of approval. Other than breakfast, I had yet to eat. Time had flown right by—a hazard of investigation, I was quickly learning. "Where do you want to go?"

Dad led me toward the door. "I heard about this place in town that's supposed to have really good food. I think it's called J&E's . . ."

22

By some miracle of fate, Judith Banyon wasn't at J&E's Banyon Tree when we arrived. I was thankful because the ownership wasn't exactly thrilled with me. Judith accused me of stealing her customers, because before I opened Death by Coffee, the Banyon Tree was the place to go in Pine Hills for your morning cup of joe. I'd been chased from the premises more than once now, and fully expected to have it happen again.

We picked a table by the window and sat. I was so intent on keeping an eye out for Judith or her husband, Eddie, that I didn't notice who our waitress was until she cleared her throat and gave me an expectant look.

"Hi, Shannon," I said, plastering on a smile. "I'll take a Coke."

She gave me a strained smile and then spun and walked away, Dad having already ordered his drink.

"You two know each other?" he asked.

"It's a long story."

Shannon came back a moment later, drinks in hand. She set Dad's tea down carefully. My Coke came down with a smidge more force.

"What can I get you?" she asked, pointedly not looking my way.

I felt bad. Shannon seemed like a nice girl, but we'd both fallen for the same man. And while I was no longer interested in Paul Dalton—shush, I'm not!—Shannon still was. I've never been the woman who'd come between a couple before, and didn't know how to handle it now.

Dad and I ordered. Shannon remained professional, but I was definitely feeling a chill coming off her. I knew her relationship with Paul was on the rocks, and I sorely hoped it didn't have anything to do with me. I was with Will, so there was no reason why it should.

Dad looked at me curiously when Shannon departed. I only smiled, shrugged, and sipped at my Coke. I was definitely not going to get into it with my dad.

Somehow, we didn't discuss Rick's murder during lunch, despite what he'd said. I can't say I wasn't relieved. Every loud sound caused me to jump, and once, when an older woman passed by, I just about leapt from my chair and hit her upside the head with my purse, thinking Judith was trying to sneak up on me.

"You ready to go?" Dad asked, half his sandwich still sitting on his plate. "You seem tense."

"Yeah," I said. I don't think my nerves could have taken much more.

Dad paid the bill, refusing to let me chip in.

Shannon's smile was icy when she gave him his change and told me to have a good day. Someday soon, I'd have to have a sit-down with her to clear the air. I didn't want there to be any bad blood between us, especially since she was once one of the only people in J&E's who treated me with an ounce of respect.

Dad and I had taken separate cars to the Banyon Tree, so my drive back home was quiet. I thought a lot about what I'd learned today, and wondered how best to approach it moving forward. How could I talk to Harland without him getting angry? Who jumped out of Rick's window? What about Joel? Could he have anything to do with Rick's death? And what wasn't Cameron telling me earlier? I swear he knew more than he was letting on.

When I got home, Dad was already there, in the bedroom, making a few calls. He sounded stressed when I peeked in on him, though he smiled when he saw me. In all of this, I kept forgetting how hard this had to be on him, and not just personally, but career-wise. The man who'd placed his books with publishers was now gone. He'd have to find someone new if he wanted to continue writing, because there was no way Dad was going to negotiate contracts on his own. I got my money sense from him, if that tells you anything.

While he conducted his business, I tried to keep myself busy with puzzles. Misfit sat on the counter next to me, watching my pen, which remained mostly motionless. I couldn't focus. I kept thinking about my three best suspects: Cameron, Harland, and Joel. One of them had to have done it, and quite possibly, more than one of them could be involved if they were willing to work together. Could Cameron have convinced the two writers to take Rick out with a promise to sign them on later? It was a stretch, but people *have* killed for less.

A knock at the door pulled me from my ruminations. I shoved my pen in my purse so Misfit wouldn't make off with it, and then headed for the door. It was late afternoon, and I wasn't expecting company. I peeked out the window to see a bright pink suit, before opening the door to a clearly distressed Jules Phan.

"Jules?" I asked. "What's wrong?"

He looked as if he was about to break down in tears. "It's terrible!" he wailed. "It's ruined!"

I stepped aside to let him in. "Are you okay?"

"I'm fine." He sucked in a breath and walked into the house. Misfit bolted to his feet, on the lookout for Maestro, but Jules hadn't brought the little dog with him. "But Phantastic Candies isn't."

"Oh no! What happened?"

"A waterline broke in the bathroom. I was out front and didn't hear anything because I'd turned the music up for the kids. It wasn't until I saw a girl playing in the water that I realized something was amiss. By the time I tracked down the source, it was too late! The whole place is flooded!"

My heart clenched, thinking of all the candy that was now soggy and ruined. I have an admitted sweet tooth, and the thought of all that sugar and chocolate being thrown into the garbage was a travesty of the first degree. Add to that the fact that Phantastic Candies was Jules's lifeblood, and we had a near national disaster on our hands.

"Did you get the water shut off?" I asked, glancing down at Jules's feet. Sure enough, his lower legs were damp to midcalf.

"I did," he said. "But we have to close until everything dries out. I'm afraid I'm going to have to replace the floors, and one of the candy chutes is now clogged with so much gunk, I don't think I'll ever get it out."

"You have insurance, right?"

He nodded, seemingly relieved. "I'll still be responsible for some of it. And the fact that I won't be making any money while they get it fixed is going to make things tight around here. Lance is on his way back home, but there isn't anything he can do." He closed his eyes and put a hand to his forehead. "Krissy, what am I going to do?"

I wrapped him in a hug. "It'll be fine," I said, hoping it was true. Jules was a good friend, and his candy store was a place the kids could go for some good cheer. "Maybe once everything is fixed, you can have a grand reopening event. It might bring in lots of customers that will make up for the lost time." I knew I'd go, and I was pretty sure most of the town would turn out as well.

He stepped back, eyes lighting up. "You're right! I could hang banners, hire a live band to play for all the kiddies." He clapped his hands together. "There could be balloons and I could set up stations for the kids to make drawings and hang them on the wall."

I nodded along, smiling. With Jules, everything was big. He truly cared about the kids he served, and I knew he would make the entire event about them, rather than himself. The celebration was probably going to be the go-to event of the year here in Pine Hills.

"I could always help out if you need me," I offered.

"Thank you." He enveloped me in an enthusiastic

hug. "Maybe we could get the entire street involved. We could turn it into a block party of sorts. I have to make some calls!"

Jules hurried out the door and over to his house, a skip in his step. With how I always seemed to turn other people's mood sour when I was around, it was nice to know I could make a positive difference in someone's life occasionally. I watched him until he stepped inside, calling, "Maestro! Krissy has given me a fantastic idea!" And then his door closed, and he was gone.

"Who was that?" Dad asked, coming out from the bedroom.

"Jules Phan," I said, closing my own door. "He's my neighbor. He owns the local candy store."

"Ah. Is everything okay? He sounded upset when he came in."

"I think so." I crossed the room to pet Misfit, who was still on high alert, searching for Maestro. "Did you get things sorted out?"

"I'm working on it." Dad sighed. "There are some details I'm going to have to work out with my publisher now that Rick's gone, but I don't think there will be any problems." He sat at the island counter as if the weight of the world was dragging him down. "This is a mess."

I sat down next to him. "We'll get through it."

"I know. I just wish there was more I could do."

"Yeah." I looked guiltily away before patting his hand. "I swear Cameron knows more than he's letting on, but he's not going to say anything that's going to get himself into trouble."

Dad smiled wistfully. "If I was Bobby Drake, I'd have

no qualms about breaking into someone's house to dig for clues. It's so much easier in books."

"Well, this isn't one of your novels," I said, flushing. I'd had my own Bobby Drake moments in the past, though I didn't want him to know that. Breaking and entering wasn't something you shared with your father. "Besides, Cameron doesn't live in town. He's staying at a hotel somewhere, so it isn't like we can break into his place, anyway."

"I do know where he's staying," Dad said. There was something in his tone I didn't like. "His room was two doors down from mine when I stayed at the hotel."

Our eyes met. "You don't think he'd have anything there that would help solve the case, do you?"

"He might." Dad rubbed thoughtfully at his chin. "If he killed Rick, we might find something there. Bloody clothes. An incriminating e-mail on his laptop."

"Or, if he knows who did it, he might be in contact with him or her. Maybe he's planning to blackmail them. Or perhaps he had a hand in orchestrating it."

Dad's mouth crooked in a mischievous smile. "What do you think about paying Cameron's room a visit tonight?"

Something in the depths of my brain screamed at me to say no, but instead, I gave him a crooked smile of my own. "Sounds like fun."

Dad clapped his hands together and laughed. "It's a date, then."

"Wait!" A new thought shot through me. "What if he's there when we get there?"

"We could tell him we're stopping by to see how he

is. Or maybe I could talk to him about my plans. I *will* need a new agent eventually."

"But we can't snoop around if he's there. Even if you are trying to distract him, there's no way he's going to let me riffle through his room."

Dad frowned. "So, now what?" He sounded disappointed.

My mind raced. While breaking into Cameron's hotel room was definitely a bad idea, it also might help prove one way or the other if he was involved in Rick's death. To be honest, I didn't want him to be. He seemed like a nice guy, albeit something of an opportunist.

To this point, all I'd really done was spin my wheels, making no real progress on the case. Since Paul hadn't come around asking me any more questions, and I hadn't seen a hint of him or Buchannan since they'd released Rita, I was pretty sure the police were just as stumped as I was. Checking Cameron's room for clues could only help, right?

An idea trickled through my brain then. Cameron was doing his best to take on his former boss's role as a literary agent. He wanted to work with some of the local authors in the hopes of finding a gem in the rough. I was pretty sure I could use that.

I snatched my phone out of my purse and dialed before I could reconsider.

"Hi, Rita," I said when it was picked up on the other end. "I have a favor to ask of you."

"I'm terribly busy at the moment, dear."

"It's about Cameron."

There was a pause before she said, "I'm listening."

"I was wondering, do you happen to have his cell phone number?"

"Well, of course I do! I convinced him to give it to me in case I made any changes to my manuscript that he just *had* to know about. You know, he's going to get me published and James Hancock and I are going on a world book-signing tour together. I've already started picking out the locations and dates!"

I rolled my eyes, but didn't burst her bubble. I needed her for this. "That sounds great. What do you say to calling Cameron up and setting up a meeting with him tonight?"

"Why?" Suspicion practically dripped from the question.

I could lie and tell her a tall tale about Cameron telling me he wanted to discuss her novel with her because he thought it had potential, but it would take all of two minutes of them talking before they'd both realize they'd been had. I'd never hear the end of it, and she'd likely find a way to get me into trouble afterward, out of spite. Besides, we needed time. And to get it, they needed to stick together for a lot longer than a couple of minutes.

So, against my better judgment, I opted for the truth.

"Dad and I want to make sure Cameron had nothing to do with Rick's murder," I said. "To do that, we need to get into his hotel room while he isn't there."

"You really don't think Mr. Little had anything to do with that horrible business, now do you?"

"I hope not," I said. "This is our way to clear his name. You call him, ask him to meet you for dinner to discuss your novel, and while he's gone, Dad and I slip in, take a look around, and then get out before your dinner concludes. You'll get alone time with him, so you'll benefit from it, too."

"It could work. . . ." Rita sounded interested, as I'd known she'd be. "It's just like your father's novel—"

I cut her off. "Exactly. Can you help? James Hancock would appreciate it."

He gave me a strange look as Rita squealed into the phone. "Of course, dear, I'll help. Now you just give me five minutes to make the call and I'll get right back to you. This is so exciting! I'm helping in a real murder investigation with James Hancock." She actually sighed into the phone before hanging up.

"Well?" Dad asked as I set my phone down onto the counter. I felt bad for coaxing her the way I had, but it had produced the desired result.

"Rita's going to see if he'll meet her. She'll call back once she knows."

My stomach was in knots as I waited. No matter what happened, I was worried about the consequences. If he refused to meet her, then we weren't going to get into his room tonight, which meant evidence might never be found. If it did work, then we'd be committing a crime, one that would likely end with the both of us sitting in a jail cell, with Officer Dalton yelling at me for being irresponsible yet again.

But could I really let this opportunity pass me by? It meant so much to my dad. He looked at least five years younger every time we discussed the case, and now that we were planning to take action, he looked even younger still.

My phone rang, and I snatched it up off the counter. "Well?" I asked, not sure what I was hoping for.

"We're meeting tonight at seven," she said. "I think he's sweet on me, though all I want is a purely business relationship."

"Great!" I gave Dad a thumbs-up. He pumped a fist

into the air and winked. "Try to keep him at least an hour. More, if you can manage it."

"I'll have that man turned into putty if that's what it takes."

I blocked the mental image of Rita trying to seduce the much-younger Cameron. "Thank you, Rita. You're being a big help."

"Tell James I'm doing this for him."

"I will."

We hung up, and I looked at the clock. "We have about three hours before we should go," I said, calculating travel time.

"Okay, great. Let me hit the shower and get changed." Dad started for the hall, stopped, and turned back to me. "I appreciate you doing this. I know we shouldn't be doing anything at all, but there's something exhilarating about being a part of an investigation like this. I haven't felt this alive in years."

"Trust me," I said. "I know the feeling."

With a wink and an excited clap of his hands, Dad headed for the bathroom. I looked at Misfit, who was watching me with his head cocked to the side, as if questioning my sanity.

"What am I getting myself into?" I asked him.

I swear, he shrugged before he jumped down and headed to his food dish. Apparently, he wasn't convinced I'd be coming back home to feed him later.

"I don't blame you," I muttered, rising to feed my cat for what I hoped wouldn't be the last time.

23

"This is it."

I turned in to the indicated lot and parked. The hotel Cameron was staying at wasn't one of those big chain hotels you saw everywhere, but rather, it was a small, family-owned one that looked more like a cheap roadside motel than anything. We wouldn't have to go inside a main building to reach his room, which could only help our chances of getting in unseen.

"At least it's kind of dark," I said, still buckled in. I was warring with myself on whether or not we should carry through with our plan or if we should turn around, go home, and share a tub of Rocky Road. The overcast sky was doing little for my nerves.

"Light's burned out," Dad said, nodding toward the light in question. "Noticed it when I stayed here. His room is just under it."

"Not exactly a high-quality establishment," I muttered, eyeing the building. More than one light was burned out, actually, and one of the doors was boarded shut. I didn't take it as a good sign.

"No, it isn't," Dad chuckled.

Besides my car, there were only nine other vehicles in the lot. From where I sat, I counted at least twenty rooms, with more around back. It was a wonder the place hadn't gone out of business yet. Pine Hills wasn't exactly a vacation destination. Maybe it *did* double as a long-term motel for some of its guests. It was the only way the place could stay afloat, I imagined.

"You should have told me you were coming," I said. "You shouldn't have stayed here."

"It wasn't so bad," Dad said with a shrug. "It has . . . personality."

I gave him a sideways stare before unbuckling. "I guess we'd better get started." I glanced around the lot at the cars. "Do you know what Cameron drives?" I asked. "I want to make sure he's already gone."

Dad shook his head. "I don't know. I never paid attention."

Knowing my luck, Cameron was probably sitting in his room, watching us.

We got out of the car and slowly made our way to the front of the hotel. The place didn't even have a real name; just a big sign proclaiming it to be HOTEL, done in all caps. A VACANCY sign blinked below it. No one was outside, guests or employees. The door to the office was to the left of the building, and we were headed to the far right. From my vantage point, I saw no one inside the office, but that didn't mean they weren't there.

Dad led me to room 119, which was on the lower floor. A metal grate stairwell led upstairs to the only other level of the motel. If anyone were to step outside above us, we'd hear them.

"Wait!" I said, stopping right before the door. "We don't have a key. How are we going to get in?" I was almost relieved we wouldn't have to do this. There was no way I was going to break a window or try to bash in the door.

"No need," Dad said, a grin a mile wide spread across his face. He reached into his jacket pocket and came away with two thin pieces of metal.

"Are those lockpicks?" I asked in a high-pitched whisper. "How did you get lockpicks?"

"Tools of the trade," he said, kneeling in front of the door. "We're lucky this place still uses old-fashioned keys. Keep a lookout for me, would you?"

I spun to face the parking lot, heart hammering in my chest. Not only were we sneaking into a room we had no right being in, we were legitimately breaking and entering. "Tools of the trade?" I said in disbelief. "You're not a thief; you're a writer. Why do you have lockpicks?"

Dad was silent a moment, the only sounds being the click of the picks entering and moving in the lock. Then he said, "When I first started writing Bobby Drake, I wanted to know how to pick a lock like he did so the story rang true. I found a professional willing to teach me. He showed me how it was done, and then gave me the lockpicks as a gift afterward. I named a character after him, you know?"

"And you just happened to have them on you?" I asked, unable to believe he'd never told me about this before.

I glanced back just as Dad shrugged. "You never know when you'll need them." Another definitive click. "There!" He stood, smiling like he'd just cracked a safe at Fort Knox. He turned the knob and pushed the door inward with a bow. "After you."

I gave my dad an incredulous look before stepping into the room. He slid in behind me and quietly closed the door before flipping on the light. After a moment's thought, he locked the door.

"Just in case," he said.

"There's not much to see," I noted, looking around the small room. The bed was a single that sagged in the middle, though the sheets looked clean. There was an end table with a lamp on it, and a small three-drawer dresser with an old box television atop it.

And that was it. No extra amenities here. The closet was closed, and another door across the room led to a bathroom that had only a stand-up shower, a toilet, and a tiny sink. One of the two lights inside was burned out, but at least there was a window to let in a little extra light.

Unsure where else to start, I started there, in the bathroom. Cameron's shampoo, a bar of soap, and a small black bag sat on the floor next to the shower. There was no room on the tiny sink for any of it, not even a razor. I opened the bag to find his deodorant, toothpaste, and toothbrush. Nothing else was in the room, not even a trash can where he might have tossed an incriminating document.

I returned to the bedroom as Dad stepped out of the closet, carrying a suitcase. He set it atop the bed, glanced at me, and then opened it.

"Just clothes," I said, peering over his shoulder. He sorted through them quickly, checking the bottom of the suitcase to make sure Cameron didn't keep his secrets hidden beneath his boxers.

"Nothing," he said, zipping the suitcase closed and

carrying it back to the closet. "Not even a hidden compartment." He sounded almost disappointed.

"Was that all that was in there?" I asked, checking my watch. We'd already been there for twenty minutes. I couldn't believe how quickly time had passed. While I hoped Rita would keep Cameron busy for the next hour or so, I wasn't counting on it.

Dad stood on his tiptoes and checked the top shelf of the closet. "Nothing else but this." He showed me a plastic hanger that had been broken in two and discarded.

I huffed and glanced around the room. "If he is reading the local authors' manuscripts, where would he keep them?" I wondered aloud.

"Maybe he has them in his car," Dad said, pushing both his palms into his back and wincing. "He doesn't spend a lot of time here. It would be a lot easier to keep them in his car in case he needs them while at your shop."

"Maybe," I said with a frown. "But wouldn't he read them here?" I walked over to the bed, and then on a hunch, dropped to my knees. I flipped up the skirt and peered under the bed. "Bingo!"

The manuscripts were stacked by twos, right where I'd found the ones in Rick's room at the bed-and-breakfast. I pulled them out and set them atop the mattress, heart now racing. Was there a reason that I'd found them hidden under the bed in the exact same way as the ones in Rick's room? Or was it simply a convenient storage space for bulky manuscripts?

I sorted through them quickly. I wasn't sure what I was looking for, but felt it was important.

Most of the names across the top were the same

as the ones I'd found at Rick's. Rita's was missing, though I assumed Cameron had taken it with him, since he was meeting her for dinner to discuss the novel. Harland's novel looked a bit worse for wear, which didn't surprise me, knowing the man. The paper was thick, and it had obviously been typed on a typewriter, rather than on a computer. The front page had a coffee ring on it, as if he'd used it as a coaster before turning it in.

I set it aside, exposing the one beneath.

"Barrett Drummand," I said, reading the name across the top. A worn rubber band held it together. With a frown, I reached into my pocket and removed the one there. They were the same tan color.

I did a quick check of the rest of the manuscripts to see if Theresa's was among them. I found it at the bottom of the stack.

Out of curiosity, I flipped to the same page as the one I'd taken from Rick's room, starting with Barrett's. Instead of the single line, there was a wall of text. Theresa's, however, held the same single line: "to the death!"

My eyes drifted to Harland's manuscript and its bent and dirty pages. The rubber band was the same tan color and was old, though not nearly as cracked and ancient as the ones the Drummands used. Was there a reason for that? Could Harland have jumped out of the window, manuscript in hand, having accidentally broken Theresa's rubber band? He would have been sweating, and likely in a panic, so it was unlikely he would have been too careful of the pages while on the run, hence why they looked so beat up.

But if he'd taken his manuscript with him after the

murder, why go back later? Had Justin seen another
fat man that day, not Harland? I had no way of knowing for sure.

"Hey, Buttercup." I looked up to see Dad holding
a laptop. "Look what I found."

I restacked the manuscripts and returned them to
their hiding spot under the bed before joining Dad.
He glanced at me once and then opened the laptop
lid. A quick swipe of the screen, and then a blinking
cursor awaited input of a password.

"Now what?" I asked.

Dad focused on the screen. "We figure it out." He
quickly typed something into the space that came up
all asterisks, so I had no idea what word he'd attempted to use. Whatever it was, it didn't work.

"We should probably go soon," I said, glancing at
my watch. Surprisingly, another twenty minutes had
passed. I tapped my watch face, wondering if it was
running fast. It sure hadn't felt like we'd been there
for forty minutes.

"I can do this." Another password, and another
failure.

"Did you hang out with a hacker at some point and
learn trade secrets from her?" I asked. "Because, if
not, there's no way you're going to be able to guess
his password."

Dad glanced at me. "That's a good idea. I might
have to see what I can set up before I work on my
next book."

I hadn't meant to give him ideas. "Can we go now?"

"Give me a few more minutes." Another attempt
equaled another failure. "I might not be an expert,
but I do know most people aren't as careful choosing their passwords as they should be. People will

sometimes use things like '12345.'" As he said it, he typed it in. Another failure. "Or 'qwerty.'" It didn't work, either.

"They also use the names of family members and pets," I said. "Do you happen to know his cat's name?"

Dad tapped his fingers on the keys in thought. "What do we know about him?"

"He was, up until a few days ago, Rick Wiseman's assistant. Other than that, I've never met him before."

Dad typed in "Rick" and then "Wiseman." Both failed.

"He's now an agent himself." My eyes widened. "Wait!" I grabbed my phone out of my pocket and brought up Cameron's Web site. I went to the "About Me" page and scrolled down, turning the phone to my dad.

He smiled and typed in "Brony."

"And we're in."

The laptop began booting up as Dad and I shared a high five.

"What do you think we'll find?" I asked, excitedly. There might be a confession inside, or perhaps a detailed diary discussing Cameron's dissatisfaction with Rick's treatment of him. Maybe there would be links in his browser's history, leading us to sites on how to kill your boss. The possibilities were endless.

The laptop finished booting up. Dad used the trackpad to open the first folder there. The files were all JPEG, titled by date. Dad and I glanced at one another before he opened the first.

The photograph was grainy, hard to see. It looked as if it had been taken through two windows—a car's and a house's. Squinting, I was able to make out Rick's face . . .

And far more of him than I ever wanted to see.

"Close it!" I said, turning away.

"I think I know her," Dad said, looking closer instead of closing the photograph. I heard him click over to another photo.

"Is it similar to the last one?" I asked, not daring to look.

But before he could tell me, we were interrupted by the distinctive sound of a key entering the lock of the hotel room door.

24

There was no time to think.

The only window in the room faced the front door, which meant it was completely useless to us. Both Dad and I were on our feet, the laptop on the bed, forgotten. We could stand there and wait for Cameron to walk in and catch us in his room, or we could try to find another way out.

I, for one, didn't feel like trying to explain this to the cops.

"The bathroom," I hissed, grabbing Dad's arm and dragging him toward the tiny space. The window there was small and high up, but it was our only chance of escaping notice, unless we wanted to hide under the bed all night and wait for Cameron to leave.

Dad jerked the bathroom door closed behind us just as the front door opened. I held my breath and listened, eyes wide, heart pounding so loud, it was practically all I could hear. Dad held his finger to his lips needlessly, ear pressed to the door. Muttering came from the other side, but I couldn't tell for sure if it was Cameron, or perhaps the killer come to finish off yet another literary agent.

There was no telling how long we had before whoever was in there decided to check the bathroom, so I turned to the window. It was just as I remembered it, small, and set high up on the wall. I thought that if we sucked in our guts, Dad and I might be able to squeeze through. The drop would be a big one, but not so bad that I thought we'd get more than a few scrapes and bruises.

I glanced back at Dad and reevaluated my assumption. I might be able to get out through the window. Dad, however, looked as if he'd end up getting stuck.

But it was our only shot.

I pointed toward the window. He nodded in understanding, though he looked skeptical. I couldn't reach the frame from the floor, so I carefully stepped up onto the toilet. The cheap plastic lid groaned and sagged inward from my weight. I prayed it would hold as I gingerly tested the window. I was afraid it wouldn't open, but when I pressed on it, it squeaked outward. Cool air blasted me in the face, and I sucked it in greedily. Freedom was so enticingly close, I could smell it.

"Boost me," I whispered. I grabbed the window frame and waited for Dad to give me a good shove on the rump.

"One," he said, placing his hands on my butt. "Two . . ."

The bathroom door opened, and the light flicked on. "What are you doing in here?"

Dad's hands vanished, and I just about fell over backward at the loss of support. I scuttled off the toilet and turned to face Cameron, who was standing in the doorway, small pocketknife in hand. He looked confused, rather than angry, which I hoped meant we might be able to talk our way out of this.

I raised my hands to show him they were empty. "Uh, hi, Cameron!" I said, mind racing for something to say that wouldn't get Dad or me stabbed. "We stopped by to say hi and saw the door was open. When you weren't here, we thought maybe someone broke in and we were checking the place out for you." The lie fell clumsily from my lips.

Cameron's face bunched in further confusion as he looked at me. He then glanced down and seemed to realize he was holding the knife out toward us in what could easily be construed as a threatening manner. He flushed and closed it before shoving it into his pocket. "And you were halfway out the window, because . . . ?"

"Checking escape routes?" I supplied, unconvincingly.

Dad actually rolled his eyes at me, but it was the best I could do while under duress.

Cameron's eyes moved from me to Dad and back again. I thought we might be able to rush him, knock him over, and get out before he could right himself if it came to that. I couldn't tell if he was trying to decide how much of our story to believe, or if he was debating on the best way to kill us.

Before I could spring into action, however, he heaved a sigh and turned away. "Come on out of there so we can talk."

Dad and I exchanged a glance before following him into the bedroom. I took a quick look around for something I could use as a weapon, just in case he came after us. Cameron had sounded so resigned, it made me wonder if he was about to confess to Rick's murder. Anytime someone admitted anything like that to me, a violent escape usually followed. I wanted to be prepared.

Cameron sat on the edge of the bed, next to his laptop. He glanced at it, shook his head, and then said, "I didn't kill Rick."

"Why would you say that?" I asked, feigning surprise.

"I know about you," he said. "Rita wouldn't shut up about it at dinner. We were supposed to talk about her book, and all she kept talking about was how she based it on your life."

"*My* life?" I asked, not quite believing what I was hearing.

"She kept saying you are some kind of genius when it comes to solving crimes." He shoved his glasses up onto his nose and then glanced at Dad. "The both of you."

"I just write stories," Dad said, holding his hands up as if warding away the compliment. "This is my first time."

Cameron gave him a wry smile before continuing. "While we ate, she said you were currently trying to solve Rick's murder, which I was happy about. At least I was until she started asking questions. Something about her demeanor made me realize that things weren't exactly on the up-and-up." He shrugged. "So I came back here."

I winced. "We weren't going to take anything," I said. "We wanted to eliminate you as a suspect if you were innocent."

Cameron gave me a long look before shrugging. "I

get it. I don't like that you broke in here when you could have simply asked to have a look around. I have nothing to hide."

I glanced at his laptop. He followed my gaze and flushed. Dad hadn't closed the last photo he opened, which was an embarrassingly revealing close-up of Rick and his lover.

"I can explain that," he said.

I crossed my arms over my chest. "Please, do."

He licked his lips and cleared his throat before speaking.

"Rick didn't pay well," he said. "In fact, he had no problem withholding money from my check if he thought I didn't perform up to expectations, which happened a lot more than was warranted. I sucked it up because I really wanted to learn, and despite his quirks, I was learning." He sighed. "Then, one night, I found out he was sleeping with an editor from one of the small presses."

"That's where I know her from!" Dad said, snapping his fingers. "I've seen her at some of the conventions I used to go to, but that's been years now."

Cameron nodded. "When I realized he was using her to land contracts—all small-time—for some of his less-than-talented clients, I figured I could use it against him to get him to pay me more."

"You mean you were blackmailing him," I said.

"No." Cameron shook his head. "I couldn't bring myself to do it."

"Then why do you have the pictures?" I asked.

"I followed them a couple of nights, and took the pictures, I admit, but I never showed them to him. Knowing Mr. Wiseman, he would have fired me on the spot, his reputation be damned. It wasn't like people liked him, anyway. I realized I was more likely committing career suicide than accomplishing anything, so I decided not to press forward with my plan."

"But why keep them?" Dad asked.

Cameron took off his glasses and used his shirt to clean them before answering. "Security, I guess. I don't know. If he fired me, then maybe I could use them to get back at him. It's spiteful, but Rick Wiseman tended to bring that out in people."

He was so earnest, I actually believed him. "When he died, why not get rid of the pictures?" I asked. "What if the police found them? They are pretty incriminating."

He looked abashed when he said, "Honestly, I didn't think about it. I was distraught about his death at first, and then was so excited about the opportunity, I simply forgot I had them. I know," he said when he saw me glance at the laptop. "I didn't even *see* the folder I kept them in when I worked. I'm so used to it being there, I simply overlooked it."

"Then why not tell us this from the start?"

He snorted a laugh. "Right. I'm trying to start my own agency here. Blackmail, even if I didn't actually go through with it, wouldn't look good on me." He lowered his gaze to his folded hands. "I know I should be mad at you for breaking in here and going through my stuff." His shoulders slumped. "But I'm not. In fact, I'm kind of glad you did."

My eyebrows shot skyward. "You're happy we broke into your hotel room looking for clues to Rick's murder?"

"If it means you can dismiss me as a suspect, I'll go through any indignity." He stood and picked up his laptop. He weighed it in his hands a moment before holding it out to me. "Here. Take it. You've apparently already figured out the password and have found the only thing on there I'm ashamed of."

I took the laptop from him, sure this was some sort of trick. "Why?"

"Other than those photos, there's nothing on there that could implicate me in Mr. Wiseman's death." He raised his chin defiantly. "In fact, you can go through all my e-mails, poke through every document. The passwords are all the same. You'll find everything in order, including e-mails with the man who did my Web site for me. I have been completely honest with you, and I want you to see it for yourself."

It was all said so shockingly straight, I felt he had to be telling the truth. Why hand over evidence if he thought there'd be something on his laptop that would prove he killed Rick? He wouldn't. Sure, he could have deleted the incriminating evidence, but if that was the case, taking his laptop wouldn't do a lick of good. I could hand it over to the police and maybe they could do whatever it was they did to find documents thought scrubbed from hard drives, but then I'd have to explain how I'd come to be in possession of the laptop. All he would have to do was tell them I'd broken in, which was the truth, and my goose would be cooked.

I looked at the laptop in my hand and then held it back out to him. Cameron took it with a grateful smile.

"Thank you," he said. "If you'd taken it, it would probably ruin me. Since I'm just starting out, I need it so I can keep on top of prospective clients, but I figured if it proved my innocence to you, then I'd suck it up and deal with the consequences."

"You might have been the last person to see Rick alive," I said, not sure if it was an accusation or me trying to sort through the facts.

"Actually," Dad said. "I think I was." He paused. "Other than the killer, of course."

I kept forgetting about that. "Well, you were with him much of the night," I amended.

"I was." Cameron hugged his laptop to his chest. "He was angry about everyone bothering him. I tried to tell him I could go through the manuscripts for him and would pass on only the ones I thought he might like, but he refused to consider even that. He said he'd burn them first. His only reason for being in Pine Hills was for the two of you."

I winced inwardly. He might have been here for Dad's novel announcement and signing, but the only thing he wanted from me was, well, me.

"I convinced him to at least take them into his room, just in case. I left them on the desk and packed up for the night. He was alive when I left him, I swear. When I showed up the next morning to pick him up, and he didn't come downstairs to meet me, I figured he might be mad at me for forcing the manuscripts on him. I should have gone in to check on him." He sat down heavily on the bed as if the weight of it was simply too much to bear. "I was going to finish out the year and then move on to my own agency. I'm not sure I can handle this." He made a vague gesture toward the floor next to where the manuscripts were hidden under the bed.

"You'll be fine," I said, feeling bad for him. If he wasn't the killer, then he had just lost his boss, as well as a mentor. While Rick's death might have accelerated his career change, it also put more pressure on him, pressure that could very well break him.

He looked up at my Dad. "I was hoping I'd find a way to impress you," he said. "I thought if I showed you how hard I worked, you might consider taking me on as your agent. I know I'm inexperienced, but I also know Rick's methods and his contacts. I answered a lot of his e-mails for him. I can do this." He looked at his laptop and tossed it onto the bed. "But after this, I'll understand if you want to have nothing to do with me."

Dad was silent a long moment before he spoke. "You know, it *would* be a much easier transition if I signed with you."

Cameron's eyes lit up, while mine widened in alarm. Just because Cameron didn't appear to be the killer at the moment, it didn't mean he wasn't.

"Dad," I hissed out of the side of my mouth. "We should talk about this."

"There's nothing to talk about. At least, not right now." He stepped forward and put a hand on Cameron's shoulder. "Now isn't the time to make important decisions like this," he said, in what I thought was the understatement of the year. "Once everything calms down and Rick's killer is behind bars, you'll be the first person I call."

"Do you mean that?" Cameron sounded like he might break down into happy tears.

"I do."

"Oh, God." I could see the headline now: MYSTERY AUTHOR'S NEW AGENT A CONFIRMED KILLER! Then again, it would probably increase his book sales. Controversy always did.

"We'll be going now," Dad said. He raised his hand

to silence me when I started to protest. There was so much more we could learn from him. "Thank you for not calling the police on us and cooperating with our investigation. You've been a tremendous help."

"It's my pleasure, Mr. Hancock." Cameron glanced at me. "Ms. Hancock."

Dad led the way out of the room. I trailed behind, pouting. I had more questions for Cameron about that night, like if he'd seen anyone, or if Rick had said or done anything that might have led to his murder. But I knew Dad was right. We'd overstayed our welcome already, and had put the poor man through enough. Besides, Dad had managed to smooth things over to the point I was pretty sure Cameron wouldn't jump on the phone to the cops the moment we were out the door.

I supposed that all in all, our trip to Cameron's room was a success. We'd learned what it was he'd been hiding from us. And while it was unsavory, I believed him when he said he hadn't gone through with the blackmail. If he had, Rick wouldn't have treated him like he had in front of everyone.

So that left me with two more solid suspects: Harland Pennywinkle and Joel Osborne, with Harland topping the list. I had yet to get a chance to talk to him, and when Rita had tried in my stead, he'd called the cops. While it might have been justified, I still found his behavior suspicious.

"That went better than expected," Dad said as we got back into my car.

"We got caught," I pointed out, in case he'd forgotten.

"We did," Dad said. "But we also learned a lot." He buckled in and sat back, smiling. "I sure did work up an appetite, though. I never realized how exhausting sleuthing could be."

Sleuthing? I stared at him, surprised. He was actually enjoying himself, far more than I would have thought.

"What do you say we go back home and I'll whip us up some pancakes," Dad said. "Breakfast for dinner was always a favorite of mine, especially after a hard day's work. I think we both deserve that, don't you?"

I immediately buckled in and started the car. "I want chocolate chips in mine."

"Of course," he said with a knowing chuckle.

25

After our pancake dinner, both Dad and I went straight to bed. I was asleep the second my head hit the pillow, my belly full and content. I slept straight through the night, and when I woke, I felt refreshed and ready to face the day.

Dad was still asleep by the time I'd finished my morning routine. I fed Misfit his breakfast, downed the remains of my coffee, and I was out the door. It was my turn to open, and I was going to be doing it with Vicki, something that was slowly becoming a rarity. With Jeff coming along nicely, and Lena able to handle most of the early-morning duties, we could now have one of them open to prevent either Vicki or me from having to spend the entire day there, from open to close.

But today, it was going to be like old times: just the two of us to start the day.

I parked a block down the street and walked the rest of the way to Death by Coffee, once again wondering if we should invest in a parking lot. It might be a strain on our budget for a time, but having somewhere for the guests to park would likely increase business. On-street parking was fine sometimes, but during the rush, many of our guests had to walk quite a ways. When it rained or snowed, I noted a definite decline in people coming through the door.

My mind was still on the logistics of buying a space without going bankrupt in the process as I reached Death by Coffee. I yanked on the door, and was surprised to find it locked. A quick glance at my watch told me I was three minutes late, meaning Vicki should have already been inside, setting up. Even when I was on time, she was always there bright and early. I'd never known her to be late.

Worry for my best friend had me scrabbling for my phone. I nearly dropped it twice as I dialed her number. I was terrified something had happened to her.

"Come on, Vicki." I stood outside, trembling, watching the street for anyone who looked out of place. If the killer had come after Vicki, then he or she might want to watch my reaction, or worse, come for me next.

My stomach soured so much at the thought, I was very nearly sick. While her absence could be explained simply—like an alarm not going off—I just couldn't see it. Vicki was the epitome of a morning person. She woke up radiant and smiling, with or without an alarm. It used to annoy me to no end how cheery she could be, even on the gloomiest of mornings, but right then, I'd give anything for that cheer.

Just as the call went to voice mail, a car pulled up in front of the shop. The passenger door opened, and Vicki stepped out. She leaned in and kissed Mason before she opened the back door for Trouble's cat carrier. She kissed her boyfriend one more time, and then turned to find me standing there, phone in hand, gaping.

"Oh!" she said, flushing. "What time is it?" She looked at her watch and winced.

"I thought something happened to you." I wasn't sure if I should be mad or relieved.

Vicki's flush deepened. Unlike with me, the color looked good on her. "I'm so sorry. I didn't mean to be late. Time sort of got away from us this morning."

"Hi, Krissy," Mason called from the driver's seat of his car.

I waved at him, but kept my eyes on Vicki. It wasn't until he honked and drove off that the pieces started coming together.

"Wait a minute," I said, watching as Mason vanished down the street. "Is there something wrong with your car?"

"No." Sly grin.

"So, if your car's fine, and Mason is driving you to work . . ." I grinned at her.

Her smile lit up her entire face as she moved to the door to unlock it. "Mason and I had dinner last night." She pushed the door open and waited for me to go in before continuing. "It ran later than expected."

"I'd say. Did you get any sleep at all last night?"

She laughed and carried Trouble upstairs to release him. I flipped on the lights and met her back behind the counter.

"I'd say I managed about two hours," she said, smiling.

I was insanely jealous that she could look and sound so good after so little sleep. And that's not to mention the fact her love life made mine look depressingly pedestrian. What I wouldn't give to wake up next to someone I loved each and every morning. Maybe I'd have a better outlook on life more often.

"How are things with Will?" she asked, as if reading my mind.

"Good, I think."

"You think?"

"With Dad being in town, and Rick's murder, we haven't spent much time together." Of course, his job had a tendency to dictate how much time we spent together more than anything. Even if Dad hadn't come, we still might not have seen each other for much more than that single dinner.

"Well, let me tell you, love is marvelous." Vicki floated into the dining area to take the chairs off the tables.

We were bordering on too mushy for my liking—especially since it accentuated my own pitiful state—so I changed the subject.

"Dad is going to be coming in sometime after he wakes up," I told her. "He wants to do the signing today, despite everything."

"You sure?" she asked. "If he wants to cancel, I'm okay with it. I can put a sign on the door, apologizing for the inconvenience, but still sell the books for him if he'd like. It's been a rough couple of days."

She didn't know the half of it. "He's sure. He figures it might help raise spirits—mostly his, I think.

And now that he's seriously considering taking Cameron Little on as his agent, he hopes a lot of the authors will show up, too. I think he views Cameron as a project and wants to do whatever he can to help his career along."

"That's nice of him." Vicki paused halfway through putting a chair on the floor. "So, this Cameron guy isn't a suspect, then?"

I thought about it and then shook my head. "I don't think so. I haven't talked to Paul to know what the police think, but if I had to put money on it, I'd say someone else did the deed."

"Huh." She finished with the chairs and met me behind the counter, where I was getting the morning coffee started. "Maybe I should have left Trouble at home today. It's going to be busy and you know how he can get when the crowd gets too big. I'd hate for him to get underfoot."

"He'll be fine." I caught a glimpse of the black-and-white cat. He'd already found himself a spot on top of one of the bookshelves and was settling down for a nap. "He adds a little something special to the place."

Vicki went into the back to get the registers in order, while I finished up the morning food prep. Conversation drifted off since she was busy counting and I was running back and forth from the oven to the front, making sure the food and drinks were in order. Thirty minutes later, everything was in place, the doors were open, and we were ready for business.

Dad's signing wasn't scheduled to start until noon, so I spent the morning rush promoting it as I served coffee. Lena came in an hour after rush, taking my place at the register, which allowed me to slip out into the dining area to clean tables, and to put on fresh coffee. Jeff was due an hour after that, which would give me a chance to help Dad finish his own setup.

At a little past eleven, Dad arrived, but not in his rental like I'd expected. The front door opened, and in he walked, Rita Jablonski hanging off one arm. She smiled at me in a way that made my stomach churn before she walked over to the counter, still clutching at Dad's arm.

"Hey, Buttercup," he said. "It's a nice morning to be out today, don't you think?"

"Very nice," Rita said, looking into Dad's eyes.

"Dad, can I speak to you for a moment?"

He gave me a quizzical look before nodding. "Sure, Buttercup. Is everything okay?"

I didn't answer. I walked around the counter and headed for the stairs.

"I'll get us both something to drink," I heard Rita say, which thankfully meant she wouldn't be following us upstairs, at least not right away.

I stopped beside the table where Dad would be signing his books. Some of the early-morning customers had already purchased their copies and were waiting downstairs for the reading portion of the event to take place. They watched us with interest, so I made sure to stand far enough away that no one would be able to overhear us.

"Why are you with Rita?" I asked in a whisper as Dad joined me.

He looked confused when he answered. "She called this morning and offered me a ride in when I told her I was still holding the signing. Since she was coming here too, she offered to stop by on her way in."

"My house isn't on the way from Rita's," I said. "In fact, she had to go well out of her way to get you."

He shrugged. "She was just being nice."

I narrowed my eyes at him. "How nice was she being?"

His brow furrowed before he realized what I was implying. He chuckled and gave me a hug. "Don't worry yourself, Buttercup. She's just a friend."

"Are you sure?" I asked, wanting it to be true, but I was afraid he was only trying to ease my mind. He *had* said he was looking to get back into the dating market. "I can't see myself calling Rita 'Mom.'"

He laughed again, finding humor in my discomfort. "I don't think I could ever date someone who was a fan of my work before I met them. I'd always wonder if they were interested in me as a person, or if they only cared about my writing."

I breathed a sigh of relief. "But why does she have your phone number?" I asked.

"She's your friend and she works with the authors in town. I figured I'd give her my number in case she needed me for anything while I was here. Despite how the evening turned out, I did enjoy the writers' group meeting."

Okay, that made sense. I took a deep breath and stepped back, glad I wouldn't have to watch my dad walk down the aisle and marry Rita. My life was already complicated enough, thank you very much. I liked Rita and all, but I didn't see her as stepmom material.

"You sure you want to do this today?" I asked, changing the subject so I wouldn't have to think about it anymore.

"I'm sure." He glanced at the table. "Speaking of which, I should start setting things up. I want everything just right." He paused, and looked sad for a moment before saying, "Rick would have wanted it that way."

I left him to it and headed downstairs to finish up my own work. Rita passed me on the way, carrying two cups of coffee. Dad might not think there was anything between them, but I could tell by the gleam in her eye that Rita didn't feel the same way. I hoped she wouldn't take it too hard when Dad let her down. In fact, I hoped he wouldn't even have to do that. He was going to have to go home, and there was no way she was going to follow him. She could remain here and cherish the memories of their time together in Pine Hills, limited as they might be.

Jeff arrived and paused to let Cameron in before taking his place behind the counter. I waved at the newly minted agent and was rewarded with a warm smile and a wave. It didn't appear as if he was going to hold my transgressions against me or my dad. A big part of me was relieved. If he turned out to be innocent, and Dad did take him on as his agent, I thought we could eventually become friends.

I turned away just as the door opened yet again, and Paul Dalton walked in.

My mind immediately leapt to the worst-case scenario. Why would he be here if he wasn't about to arrest someone? And who else would he come to Death by Coffee for, but me or my dad?

I stomped over to him. "What do you think you're doing here?" I demanded.

He stepped back, startled. "Hi to you, too," he said.

"I came in for a cup of coffee, if you still serve it." He glanced around the room, eyes lingering on where Dad was arranging his books, before looking back at me.

"A cup of coffee?" I almost laughed, thinking it ludicrous, but then realized we *were* standing in a coffee shop. "Okay, that's fine." I felt bad for snapping at him.

"Why else would I be here?" he asked, blue eyes smoldering with something I didn't want to think about. It was like he was trying to tell me something with that stare, to reach into my brain and not just leave something behind, but sort through the jumble of emotions that had me practically stammering every time I looked at him.

"I don't know," I said, forcing myself to look away before I completely lost it. "I thought maybe you'd come to arrest Rick's murderer."

He shook his head and frowned. "Honestly, we aren't making much progress. No one saw anything, or at least, no one is talking. There wasn't much evidence we could use at the scene, either." He sighed. "But we'll figure it out. I promise you that." His eyes once more strayed to Dad. I couldn't tell if there was an accusation there or not.

"So, you have nothing?" I asked, disappointed. While I didn't want him coming to arrest Dad or me, I'd hoped he'd made *some* sort of progress because, quite frankly, I was getting nowhere.

"I wouldn't say that," he said. "We have some leads, but I can't talk about them now." He glanced past me, eyes lighting up. "Thank you."

"No problem," Lena said, handing him a to-go

cup. "It's your usual. Someone has already paid for you."

An older man by the counter saluted as both Paul and I looked. Lena gave me a wink before heading over and handing the gentleman his own coffee.

"Well, I hope you figure it out," I said, turning back to Paul. "Rick's killer needs to be caught. I knew him." I stopped short of saying he was a friend.

"I'll get him." He clasped me on the arm with his free hand. It was warm, comforting, and reminded me of all those times when we'd been alone. The spark I was trying hard to deny lit between us. Before it could fully ignite, Paul stepped back. "I'm glad you're staying out of it this time."

I reddened and covered it up by looking at my feet. "I'm trying."

Paul chuckled. "I'm glad." He heaved a sigh. "I'd better get back to work. You be good, all right?"

I nodded, refusing to look up again until I heard the door open and close. I watched Paul get into his cruiser, his slacks hugging tight to his hips and butt. It was times like these I wished life had a slow-motion button. And maybe a rewind. Yeah, I could definitely go for that.

I cleared my throat and looked guiltily away. I was going to have to do something especially nice for Will after those traitorous thoughts. While there was nothing wrong with looking, I knew I wouldn't like it if Will were to ogle every good-looking woman that passed. And with how my body felt all warm and tingly where he'd touched me, I was pretty sure I was doing more than simply looking.

Turning away from the door, I returned to my place

behind the counter. I didn't meet anyone's eye,
though Lena tried. She knew there was more to our
relationship than I wanted to admit. I, for one, didn't
want to see confirmation of it in her gaze.

The doors opened. Guests started pouring in,
which took my mind off Paul and my confused feelings for him. It was early, but people had already
started to head upstairs to shake hands with Dad
and pick up copies of his books. It wouldn't be long
before he'd come downstairs and begin reading to
what I hoped would be a room full of his adoring fans.
I didn't have time to worry about my personal life
anymore, and for that, I was thankful.

26

After the reading, Dad's line was steady through the afternoon, as were the lines at both the down-stairs and upstairs registers. It took two hours before they tapered off, allowing all of us to take a breather. There were still quite a lot of people milling around, many simply wanting to talk to the semifamous author who'd decided to pay a visit to our quiet little town. I'd seen book signings where only five or six people showed up—and they were often friends or family of the author. Today, however, it felt like nearly the entire town had stopped by.

Dad took it all in stride, smiling practically nonstop as he shook hands and chatted with those who'd taken the time to visit with him. I did my best not to take any of it personally, but come on, it was my *dad* we were talking about here. I was proud of him, and was proud to be his daughter. There was nothing wrong with basking in his glow while I could, even if it might be a little tacky.

"I'll be back in a few minutes," I told Jeff and Lena, who'd been handling most of the serving behind the counter. I filled a coffee cup and carried it upstairs to Dad.

"Thanks, Buttercup," he said, taking a sip. He was still smiling, but it was becoming strained. I could see the exhaustion building behind his eyes. Between our not-so-official murder investigation and the book signing, he had to be running on fumes by now.

"You doing okay?" I asked him, holding up a hand to the woman who'd come up to the table with at least ten books in her arms, ready to be signed. She huffed, but waited.

"I'm fine. Hand's getting a little sore, but I'll make it. It's been a while since I've had to sign so many books at once."

"If you want a break, just let me know. I can make up a sign real quick and set it up." This earned me some hard looks from a few nearby fans.

"No, I'll be fine. I figure I can break for a quick bite to eat in about an hour." Knowing Dad, he'd completely skipped lunch before the signing started. "I might come back for a little while after that, but we'll see how I feel after I eat. I may need a nap." He chuckled.

"If you're sure . . ."

"I am." He smiled, winked, and then turned to the waiting woman, who immediately broke into a spiel about how important his books were to her.

Dismissed, I stepped away from the table with a frown. Dad was putting on a strong face, but he was tired. He wasn't as young as he used to be. It was clear it was wearing on him, but he was too proud to admit it. I just wasn't sure how to convince him that stopping wasn't a sign of weakness.

I was on my way back to the counter, thinking I

might call the signing done in the next half hour, when I noticed Joel Osborne sitting alone at the table by the stairs. A quick glance at Lena and Jeff told me they weren't busy, so I made a detour over to him.

"Hi, Joel. Get a book signed?" I asked, knowing he had. He was holding what looked to be a first edition of Dad's first Bobby Drake book, *The Withered Sparrow*.

"I did." He beamed at me as he flipped to the first page, where Dad had scrawled not just his name, but a short personalized message. "I can't express how happy I am about this." He reached up and touched his fedora. I was beginning to wonder if he would ever take the thing off.

"It must be nice to meet someone whose books you love."

"It is." He closed the paperback and hugged it to his chest like it was his most prized possession. "I hope that I'll someday have a novel published as well. I'll send Mr. Hancock a free copy, just to show him how much I appreciate all he's done for literature. Without him, I'd never have considered writing."

"It's a shame about his agent, though," I said, mentally wishing I'd had a better line, but it was the best I could do.

Joel frowned. "I'd hoped he would take me on because then I would have been represented by the same agent as the man whose novels I love. But now"—he shrugged, eyes going to Cameron—"I suppose he'll have to do."

"You aren't interested in being represented by Mr. Little?"

Joel sighed and sat back, a look on his face like he was actually thinking hard about the question. It struck me as odd since he'd just said how much he wanted to publish a novel.

"I guess it wouldn't be all bad," he said after a moment. "But Mr. Wiseman was the agent to James Hancock. There's no beating that."

"Well, Cameron might be taking Dad on," I said. "So, if it's important to you, there's still a shot at being represented by the same agent."

"I suppose." He didn't sound as excited by the prospect as I thought he'd be. "It just isn't the same. Mr. Wiseman was the one who placed these novels." He looked down at the book in his hands. "I can't imagine why anyone would want to kill him. He was my best chance of getting published the traditional way. There are some authors here who are now considering the self-published route. I'm not one of them."

I was about to ask him who he might be referring to, though I wasn't sure how it would relate to Rick's murder, when I caught a glimpse of one man I'd been wanting to talk to since this whole thing started. He looked as if he was getting ready to leave, and I didn't want to miss my chance yet again.

"Thank you for your time," I told Joel, who immediately went back to admiring Dad's autograph. "Harland!" I called, hurrying over to the fat man. "Hold on a sec."

He glanced at me and scowled, but at least he didn't walk away. "What?"

"I was hoping to talk to you. I haven't had a chance since that night at the meeting."

"So?" He crossed his arms, glare deepening.

Okay, so this wasn't going to be a friendly conversation, no matter how nice I was trying to be. "I was curious to know how you're holding up. You took a manuscript to Mr. Wiseman before his death, didn't you?" I wasn't sure why I asked, considering I hadn't seen one beneath the bed.

He narrowed his eyes at me. "So? Everyone did."

Hmm. Interesting. "Were you upset with the way he treated you? Rick wasn't very nice to many people."

Harland licked his lips slowly, eyeing me. "And? He was a busy man. You think I killed him, don't you?"

"Did you?" No sense in hiding it. There were tons of people in Death by Coffee, so if he tried anything, I was pretty sure someone would leap to my aid.

"Why would I?" he asked. "I gave him my novel. He was my best chance out of here. I might have called him a name or two, but not to his face. The guy owed me for how he treated me, and I expected him to pay me back in the form of representation. It was the least I deserved."

Cocky much? I decided to go for broke and play my ace card. "You went back to Rick's room after the murder, didn't you?"

I expected Harland to go motionless, or to break into a sudden rage, having been caught. Instead, he simply shrugged. "So?"

"Why go back?" I asked him. "Did you kill him and then realize you left something behind that could tie you to the murder?"

He snorted. "You're not that bright, are you?" Before I could form a response, he went on. "I went back because I gave the bastard the only copy of my manuscript. I needed it back to give to that bozo." He jerked a thumb toward Cameron. "I wasn't going to let another opportunity pass because the idiot went and got himself killed. Now, if you'll excuse me, I have more important things to do than stand around answering to the likes of you."

I watched Harland go, really wanting him to be the killer. He was one of the most unpleasant men I'd ever met, but that didn't make him a murderer. His story rang true, even if it was a bit selfish. I mean, who in their right mind would walk into a dead man's room and take something, even if it belonged to them?

Of course, this was a man who typed up his novel on an old typewriter, rather than a computer. You didn't see that very often these days. I could see why he would want his manuscript back.

I turned and found both Theresa and Barrett Drummand walking away from Cameron. Since I was on a roll, I figured I might as well go for broke and bother them, too. Maybe they'd have something interesting to say.

When Barrett saw me coming, he took Theresa's arm and tried to steer her away. I managed to trap them between the stairs and where Joel sat.

"I just want a few moments," I said when Barrett tried to turn around and walk away. "Please."

Barrett sighed and turned back to face me. Theresa lowered her own gaze and wiped at her eyes.

"Is everything all right?" I asked, directing the question at her.

"She's fine," Barrett said. "It's been a stressful couple of days. We'd like to go home now so she can get some rest."

Theresa looked up long enough to give me a wan smile, and then nodded her head ever so slightly, as if thanking me for asking. She went right back to looking at her feet.

I pressed on. "I was wondering if either of you happened to speak to Rick Wiseman before he died? You left your manuscripts with him, didn't you?"

Theresa nodded, but it was Barrett who answered. "Theresa did. A lot of good it did her."

"But not you?" It tracked with what I'd seen. "Why not?"

"I changed my mind," he said. "There's nothing wrong with that." His hand tightened on Theresa's arm, and she sucked in a breath. "The man wasn't worth the time or effort."

"I thought you left yours, too?" Theresa spoke at barely above a whisper.

"I didn't." Barrett tightened his grip even further, causing her to squirm. "I gave my copy to Mr. Little. You can ask him if you'd like."

"Excuse me." We all glanced down at Joel, who was still sitting where I'd left him. "Barrett, I swear I saw your name when I turned in my own manuscript."

"You must be mistaken." Barrett spoke through clenched teeth.

"No." Joel stood, book still clutched at his chest. "No, I don't think I am. I saw your name as plain as day. It was right there on the top of the stack."

"Barrett?" Theresa stepped back from her husband, his hand falling limply away. "What is he implying?"

Barrett laughed, but it was a strained, forced sound. "Never you mind him," he said. "I didn't leave my novel there. I only gave it to Mr. Little. You saw me do it."

"I also saw you place yours on top of mine." She said it at a near whisper, as if she was afraid he'd hurt her for contradicting him.

"I found a rubber band," I said, cutting in. "It was

outside Rick's window, right where there were marks indicating someone had jumped."

Theresa's eyes widened as she looked at her husband. "Barrett? Did you . . . Could you have . . . ? When you left, I thought you were going for a walk. And when you said you'd fallen and gotten dirt on your jeans . . ."

Barrett looked from his wife, to Joel, and then, finally, to me. Death by Coffee had fallen deathly silent. Even Dad had stopped signing and was standing at the top of the stairs, watching us.

"It's all a misunderstanding," Barrett said before squeezing his eyes shut. "He was so damn frustrating." When he opened his eyes, he was looking at his wife. "He shouldn't have talked to you like that. I'm the only one who has that right."

"Barrett . . ." Theresa clasped a hand over her mouth.

"I'm sorry." Wild-eyed, he looked around the room as if seeking an escape. Dad was moving slowly down the stairs, while a few others were backing away, not wanting to get involved.

Rita stood from where she'd been sitting by the door. "You killed him!" She wagged a finger at him. "Shame on you, Barrett Drummand!"

"Maybe you should sit down," I said. "It's over." I patted my pockets and cursed my luck. My cell was in my purse, which was in the office. "Someone, call the police."

"I'm not going to jail." It was spoken in a whisper, but I heard the heat in it.

"Barrett, be reasonable."

Of course, reason had fled the moment he'd gone to Ted and Bettfast to kill Rick Wiseman.

With one last frantic look around the room, Barrett made his move. He was quicker than he looked. His elbow shot out and connected solidly with my gut, bending me double. He shoved me backward, causing me to fall into Joel, who was knocked back into his chair, with me landing in his lap.

It was all the opening Barrett needed.

He bolted for the door, pushing Rita aside as he went. She went sprawling, hitting the floor hard with her backside.

"Someone, stop him!" Dad shouted. He rushed over to me as I painfully worked my way to my feet. Joel's arms were wrapped around me, holding on to me like he might a lover. It took me a moment to extract myself. "Are you okay?"

"I'm fine." I sucked in a pained breath and did the one thing I loathed above all else.

I started running.

Now, I'm not a good runner. Even on my best days, I can only handle a few dozen steps before I'm winded. So, saying I ran might be stretching it, considering Barrett had knocked the wind right out of me before I'd even gotten started. At least I tried, which was more than I could say about the onlookers.

I lumbered my way to the door, Dad protesting behind me. I heard someone shouting for someone to call the police already, and vaguely wondered if anyone would actually stop recording us on their phone long enough to make that call. I didn't find it likely.

I staggered out the front door, half the store hot on my trail. A quick scan showed me Barrett, already across the street. He whipped out his keys, thumbed the fob, and had his car door opened before I could even think about giving chase.

"Someone, stop him!" I wheezed, but to no avail. It was already too late.

With a roar, Barrett's blue Honda flared to life. I planted my hands on my knees, praying Paul would come tearing around the corner and block him off before he escaped, but instead, it was the Honda engine that revved as Barrett shot out of his parking spot, barely missing an oncoming bus as he fought for control of the wheel.

And then he was gone, around the corner, and out of sight.

27.

"I let him get away!" I paced back and forth in front of my family and friends, as distraught as I'd ever been. "I should have been faster. As soon as I figured out it was him, I should have done something to keep him from leaving. I could have had someone bar the door, or . . . or . . ."

"You shouldn't keep blaming yourself, Buttercup," Dad said, putting a hand on my shoulder. I paced out of it, not wanting to be comforted, not when there was still a killer on the loose thanks to me.

"You could have gotten hurt," Vicki chimed in.

"*I* did get hurt!" Rita wailed, rubbing at her backside and elbow.

Nothing anyone could say would change my mind. I should have suspected Barrett long before now. All the evidence was there, if I'd really looked hard at it. I'd been too distracted by Harland's return to the crime scene and Cameron's sudden rise to success to pay much attention to the smaller things.

Then again, what did I really have on Barrett? Some scattered manuscript pages and a broken rubber band, all of which belonged to his wife? That wasn't a smoking gun. It wasn't even a pointy stick. Now that I knew Barrett was the killer, I could easily say I should have figured it out, but the evidence was so circumstantial, it was no wonder I'd overlooked it.

"I should have known," I grumbled, unable to ease my own mind. This was the sort of puzzle I lived for, yet I'd screwed it up.

"It's really not your fault," Dad said for what had to be the twentieth time since Barrett escaped.

I sat down heavily. Had it really only happened a few minutes ago? Theresa was still crying in the corner, being comforted by Joel and Cameron. There were people who were still recording the proceedings so they could post the videos online later. He might have fled, but that didn't mean he'd gotten far.

There was still time to fix this.

I shot to my feet and ran to the office without explanation. I went straight for my purse, yanked out my phone, and dialed.

"Krissy?" Paul sounded stressed. "I'm busy at the moment, so please tell me this is important."

"It is." I paused. "To me, at least."

He sighed. "One of your employees called me. She said Barrett Drummand killed Rick Wiseman. Said you gave chase, but couldn't stop him."

"He got away." I practically wailed it. "I did everything I could, but he got into his car and drove away."

"That's what she said." It was his turn to pause. "Are you okay?"

"My pride is bruised, but I didn't get hurt." I considered telling him about Rita, but decided that was a story better saved for another time.

"I went to the Drummand residence. Barrett isn't

there. I doubt he'll show either, but I left someone watching the place, just in case. I'm on the way to his workplace now, but I don't think I'll get lucky there, either. He's probably heading straight out of town. I have people looking for him. We'll get him."

"It's my fault," I said, the pity party still in full swing. "I let him get away."

"Now, Krissy," Paul said, sounding a lot like my dad. "You did what you could—more than you should have done, really. I don't know how you figured out he was involved, and honestly, I don't think I want to know. I just"—he coughed, cleared his throat—"I'm glad you solved it."

Wait. Was that a compliment? From a cop who'd spent the last few days telling me to stay out of the investigation?

I knew it shouldn't have mattered, especially since Barrett was on the run, but that one little compliment had me just about dancing in place. I felt vindicated, even if in the end, the suspect was currently still out there, a free man.

"Please find him," I said, trying to hide the pleasure in my voice. "He needs to face justice."

"I will." A horn honked, and I heard an engine rev, though I couldn't tell if it was Paul's car or not. "I've got to go. Buchannan is on his way there. Tell everyone to stay put so he can get their statements. And Krissy . . ."

"Yes?" As sweet as could be.

"Please, stay there. I don't want you going after this guy, okay?"

"Sure thing." I wasn't in the least bit shocked that my fingers had somehow crossed on their own as I said it.

I hung up and took a moment to compose myself before I left the office. The glow from Paul's compliment had already worn off, and I was back to being a near nervous wreck. I smoothed down my hair, took a deep, calming breath, and then headed back out into the dining area to find that a good number of the guests had already left. Buchannan wasn't going to be happy about that, but there was nothing to be done about the departed.

But I could still do something about the people here.

"Lena, would you watch the door, please?" I asked before raising my voice to be heard over the murmur of the crowd. "The police are on their way and will want to talk to everyone. Sit tight until they get here. We'll still be serving coffee and cookies while you wait." I motioned toward where Jeff stood in a corner behind the counter.

A grumble worked its way through the crowd, but at least no one made as if to leave. Lena took her spot by the door and flipped the OPEN sign to CLOSED. She crossed her arms and tried to look imposing, which would have been cute, if the situation hadn't been so dire.

I tried not to think about how the latest disaster might affect business as I crossed the room to join my Dad. Would people keep coming here if murderers kept popping up? I know I would be hesitant.

"Are you feeling better?" Dad asked, as I came to a stop next to him.

"I am." I smiled at him to prove it. "A policeman is on his way here. The cops don't have Barrett in custody yet, but they're looking."

"I can't believe he could have killed Mr. Wiseman," Rita said. I hadn't noticed she'd moved to sit in the chair next to Dad. She was holding her arm as if it were broken, though the skin wasn't even red anymore. "I've known Barrett for a long time." She shook her head sadly. "It's a shame. A real shame."

Across the room, Theresa stood. Only Joel was with her now. I debated on whether or not to leave her be. She'd just received what had to be the shock of her life, learning her husband was a murderer. Cameron was watching her from a nearby chair, but made no move to go near her.

I felt bad about it, but I started her way. There was no guarantee Paul would find Barrett on his own. If anyone knew where he might go to hide, his wife would.

"Hi, Mrs. Drummand," I said, gently. I nodded my head toward one of the tables, looking squarely at Joel. He smiled, bowed his head, and then joined Cameron.

"Theresa," she said. "Call me Theresa. I . . . I don't know if I can bear that name anymore."

"I'm sorry, Theresa." I led her away from listening ears and sat her down at an empty table. She looked lost and shaky. I was afraid she might faint, or worse, break into hysterics, if left standing on her own. "How are you holding up?"

She looked up, mousy eyes wide. "How do you think? I just found out my husband killed a man. He could have killed me next. He . . . Barrett was never nice to me, but he made me feel better about myself." Her hand went reflexively to her hair and brushed it forward so it hid most of her face. She glanced around and shrank within herself even more when she realized nearly everyone in the room was watching us.

"Do you know where your husband might have gone?" I asked, getting straight to the point. The faster this was over with, the quicker she could move on.

Theresa shook her head. "I don't know him anymore. I don't think I ever did. How could he have done such a horrible thing?"

I had no answer for her.

"He wasn't a happy man," she said. "But he tried to treat me right, in his own way. He never hit me." She looked into my eyes, begging me to believe her. "He just squeezed hard sometimes. I don't think he realized he was doing it. He mostly just talked down to me when I screwed up, made sure I understood how I'd failed."

"That's abuse, too," I said.

Her shoulders rose and fell in a weak shrug. "I suppose." She sniffed and wiped at her nose. "All Barrett ever wanted was to be a writer. It was what drew me to him in the first place. It was the most important thing in his life. I think he would have left me if he ever thought I'd get in the way of his dream"—a brief pause before finishing—"our dream."

There was nothing I could say that would make any of this any better for her, which I so desperately wanted to do. So, instead of speaking, I hugged her. Theresa stiffened at first, as if she wasn't used to being touched in a gentle way. But then she softened and leaned into me. Her entire body trembled as she whispered "Thank you" into my ear.

I held her for a good long minute before leaving her to sort through her emotions. I truly hoped I wasn't the first person ever to show her affection, though by the way she acted, I was afraid I might have been.

I looked toward Cameron, mostly so I wouldn't break down into tears thinking about Theresa. Looking at him reminded me of what he was to all of the authors here. An idea slowly started forming in my head.

When Barrett killed Rick, he must have taken his novel with him. I believed Joel and Theresa when they said he'd left it outside the door at the bed-and-breakfast. He must have tried to grab Theresa's novel at the same time, but the rubber band had broken, and in his rush to gather her manuscript, he'd scattered the pages. Knowing time was short, he was forced to leave her novel behind.

But he hadn't left his own. He could have printed off another copy, but it was his life's work, the one thing he believed defined him. There was no way he was going to leave it in a dead man's possession.

And now, Cameron had it.

I hurried over to where he sat. "Do you have Barrett's manuscript with you here?" I asked, scouring the area for a briefcase or a box of papers telling me it was. There was nothing.

"It's back in my hotel room with the others," he said. "They're too heavy to carry constantly."

"Does Barrett know where they are?" I asked.

"He asked about it when we talked. So, yeah."

My mind raced. Would he take such a risk? The novel was his life. The police were at his house, so he couldn't go get it off his computer. If he didn't save it to the cloud or have his laptop with him, then the only copy would be the one sitting in Cameron's hotel room this very moment. Would he abandon it now when everything else was crumbling around him?

It seemed like a long shot, but it was all I had.

I bolted for the back room, ignoring the questions that flew my way. I snatched up my phone again and dialed.

"Paul!" I nearly shouted it when he answered. "Where are you?"

"Looking for Barrett Drummand," he said. "Why?" He knew I was onto something, because he'd turned on his serious police officer voice.

"I think I might know where he's gone."

"Where?"

"The hotel." I frowned. Did that place even have a name?

"The one out on Parish?"

"That's the one!" I said, relieved I wouldn't have to explain it to him. "I think he went there to look for his manuscript. He knows it's there, but I don't think he knows which room." Heck, I wasn't even sure if he knew which hotel, though I didn't think there were very many in Pine Hills for him to search.

There was a pause. "I'm heading there now, but I'm clear across town."

It would take Paul far too long to get all the way to the hotel, even if he raced full speed. And who knew when Buchannan would arrive? Barrett could be long gone before either of them ever came anywhere close to the hotel.

But Death by Coffee was a whole lot closer, and I was already here.

"I've got to go."

I hung up and shoved my phone deep into my purse. Paul was going to kill me, but I couldn't risk letting Barrett escape. There was a good chance he'd already been in and out of the hotel room—if he'd even gone there in the first place—and I was wasting my time.

But if there was even the slightest possibility he might still be there, I couldn't let the opportunity pass.

My phone rang in the depths of my purse as I snatched up my keys. I pointedly ignored it, deciding to leave my entire purse in the office, instead of taking it with me. It would give me an excuse for not answering what would inevitably be Paul's warning call.

I hurried out into the dining area, where Dad stood, doing his best to comfort Rita, who was milking her "injury" for all it was worth. You'd have thought Barrett had shot her with all the whining she was doing.

"We've got to go," I said, barely pausing as I grabbed Dad by the arm and dragged him toward the door. Normally, I might have gone alone, but I figured having someone who could take Barrett one-on-one would be better than me trying to go it alone and getting my butt kicked.

"Where are we going?" Dad asked, allowing me to lead him away.

I didn't answer. I didn't want anyone overhearing and telling Buchannan when he got there.

Thinking of the grumpy policeman made me walk

that much faster. If he showed up before I was out of sight, he'd surely stop me and handcuff me to a chair. Then Barrett would get away, and knowing my luck, the blame would somehow fall onto me.

Lena pushed the door open for me and whispered, "Good luck," before taking up her post once more.

"Thanks," I muttered. I was pretty sure I was going to need all the luck I could get.

28

"Maybe we should let the police handle it," Dad said, clutching at the dashboard as I took a turn a little too fast.

"They'll be too slow." I bit down on my lower lip and cringed as a squirrel started running toward the road. It thought better of it, and I zoomed past safely. I eased off the gas a little, knowing I'd never forgive myself if I ran over any animal, pet or not.

Dad sat back in his seat, but kept his hands braced, just in case I suddenly decided to speed up again. "Do you mind telling me where we're going?"

"The hotel," I said, slowing even further as we came upon a red light. I looked both ways, and seeing no one coming, shot through it. "Theresa said Barrett only cares about his writing, and the only accessible copy of his life's work is currently sitting in Cameron's hotel room." Or, at least, I hoped it still was. Barrett had a pretty good head start on us. I was hoping he hadn't thought about his manuscript right away, and was just now arriving. Either that, or he'd gone to his house first, and was currently sitting safely in police custody.

"Do you really think he'd risk it?" Dad asked. "He could always write the book again if it means so much to him."

"Don't talk like that." I paid him a quick glance before gluing my eyes to the road. If Barrett wasn't going to turn himself in, and he didn't go to the hotel for his novel, then there was no chance I was going to catch him.

The HOTEL sign came into view. I flew into the lot and came to a screeching halt across three spaces. I'd already broken at least a dozen traffic laws on my way there, so what was one more? It wasn't like anyone was going to give me a ticket.

"I don't see it," I said, heart hammering as I scanned the vehicles in the lot for Barrett's car. "Do you see a blue Honda anywhere?"

Dad looked around and shook his head. "Maybe he didn't come."

My heart sank. His car wasn't there; I was sure of it. Paul was probably racing here now, thinking I'd given him a lead, when all I'd done was send him on a wild goose chase. And since I didn't bring my phone, I couldn't call him. When he got here, he was going to kill me.

My eyes strayed to Cameron's hotel room door. It was hanging open a crack. There were no indications that anyone was inside.

"We're too late," I said, staring at that tiny sliver of darkness. "He was already here and we missed him."

Dad put a hand on my shoulder and gently squeezed.

"You tried. It's all you can do sometimes. At least now the police will have somewhere to start."

Trying wasn't good enough for me. "Maybe he left a clue inside that will tell us where he went." I pushed open my car door, thinking that if he did, then perhaps I could give chase. All wasn't lost, at least not yet.

"Kristina!"

Dad almost never called me by my full given name, and when he did, I'd always taken heed.

But not today. I got out of the car, fully intent on the open doorway. I doubted Barrett would have left incriminating evidence on where he was going. It wasn't like he'd leave a forwarding address so Cameron could contact him about his novel later, once things calmed down. Murder didn't simply blow over.

But I refused to believe the trail ended here. There had to be *something* that would help me find him.

A door opened down the line of rooms. A man poked his head out, squinted at me as if trying to determine who exactly I was, and ducked back inside without a word. No one else moved, no doors opened. It was just me and the waiting empty room.

I crept toward the open doorway, not sure what to expect when I got inside. Would Barrett have ransacked the room in search of his manuscript? He had no way of knowing where Cameron would keep it. Thinking back, I was starting to doubt Barrett was the one who'd shoved the manuscripts under the bed. There *had* been a stack on the desk when I'd found Rick, and I didn't believe the police took them. Harland might have been the one who'd moved them.

If that was the case, then perhaps Barrett hadn't

found his novel. Maybe he would come back later, or go looking for Cameron. There still might be a slim chance he hadn't left town yet, which could very well spell his doom.

The car door opened behind me. I held up a hand and hoped Dad would stay back. It was bad enough I'd dragged him out here in the first place. I'd risked his life by driving like a lunatic, bringing him to where I'd thought I might find a killer. I didn't need to get him into any more trouble, be it a breaking-and-entering charge, or worse.

I took a deep breath and made for the door, though I did move slower than I had been. Barrett was long gone, so there wasn't anything to be afraid of, yet I couldn't help but be cautious.

Loud music played in one of the rooms down the row. A car zipped by on the road behind me. I glanced back to find Dad standing by my car, a concerned expression on his face. He nodded once, as if to tell me I had his permission to keep going, which meant a lot. I turned back to the door, straightened my back, and reached out to push it open the rest of the way.

Before my fingers could so much as brush the wood, the door jerked inward and I came face-to-face with Rick Wiseman's killer.

"Oh!" It came out as a surprised gasp.

"Ah!" Barrett's had a little more life to it as he jerked back in surprise.

We eyed each other, neither moving. Barrett had his manuscript clutched to his chest, fingers holding so tight, his knuckles were popping white.

"Barrett," I said, swallowing back my fear. The man

had killed once; he could very well decide to do it again. "Let's think about this."

"There's nothing to think about," he said. "Get out of my way."

"Please." I licked my lips, which had gone completely dry. "You made a mistake. We all make them." Like me coming here without a weapon. "Think about Theresa."

"I *was* thinking about her," he hissed. "That's why I'm in this mess." His eyes flickered over my shoulder, to my dad, and then back to me. "She only wanted to talk to him, and that man treated her so horribly. I . . . I didn't like it. It made me realize how."—his jaw bunched—"It wasn't right."

"Of course it wasn't." I needed to stall. If I could keep Barrett there until Paul arrived, I could step aside and let the man with the gun take care of him. If Barrett were to push the issue, there was no way I was going to be able to stop him.

Barrett shook his head angrily. "You can't possibly understand. He liked you." He said it like it was a curse. "Everyone knew it. If you would have asked him to look at our novels for us, I'm sure he would have done it, just to get on your good side." He looked me up and down, disgust painted all over his face. "But you wouldn't have helped us, even if we'd asked. No one was willing to stand up for us. If it wasn't for the fact he wouldn't open the door, I would have knocked him flat when he'd yelled at us that night, just to show him he couldn't treat people that way and get away with it."

"You didn't have to go back," I said. "You could have left your manuscript and hoped for the best like everyone else. You could have left well enough alone and made your wife feel better about herself, instead of making things worse."

His eyes flashed in anger. "It wasn't that easy." His grip tightened on the pages in hand. It was a wonder his fingers didn't pop through the stack.

"Did you go there that night to kill him?" I asked, wanting to understand. And buy more time for Paul to get there.

Barrett barked a bitter laugh. "I went there to put him in his place. I slipped in when no one was looking and beat on his door until he answered the damn thing. He was sporting a swollen eye and a busted lip already, so I wasn't the first one who'd grown tired of his attitude."

That would have been Dad, of course. "What happened, Barrett?" I put as much sympathy into my voice as I could. As long as he was talking, he wasn't running. Or stabbing me. Both were a win. "Did he threaten you? Make as if to call the cops?"

Barrett shook his head, and for a moment, I thought I saw regret in his eyes. "He let me into his room and I gave him a piece of my mind. He just stood there, looking at me, almost like he was bored. When I finished my rant, all he said was, 'Are you done?' I couldn't take it. He was so damn smug. So . . . I . . ." He swallowed hard, seemingly unable to go on.

"You snapped," I finished for him.

"I grabbed one of those coffee mugs off his desk. It was already filled, so I threw it in his face. It burned him—I could see his skin redden—but he only laughed at me. There was a pen sitting there, so, I . . . I . . ." His jaw hardened. "I need to go."

"Don't do this," I said, glancing back at Dad. He was still by the car, watching us.

"Get out of my way." He took a step forward, out of the hotel room, right into my personal space.

Reflexes took over. I mean, when someone walks toward you, you don't just stand there. And since I didn't want him to escape, I wasn't going to simply step aside.

So, instead, I planted my palm square in the middle of Barrett Drummand's chest in an attempt to stop his forward momentum.

He stopped all right. For all of the two seconds it took for him to grab hold of my wrist with one hand and twist.

I cried out as pain shot through my arm, up into my shoulder. I went straight to my knees, and no matter how I fought, I couldn't break his hold.

"You need to learn your place," he whispered at me, his tone harsh and uncaring. I imagined Theresa had heard that exact same line, spoken in the exact same way, at least a hundred times. "All women do."

Any sympathy I might have had for him vanished right then and there. The man treated women like they were beneath him. He might have gone to confront Rick about how he'd treated Theresa, but it had been for entirely selfish reasons, not out of any sense of manly duty.

Tears blurred my vision, but I could still see well enough to note the way the rubber band holding Barrett's manuscript was straining. With my free left hand, I reached up and gave it a quick tug, while allowing myself to fall backward, right hand jerking away from where Barrett held it.

Pain just about made me black out, but my action had the desired effect.

Barrett staggered forward a step as the rubber band snapped. Pages flew everywhere, slipping from his grip.

"No!" He released me as he tried to snatch the fluttering pages out of the air.

The sudden release caused me to fall over onto my butt, but I was free. Sirens rose in the distance, and before I could right myself, Barrett's head snapped up, eyes wide. He looked at the pages fluttering along the parking lot pavement, and then in a split second, made up his mind.

Ignoring the loss of his life's work, Barrett scrambled to his feet and ran for a white Chevy parked only a few spaces away from my car. He was so intent on his escape, he didn't see my dad coming.

James Hancock, mystery author and father to yours truly, leapt at the fleeing murderer, much like his character Bobby Drake might have done in one of his novels. He hit Barrett on the side, using his weight to drive the other man to the ground. They rolled over once, Barrett on top, and I was sure he was going to jam an elbow into Dad's gut and complete his getaway.

But Dad had other ideas.

He flipped the other man, somehow gaining hold of Barrett's arm in the process. Barrett landed on his stomach with a grunt, Dad rolling to sit on his back, bending his arm up nearly to his shoulder blades. Barrett cried out as Dad's knee became firmly planted on his kidneys.

I got to my feet and stared at the man I'd lived with nearly my entire life. It was like I was truly seeing him for who he was as I asked, "Where in the world did you learn to do that?"

Dad smiled and winked. "Research."

A moment later, Paul's police cruiser tore into the lot. By the time he took control of Barrett, the killer was practically begging for him to arrest him, just as long as he was out of Dad's viselike hold.

"Well, Buttercup," Dad said as we watched Officer Dalton shove the killer into his car. "What do you say we go and get some ice cream? I've worked up something of an appetite."

I glanced at him and smiled. "Sounds fantastic."

We'd have to give Paul our statements at some point, I was sure, but it could wait. Right then, Dad and I had some serious father-and-daughter time to catch up on, and I, for one, wasn't going to miss it for the world.

29

"Tell me it isn't true!" Rita clutched at my hand, squeezing until it felt like she was going to break the bones. "This can't be the end."

"It is," I said, extracting my battered appendage. "It's time for him to go."

She wailed and sat down heavily, rocking the chair back on two legs before settling it back down on four. She covered her eyes with the back of her hand as she spoke. "It's as if the sun will never shine again."

I rolled my eyes skyward. "I'm sure he'll come back someday." I looked upstairs, where Dad was thanking Vicki for allowing him to hold his signing here at Death by Coffee. It was just past the morning rush, and I was due to clock in in an hour to help handle lunch. Before then, I had time to say my good-byes.

I left Rita to her grief and went over to join Dad and Vicki. They broke from a brief hug as I drew near.

"Hopefully next time will be less of an adventure," Vicki was saying.

"I could definitely use some downtime." Dad smiled.

"But it wasn't all bad." He put an arm around my shoulder and hugged me close. "I got to spend some quality time with my daughter, and see how adventurous her life has become."

I hugged him back. "I could use a little less adventure myself," I said. Ever since I'd come to Pine Hills, it felt like I was always getting myself into one crazy situation after another.

"'Bye, Mr. Hancock," Lena called from behind the counter downstairs. She waved and then spun away, purple hair bouncing as she headed for the back, presumably to do the dishes.

In the dining area, Rita's wails reached a crescendo.

"I'd better tell her good-bye," Dad said, eyeing the mourning woman. He looked a little worried, like he thought she might latch on to him and never let go if he got too close.

I wasn't so sure he wasn't wrong. "Let her down easy," I said with a wink.

Dad headed over to her. I stayed where I was, not wanting to get involved. Trouble must have caught wind of my mood, because he came over to me and rubbed up against my leg. I picked him up and stroked his head twice, then put him back down before he changed his mind about me and brought out the claws.

"You okay?" Vicki asked, catching a hint of my melancholy.

I nodded. "Yeah. It was nice seeing him, but it's time he went home." I sighed. It might be time for him to go, but I was going to miss having him around.

"I heard the two of you found the killer together," she said. "It must have been quite an interesting ride."

"Tell me about it." I rubbed at my sore wrist. It was

bruised purple, but it was a small price to pay for putting a murderer behind bars.

I watched as Dad helped Rita to her feet and gave her a hug. She blubbered into his chest and grabbed hold of him as if she might drown in her own tears if she were to be let go. He glanced back at me and mouthed "I don't know what to do" before putting his arms around her and hugging her back.

I was about to go down and rescue him, when the door opened and Paul Dalton walked in, dressed in full police uniform. He glanced around the room, pausing to take in Rita and Dad. He looked mildly alarmed, but when he caught sight of me, he put them out of mind. He crooked a finger at me as he took off his hat and smoothed down his hair.

"I'd better go see what he wants," I said, knowing there was a good chance he was going to let me have it for chasing after the killer without him. He had yet to give me a firm reprimand.

"Good luck." Vicki said before heading into the stacks, Trouble in tow.

Paul cleared his throat as I neared. He looked nervous, but forced a smile when I stopped in front of him.

"You doing okay?" he asked, glancing at my wrist.

"Peachy." I tucked my hand under my arm to hide most of the bruising. "Did he confess?"

"He did. Even went as far as admitting to stealing his neighbor's truck. He figured he'd grab his laptop and go, but when he saw me at his house, he changed his mind and went after the physical pages, instead. If he wouldn't have been so worried about his book, he might have gotten away." Paul sighed, sounding relieved. "He told us he killed Rick Wiseman in a fit of rage, and swears up and down his wife had nothing to do with it."

"That's good," I said, glad he hadn't dragged Theresa down with him. "I mean, about her being innocent. She seems like a nice lady."

Paul nodded. "She's pretty upset. Not only is her husband in jail, but I guess that other agent told her he wasn't interested in her manuscript before he left. She blames Barrett for that, too." He sounded mildly amused.

"Cameron's gone?" I asked, though I supposed I shouldn't have been surprised. It had been a very long week, and if he wanted to get his business on track, he had to get back to New York soon so he could get started with all the inevitable paperwork. I doubted he could simply declare himself an official literary agent without having to sign a few papers first.

"Left last night as soon as I cleared him to go."

I felt a little bad that he hadn't said good-bye to me, but understood why. He might not have shown it while the investigation was going on, but he had to be mad that I'd ever considered him a suspect. I was pretty sure I'd hear from him again, however. Dad was almost positive he was going to sign with Cameron to help him get his career jump-started.

"What about Harland Pennywinkle?" I asked. "Is he in trouble for going back to the murder scene after his manuscript?"

Paul rubbed at the back of his neck. "I think we're giving him a pass on that. Buchannan ripped him a new one when he found out, and I figure that's good enough. What he took wouldn't have changed anything when it came to catching the killer, although, the next time he pulls something like that, he's going to spend some quality time behind bars."

There was something in his voice that told me he wasn't just talking about Harland.

"I'm glad it all worked out," I said, doing my best to act like I didn't catch his meaning. "Now things can get back to normal."

Paul went still. His eyes latched on to mine, held me there. "About that . . . ," he said, voice wavering in uncertainty.

My heart went into overdrive, and my mouth went dry. I glanced at Dad, who was trying to extract himself from Rita's grip. She was on her knees now, begging him to take her with him. I felt bad for him, but was glad she was keeping him busy.

"Yes?" I asked, turning back to Paul. It came out as a croak.

"I've been thinking a lot about how things have gone lately." He cleared his throat and paused.

Before he could continue, the door opened and in walked Will Foster. "Krissy!" he said, hurrying over to me. "I'm sorry I'm late." He barely paid Paul a glance as he wrapped me in a hug. "I'm glad I didn't miss him."

Paul sagged back, looking almost relieved. "Will," he said in greeting.

"Officer Dalton."

The two men eyed each other for a moment before they both nodded, as if coming to some sort of silent understanding.

"I'd best get going," Paul said, putting his hat back on. "Stay out of trouble, you hear?" He gave me a crooked smile before turning to my dad, who'd just joined us. He tipped his hat and said, "Sir," before turning and walking out the door.

"What did he want?" Will asked. Was that jealousy I detected in his voice?

"Just to let me know that Barrett confessed," I said. It wasn't the whole truth, but since Paul hadn't finished his thought, it was close enough.

"He didn't seem too happy about it," Dad said. "He looked kind of sad."

"Yeah, he did." There was a small ache in my heart and a part of me wanted to rush out the door to see if I could ease both of our pain by giving Paul a friendly hug. I knew it would be a mistake, however, so I stayed right where I was.

Will lifted my injured hand and gently kissed my wrist. "Well, the killer has been caught and all is well. I only wish you wouldn't have gotten hurt."

"I'm fine." And really, I was. With Barrett behind bars, life could go on. The local authors had a lot to talk about, and since Cameron was willing to work with them, they also had something to look forward to. He might not end up representing any of them, but he might instill some confidence in them so they'd submit elsewhere.

"I'd better get to the airport," Dad said, glancing at his watch.

"I can drive you if you'd like, Mr. Hancock," Will said.

"No, that's okay."

"Don't take it personally," I told Will. "He won't let me drive him, either."

"I have to take the rental back," Dad said. "Or else I'd take you both up on that offer."

"Well, I hope we get to sit down and talk again

sometime soon." Will held out his hand, and Dad shook it.

"Be good to her, okay?" He turned to me. "And you, be careful, all right, Buttercup?"

I wasn't sure if he was talking about my penchant for getting into trouble, or if he was referring to my internal war over my feelings for both Will and Paul. He was observant enough; I assumed he'd caught wind of my indecision by now.

"I will," Will said.

"I'll think about it," was my response.

Dad picked up the fedora Joel had given him, dropped it onto his head, and cocked it at a fetching angle. He winked at me before leaning in and kissing me on the cheek. "I'll see you soon."

"'Bye, Dad."

"Good-bye, my love," Rita called from her spot on the floor.

Dad beamed a smile, gave one last wave to everyone in the room, and then opened the door to Death by Coffee. He stepped outside and looked up into the sky, sucking in a deep, expansive breath.

And then with a bounce in his stride, he headed for his car.

I watched him go with a smile. He might be leaving, but life would go on.

And I was intent on living it to the fullest.

**Krissy Hancock is staying in her adopted hometown
of Pine Hills, Ohio, for Christmas this year—
and she even has a whole week off from her
combination bookstore-café. But a killer is
about to dampen her spirits . . .**

Unfortunately, Krissy's been roped into filling in for
a sick elf in the local holiday musical extravaganza.
With a demanding director, backstage gossip,
and two men in fierce competition for the starring
role, it isn't all sweetness and Christmas lights.
Then a murder puts a stop to the production,
and Krissy is faced with a pageant of suspects.

Could her ex-boyfriend, a fellow elf, really be the
culprit as the police are claiming? Or will the actor
playing Santa be trading his red suit for an orange
jumpsuit? When her behind-the-scenes investigation
starts getting dangerous, the only thing Krissy really
wants is to make it to Christmas dinner alive.
But first she'll have to finish wrapping up this case . . .

**Please turn the page for an exciting sneak peek of
Alex Erickson's next Bookstore Café mystery**

DEATH BY EGGNOG

coming soon wherever print and e-books are sold!

1

It lurked beneath the rectangle of brightly colored paper. A tail swished back and forth, causing a faint crinkling sound. Though I couldn't see them, I knew there to be two wide, yellow eyes peering out at me from beneath the nearest edge. The hairs on the back of my neck rose as the entire paper vibrated.

"Don't you even think about it," I said, hiding the ribbon behind my back. It was to be the finishing touch on my gift for Dad, though a part of me knew it was already a loss. "I knew I should have locked you up."

Misfit's tail swished once more, and then went still.

I held my breath, nervous anticipation causing my stomach to flip uneasily.

And then he attacked.

I screamed as the orange ball of fur tore from beneath the wrapping paper, eyes intent on the edge of ribbon he could just barely see from around me. Self-preservation caused me to reflexively toss the ribbon across the room, knowing if I didn't, I might lose a hand.

Misfit veered off course, eyes completely black, and snagged it from the air. He rolled once with it, slammed into the couch, and then tore out of the living room, toward the bedroom, ears pinned back, ribbon clamped firmly between his teeth. I'd have to retrieve it from him before he swallowed it, but for now, he could have it.

I rose and took a calming breath. As any cat owner knows, there's nothing more startling than a kitty in full-on psycho play mode. My admittedly soft flesh was no match for his needle-like claws and pointy teeth.

My phone rang as I was about to start cleaning up, causing me to jump. I snatched the phone off the floor where it sat beside a pair of gifts I'd wrapped for Misfit before he realized what I was doing. Dad's gift was the only one that remained unfinished, but at least it was wrapped. I planned on doing the rest of my shopping later, before my flight back home to California.

A quick glance at the screen told me it was my dad, James Hancock, calling. I grinned and answered with a chirpy, "Hello!"

"Hi, Buttercup."

There was a hesitation to his voice I ignored as I picked up the extra wrapping paper trimmings I'd cut away. "I'm just finishing up with my gift wrapping and then I'll be all packed. Misfit is making it harder than it should be." I laughed. "I can't wait to see you."

There was a long pause as he cleared his throat. "So, about that . . ." This time he coughed. "I was thinking that maybe you could spend this Christmas with Will. In Pine Hills."

I blinked, confused. "But we always do Christmas at your house."

"I know, but, well . . ." He sucked in a deep breath and let it out in a huff. "Something has come up."

Dread worked its way through my gut. "Is everything okay? You're not sick are you?" I felt faint. If Dad was sick, I needed to get out there! "I can fly out tonight. I'm sure I can change my flight."

"No, no, it's nothing like that." Dad chuckled, though it didn't set my mind at ease. He was all alone in California, Mom having died years ago. And since I moved away, he had no remaining family to spend the holidays with. "It's just . . ."

I waited, but he didn't continue. My mind conjured all sorts of horrible images better suited to Halloween than Christmas. Could he be calling me from a hospital bed, too proud to tell me he was dying? Or did the house burn down thanks to a freak electrical accident when he'd plugged in the tree?

I couldn't take his silence any longer. "What's going on?" I asked, voice pitched a few octaves higher than normal.

Dad sighed. "Remember when I told you I was thinking of dating again?"

I frowned. That wasn't what I'd expected him to say. "Yeah?"

"Well, there's this woman. Laura." He sounded a lot like I did every time I mentioned Will; sort of dreamy, and a little goofy. "She asked me to spend Christmas with her this year. She's going to the Swiss Alps, and well . . . I'd like to go."

My mind was still trying to catch up with the fact Dad had started seeing someone, so it took me a few long seconds to respond. I mean, I knew he was looking to date again, but some part of me never thought he'd actually do it. The idea of Dad with anyone other than Mom was kind of surreal.

"Laura?" was all I could think of to say.

"She's great." I could hear the smile in his voice. "She likes to travel, hence the Alps. She says it's perfectly safe. We'll be staying in a cabin, not climbing the mountains or adventure seeking. No camping in the cold for these old bones." He laughed, though he sounded nervous.

"You want to go to the Alps?" I asked, still a few beats behind.

"If you think it's a bad idea, Buttercup, I can cancel." He didn't sound like he wanted to, but was willing to do anything for his daughter.

Which, of course, made me feel like a royal jerk for sounding as if I might disapprove in the slightest. "I think it's a great idea," I said. I might have forced the cheer a bit, but that didn't mean I wasn't happy for him. I was thrilled he was finally moving on with his life; I was just bummed I wouldn't get to see him this holiday season.

"If you want, I could ask her if it would be all right to invite you along. I'm sure Laura would be okay with it."

"No, that's not necessary. You two should have fun together. I can stay here and spend Christmas with Will. Besides, I think he was a little upset I'd planned on leaving, so it works out."

"Are you sure?" Dad sounded both pleased and a little heartbroken, which made me feel better about my own feelings. I wasn't the only one who was going to have to get used to things being different this year.

"I'm sure." A thump in my bedroom reminded me

Misfit had a piece of ribbon. "I'd better go. Cat's causing some trouble. Need to rein him in before I head in to work."

"I'll talk to you later, Buttercup. And . . . thanks."

"Have fun," I said and hung up, feeling a smidge melancholy. I liked the idea of spending Christmas with Will, but I'd miss Dad something fierce. I was afraid it just wouldn't be the same without him.

I hurried into the bedroom to find Misfit in the corner, ribbon wrapped around him like he was a fuzzy, wiggly gift. He'd somehow gotten tangled in it to the point where he couldn't get out. He glared at me as if it was all my fault.

"That's what you get," I told him as I untangled him. He made a swat at the ribbon as I pulled it free. I yanked it back and stuffed it into my pocket where he couldn't reach. "Looks like we're going to spend Christmas together this year." Normally, Vicki watched him while I was gone. He'd stay with her and his litter-mate, Trouble. From what Vicki tells me, they both managed to live up to their namesakes every time they got together.

I returned to the living room and cleaned up before Misfit found something else to destroy. I put all three gifts into the spare bedroom, closing the door behind me so Misfit wouldn't get in and unwrap them early. I'd have to mail Dad's gift to him at some point, but that could wait.

Once everything was packed up, I pulled on my coat, grabbed my purse and keys, and then headed out the door.

Winter was here, but had yet to dump snow on us. There'd been a light dusting a few days ago, but it was already long gone. I hadn't paid any attention to the weather reports to know if a storm was coming since I hadn't planned on being in town to see it. As I got into my car, I mentally reminded myself to check the weather, as well as cancel my flight.

My Focus coughed a few times before starting. I gently stroked the dash, murmuring thanks as it started to warm. I so didn't need to be car shopping this time of the year, not with all the gifts I still needed to buy. I'd planned on shopping for Vicki, Will, and the rest of my friends while in California. I could get things there I wouldn't be able to find here. I added a shopping trip to my list of things I needed to do as I fished out my phone and called Will.

"Hi, Krissy," he said by way of answer. "You caught me just in time. I'm about to head back into the office."

I glanced at the dashboard clock and noted it was a lot closer to noon than expected. I wasn't going to be late, but I'd be cutting it close.

"I won't keep you," I said. I didn't like driving and talking, but wanted to call him now before he made plans. "I wanted to let you know that it looks like I'll be in town this year for Christmas."

"I thought you were flying back home?"

"Dad's got a date," I said, still not quite believing it. "I'm staying here. If you have time, I would love to get together for Christmas. I know you might have already made plans, but if you could slip me in . . ."

There was a pause and the rising sound of voices in the background. "I didn't really think much about it," Will said. "I'd love to have you over. We can solidify our plans later. I really need to go."

"Okay, that's fine. I'll talk to you later."

I hung up, feeling only a little better. He had

sounded distracted, but I chalked it up to the time of year. People did dumb things in the cold, and since Will Foster was a doctor, it was his job to fix the results of those bad choices. His waiting room was probably full of people who'd decided to take a dip in an icy pond, or slipped on some ice while walking to their car. Hopefully, his job wouldn't get in the way of our Christmas together. I was hoping we could make it special this year, now that I was going to get to spend time with him.

I parked a few blocks from Death by Coffee, the bookstore café I co-owned with my best friend Vicki Patterson. I made sure I was suitably bundled, and then hurried down the sidewalk to the store. The air temperature wasn't horrible, but the wind was bitingly cold. It stung my eyes and my nose and ears were already throbbing. It would be a great day for coffee—if you were willing to brave the cold to pick some up.

Warm, coffee-scented air blasted into me as soon as I opened the door. I all but floated behind the counter, shedding my coat along the way. Half the seats were taken by customers whose hands were wrapped tightly around their hot drinks. A few more were browsing the bookshelves upstairs. I poured myself a cup of eggnog flavored coffee, and instead of using my usual chocolate chip cookie, I used the house made eggnog creamer instead. I took a sip, and just about melted into the floor.

"How's business today?" I asked as Vicki came out of the back room, a freshly made batch of eggnog in hand.

"Good," she said, cheerily. "Both the eggnog and flavored coffees are a hit." We'd just started selling them that very day. "Can hardly keep up with the demand."

I beamed in pleasure. It had been my idea to go the eggnog route, including regular old eggnog to our menu for the holiday season.

"How does it feel to be on your last day of work?" she asked, leaning against the counter. She didn't mean to make it look seductive, but somehow, it did. Vicki was just one of those people who brightened up any room, no matter the circumstances.

"About that," I said, glancing up the stairs to where Jeff Braun, one of our employees, was ringing up a book sale. "I'm not going."

"Did something happen?"

"No. Well, yeah, kind of." I shrugged. "Dad has a date. I'm staying here."

"Oh!" Vicki's eyes lit up like I'd just told her she'd won the lottery. "What do you know about his date?"

Another shrug. "Her name is Laura and she likes to travel. They're going to the Swiss Alps."

"Really?" Vicki got a far-off look in her eye. "That sounds fantastic."

"I'm sure it will be," I said, some of the melancholy slipping back into my voice. "But it does mean I'm going to be in Pine Hills this year, so if you want to rework the schedule to fit me in, I'm willing."

Vicki came back to the here and now with a shake of her head. "No, you should take the time off. Even though you aren't leaving town, you could use the break."

"I'll just be sitting around my house, so it would be no big deal," I said, though I was hoping I'd be doing a lot more than that. It all depended on Will's work schedule and how much time he'd be able to wiggle me in for. Owning his own practice took a lot out of him, more than I was sometimes comfortable with.

I sighed and wondered how best to spend our newfound time together. Maybe next year Will and I could take a trip, see the world. I'd seen a few of the fifty states, but had yet to travel anywhere outside them.

But this year . . . I was already envisioning candlelight dinners and hot bubble baths.

Vicki was looking at me with a huge smile on her face as I came back to the present.

"What?" I asked.

"That look on your face." She laughed a good-natured laugh. "You were practically swooning where you stood."

"I was not!" I blushed, covering it up by gulping some coffee. "I was just thinking."

"It's okay. I have some pretty steamy plans this year too." She winked at me and then floated to the register to take an order.

Thoroughly embarrassed, I carried my coat and coffee into the back room. I flung on an apron, fanned myself off (what can I say? It was a pretty steamy fantasy) and then headed out front to begin the long day at work.

Or at least I would have, but I was verbally assaulted the moment I stepped behind the counter.

"It's terrible!" Rita Jablonski wailed, hurrying over to me. "It's a travesty!"

Used to her overstating pretty much everything, I didn't drop into an immediate panic. The town gossip had a tendency to overreact. I'd done a good job of late taking it in stride and not getting annoyed with her like I used to. It was just one of Rita's quirks.

"What happened?" I asked as I checked the cookie case to find it looking a little spare.

"Mandy is sick and I don't know what we're going to do! There's only two weeks until the big day and now with her out of commission, we're one short!"

I tried to follow, but she was being so vague, I could only ask, "Mandy?"

"Mandy Ortega. It's her diet, I tell you. She eats all the wrong things and it's impacted her immune system to the point that any bit of stress and she comes down sick. I knew when she was cast it was a bad idea."

A lightbulb went off in my head. "She's in a play?"

"Of course she is," Rita said with a dismissive wave of her hand. "We have it every year, dear." She stepped back and looked me up and down. "You know, you could probably fit into her costume."

This time, instead of a lightbulb, alarm bells were going off in my head. "No, I don't think so."

But it was already too late. Rita was on a roll and there was nothing that would stop her. "She was an elf in our Christmas production," she said, speaking right over me. "Not a big role, mind you. You wouldn't have to learn many lines at all. And every time you do speak, it will be a group effort, so if you flub it, it won't be that big of a deal."

"I really don't think I . . ."

"The costume *should* fit. Your diet doesn't seem to be much better than Mandy's, so there's a risk there."

"Hey!"

"There's only two weeks until the show," she went on, oblivious. "Practices have ramped up, so there is one every night, right up until show night. That shouldn't be too much of an issue for you."

"Rita, I don't know anything about acting in a play."

"If there was someone else, you can bet I'd ask them, but since there isn't . . ." She shrugged as if saying it was out of her hands.

"What about Vicki?" I asked, grabbing hold of her as she came down the stairs. "She's done plays before. She'd know what to do."

Rita took one look at Vicki and laughed. "Weren't you listening? We only have one spare costume. There's no time to have another made and you're the perfect size! She'd drown in Mandy's getup."

I knew I should have taken it as an insult, especially since Rita weighed more than me, but I was too panicked to care.

"But . . ."

"You should do it, Krissy," Vicki said. "It would be a great experience."

Gee, thanks, I thought. Betrayed by my best friend.

"Practices start at six at the community theatre. I'll let Lawrence know you'll be coming."

And with that, she spun away, leaving me gaping after her.

"It'll be fun," Vicki said before she too left me standing there, feeling as if I'd been bull-rushed.

"Fun," I said. Somehow, I seriously doubted it.

Connect with **U**s

Visit us online at
KensingtonBooks.com
to read more from your favorite authors, see books
by series, view reading group guides, and more.

Grab These Cozy Mysteries from
Kensington Books